I NOW PRONOUNCE YOU MR. AND MRS. THUG 2

TN Jones

I Now Pronounce You, Mr. and Mrs. Thug 2 Copyright© 2019 by TN Jones.

All rights reserved. No part of this book may be reproduced in any form or by any electronic or mechanical means including information storage and retrieval systems, without permission in writing from the author. The only exception is by a reviewer, who may quote short excerpts in a review.

Cover designed by Felicia Ann

This book is a work of fiction. Names, characters, places, and incidents either are products of the author's imagination or are used fictitiously. Any resemblance to actual persons, living or dead, events, or locales is entirely coincidental.

ACKNOWLEDGMENTS

    First, thanks must go out to the Higher Being for providing me with a sound body and mind in addition to having the natural talent of writing and blessing me with the ability to tap into such an amazing part of life. Second, thanks most definitely go out to my Pretty Prin; you mean the world to me. Third, to my supporters who have been rocking with me since day one, and to the lovely new readers for giving me a chance. Fourth, to King L.O. and Jammie Knight for being amazing people and helping me along the way. Y'all have provided much insight into the creation.

    Like always, I wouldn't have made it this far without anyone. I truly thank everyone from the body of my heart for rocking with the novelist kid from Alabama, no matter what I drop. Y'all make this writing journey enjoyable and have once again trusted me to provide y'all with quality entertainment.

    I hope y'all enjoy, my loves! Muah!

CHAPTER ONE

Tashima

I couldn't believe my eyes. Dom Dom was standing in front of me, looking and smelling good. He had aged but in more handsomely. As I glared into his eyes, I wanted to get lost in them, but I couldn't. The fact that he was at the threshold of the house that I shared with Dyon blew my mind; the last thing I needed was for Dyon to see that Dom Dom was free and at our home. I wanted to ask many questions, but I couldn't because that handsome motherfucker shoved his head towards mine. Instantly, our tongues seductively danced. While enjoying our intimate kiss, my knees buckled, causing Dom Dom to hold tight to me.

We had to leave the house now, I thought as our hands tenderly and passionately roamed each other's backs as my kitty purred for its first master to enter.

Breaking the kiss, I lovingly looked at Dom Dom and said, "Time to go."

"Okay. Where do you have in mind, love?"

"The beach," I breathed as I ran towards the kitchen to grab my ringing cellphone and keys.

"Nawl, I need to make love to you now. The beach gonna have to wait 'til we are done," he voiced on my heels.

"Okay," I quickly replied, nervously.

"Why are you nervous? I'm sure Momma taught you to control that," he voiced nonchalantly.

The last thing I need is for Dyon to catch you in our home, I thought as I powered off my phone and told him, "Come on."

From the time I locked and closed the door, I felt that Dyon was going to see Dom Dom and me leaving the house. My legs didn't move as fast as I wished them to, and Dom Dom took his precious time walking towards the driver's side of the idling Audi that Sonica used to drive when she lived in the States.

"Where are we going?" he asked as I ran to my car.

"Auburn. I purchased a home there six months ago," I rapidly told him as I pressed the unlock button on my key fob.

"A'ight. Hop in the Audi instead of driving yo' whip," he demanded, looking my way.

"No, I'm driving my car. Follow me," I voiced rapidly as I nervously looked around the neighborhood before taking a seat inside of my car and starting the engine.

I knew what Dom Dom was doing, and it started to piss me the fuck off. He was not about to start a damn war, and he was freshly out of prison, which I had no damn idea that he was returning home today. If I had've known, I sure as hell wouldn't have been at home.

The second he placed his behind in the driver's seat of the Audi, I placed the gearshift in reverse. Quickly, I sped away from my home. The moment three of my tires were on the road, I barely pressed the brakes before I dropped the gearshift into drive mode. As I pulled off, I looked in the rearview mirror and saw that Dom Dom hadn't left the yard. With my phone in my hand, I powered on my cellphone.

Angrily, I banged on the steering wheel as I shouted, "Bring your ass on, nigga! You up to some shit and haven't been out long enough."

As I zoomed down the road, I received a call from Dom Dom.

"Yeah?" I spoke nervously.

Laughing, he demanded, "Go to my house. We can leave yo' car in the garage, an' you gonna drive the Audi. A'ight?"

"Okay," I replied as I sighed heavily.

"You fell fo' that nigga, didn't you?" he asked as my phone chimed in my ear.

Quickly, I removed my phone from my ear and looked at the screen. Dyon was calling. My heart seeped to my ass, and I was eager to power off my phone.

"I see you ain't too quick to answer that question," Dom Dom spat, just as I placed the phone back to my ear.

"Dom Dom, what do you think? He's the only one I've been around since you got locked up. What else was I supposed to have done?" I asked in an annoyed and frustrated tone as I made my way towards his home.

"Played that nigga an' kept yo' feelin's to me an' only me. I thought I made myself clear when I said that when I got out that you were going to be mine an' mine alone," he stated in a stern tone.

I need to get off this damn phone, I thought as I smartly replied, "It would've been nice to know exactly when you were going to touch down. I would've better prepared myself to knock my feelings down about Dyon."

"It shouldn't be that damn high to begin wit', Tashima," he barked, causing me to jump as my pretty kitty became wet.

"That shit is easier said than done, Dom Dom. You and I have missed twenty-one years together whereas Dyon, and I have gained twenty-one years," I spoke, looking into the rearview mirror as my phone chimed again.

"Just get to my house," he aggressively spoke before ending the call.

I rolled my eyes and sighed as I powered off my phone. For years, I had planned how I wanted Dom Dom and me to reunite, and it surely wasn't the way that it was being done now. The way shit was taking place, it would cause confusion, stress, and unwanted pain for everyone involved, especially me. I hated that he didn't give me the heads up, or it could've been that I hated that I didn't keep tabs on his release dates like an ordinary woman in love with a man that's in prison supposed to.

From my neighborhood to Dom Dom's community, all I thought about was how to keep the confusion down between the two men that I loved. There was going to be a lot of sneaking around, and I didn't want that. I needed to be with them freely because I refused to choose whom to spend the rest of my life with.

As I approached Dom Dom's driveway, I saw the garage door open. I didn't waste any time driving my car inside. Quickly, I shut off the engine before hopping out. After I exited my car, locked the door, and sashayed towards the driver's side of the Audi, a sigh of relief escaped my mouth. However, I couldn't escape the downcast eyes of my first love. He didn't say a word to me as he walked to the passenger side of the car.

The moment we settled into the comfortable seats, his fine ass sighed sharply, leaned towards me, unbuttoned my shorts, and said, "I guess I need to remind you who the fuck you really belong to and why, huh?"

Weakly, I sat in the driver's seat with my mouth closed tightly as I spread my legs to the first nigga that ever drove me crazy with his tongue, fingers, and dick. One finger followed by two was in my wet fortress as Dom Dom sucked on my neck in a way that had me shaking from my head to my toes.

Oh, God. This feeling. I missed this. Dyon could never provide me this wonderful sensation, I thought as I cooed, "Dominiicckk."

"Yes, baby, yes," he replied as he tapped against my G-Spot.

"I miss you," I whined as I thrust my pussy onto his fingers.

"As I miss you. I'm going to reward you fo' everything you have done. I promise you I'mma give you the world an' so much mo' Tashima. But, um, I'mma need you to get that Dyon character out of yo' system," he whispered in my ear before sucking on my earlobe and applying incredible pressure to one of the most sensitive areas on my body.

How am I going to get Dyon out of my system? He makes me tick, but in his own little way, I thought as I came on his fingers all the while moaning his name.

"It's time to leave the city fo', baby. Drive ... carefully, an' let me greet my queen the right way," he sexily spoke while playing in my pussy.

From Montgomery to Auburn, Dom Dom had me singing his name, telling him that I loved him, and that I was going to be by his side regardless of what I had to do. In the back of my head, I knew that I couldn't cut Dyon loose. I just couldn't. Within those twenty-one years of not trying to love Dyon on that level, I ended up loving him just like I loved Dom Dom. I wasn't complete without them. I had to have them by my side; the issue was how to get them on board with sharing me, willingly.

When I parked the car in front of the secluded, single-family home that had a colorful flowerbed filled with summer flowers, Dom Dom rapidly removed our seatbelts before sliding my seat backward. In the front seat, we stripped naked and began sucking and kissing on each other like it was no tomorrow. The second he pushed me against the driver's door, spread my legs, and shoved his head into my hungry pussy, I lost every insight to how I was going to make those two niggas love and understand that I needed them in my life and that I wasn't going to sneak around with them.

Dom Dom's tongue felt like home. It was everything and then some. He catered to my swollen, pink bud as two of his fingers were inside of me, familiarizing and teasing. Slow flickers from his tongue sent chills throughout my body, causing me to tremble with each suck and tug on my pretty, little kitty. For God knows how long, Dom Dom was nibbling and sucking the life out of me before I told him that I couldn't take being on the wet seats.

"Get on this dick," he ordered with the sexiest expression I had ever seen on a man's face.

"Not yet," I told him breathlessly as I climbed across the passenger seat.

After I slid it backward, I shoved Dom Dom back, gazed into his eyes, and said, "Relax for me, baby."

Growling, he spoke, "Mane, I'm not feelin' this shit at all. I can't fathom you suckin' on another nigga's dick."

"Just don't think about how I learned. Just enjoy, please," I spoke as I gripped the thickest dick that had ever been in my hand.

Lord, I gotta get my pussy back to the way it was, or Dyon going to know that I had lain with someone who is three times thicker than him, I thought as I licked my lips all the while producing a significant amount of saliva.

"Manee..."

Before he could start his sentence, I licked his swollen head. He gasped as his head flopped on the headrest. Knowing that I had to take baby steps with the type of dick I was holding, I took pleasure in taking my time with the hardened tool. Dom Dom's body relaxed more in the passenger seat. While I gazed into his eyes, I saw tears forming as he mouthed that he loved me and always would. Those words amongst seeing him emotional took me on a path that I wished I hadn't gone on. I lost myself in his eyes, his words, and the feel of me sitting in between his legs with half of his dick in my mouth.

I ate that nigga dick up as he tried his best not to squirm and groan. I got the best of him as he got the best of me. With every suck and lick on his dick and balls, I thought about the first time he tasted, fingered, and sexed me. With every deep throat motion, I thought about how kind, loving, and amazing he was when he and his mother took my sister and me in. While fondling his balls and making love to his dick with my mouth, I realized how much Dom Dom meant to me. If it weren't for him, my sister and I would've been screwed by Alabama's legal system. He was there for us. Unconditional love and a sacred bond came about, and there wasn't a soul on this earth that could take him away from me or me from him. I was his, and he was mine. It was going to be like that forever!

I felt a glob of warm liquids spilling down my throat as Dom Dom's hands were on the back of my head while he groaned my name. I had zoned out. When I realized what had happened, I removed my mouth from his dick and sweetly and lovingly said, "You were the first to nut in my mouth. Now, you know where I really lie at."

"I love you, guh. I mean like I'll kill a nigga 'bout you type of love. After all these damn years, a nigga mo' in love wit' you than ever before," he softly said as I climbed on top of him.

Feeling bubbly like I did the first time he expressed his feelings for me, a huge grin was on my face as I reciprocated those same words to him.

"Can that dick still stay hard after it nut?" I joked.

"Ain't shit changed 'bout this dick," he laughed.

"Good, cause we have a meeting all damn day and night, sir," I sexily cooed as I grabbed his dick before placing it at my opening.

A bitch caught hell trying to get that motherfucker inside of me. Frustrated, I shook my head and said, "You gonna have to get on top of me, first."

Laughing, he said, "Well, hello there, my timid little fourteen-year-old boo."

As he placed me on my back, I giggled and said, "Shut up, Dom Dom."

"I will, but don't you shut up," he voiced before gently rubbing the head of his dick from my clit to my juicy opening.

"Oooh," I whimpered, twirling my pussy on him.

A feeling that I hadn't felt, since the last time we had lain together, was in full effect. It was amazing to see and feel his mouth on my body. One nipple was in his mouth as he thumbed the other. Just off him playing with my titties had me ready to rock the car. He kept teasing me before I demanded that he put his dick deep inside of me. Shoving his head toward mine, I sucked his bottom lip into my mouth as his thick, elongated dick entered my exclusively juicy hotbox.

"Dommmiinniicckk," I moaned as my legs shook instantly.

He was so thick inside of me that I could barely breathe. Dick, dick, and more dick was on that fine ass man, and I had to master it—all over again. He slow rocked my body and made promises to me, which I knew that he wasn't going to break.

Finally, I became somewhat comfortable with his size and began to thrust my kitty on him. We came together in a delightful orgasmic way. We were tangled together like snakes in a pile underneath an abandoned house.

"You still on those birth control pills?"

Please don't ask me to come off it, I thought as I gazed into his eyes while rubbing the back of his head and breathlessly replied, "Yes."

"When do you have to get another one?"

Lie to him, I thought as I truthfully replied, "Next week."

"It's time to come off. I'm home, an' it's time fo' us to have a family. It's time fo' ole boy to leave what had always belonged to me," he spoke in a boss-like manner while placing kisses on my forehead, nose, neck, heart, and finally my lips.

Oh, Lord, how am I going to pull off wanting and having Dom Dom and Dyon? I'm finna create a disaster because I will not choose between the two, I thought as he asked, "Did you hear what I said?"

"Yes, baby, I heard what you said," I lowly voiced as I placed a kiss on the side of his neck.

"Good because I really don't feel like murderin' a nigga my first week out," he voiced while shutting the car off and removing the keys from the ignition.

As my mind wondered, Dom Dom had opened the passenger door, snatched me out of the car, placed me around his waist, and rubbed his swollen dick against my clit. Not surprised that he was ready for round two, I wrapped my hands around his neck, lifted my body, and allowed him access to my nutty cat. From there, we were like wild animals in a fucking jungle. Dom Dom took my body to places it had never been. Tears streamed down my face as I loudly moaned his name and scratched his back.

Gripping a fistful of my hair, Dom Dom pulled my head backward and growled, "Tashima, I don't think I made my-fuckin'-self clear when I said that you belong to me. I feel that you want shit to go yo' way, baby, I hate to tell you this, but I ain't sharin' you wit' a nigga. That nigga had you fo' twenty-one-motherfuckin'-years, his got damn time is up! I'm motherfuckin' here, an' I ain't going no-damn-where!"

"I know. I knoowww!" I hollered sensually, super turned the fuck on.

"I'll kill him. You know I will," he voiced while spreading my ass cheeks, digging his dick deeper into my core.

I was putty in his hands, and he knew. He knew that I hadn't been fucked like that since the day the police officers arrested him. He knew that I hadn't had my hair pulled while he savagely talked to me and dug in my guts. He knew what made me tick, and I be damned if he didn't cater to my needs of having rough sex while demandingly talking to me. Before I knew what was happening, I was in too damn deep. So, deep that I didn't know if I was coming or going. I feared and was eager for the rest of the night to show face. Why? I knew our lovemaking was going to be the shit, but I knew that he was going to say something about Dyon that was going to put me right back at square one—how was I going to have them without them trying to kill each other?

"Who's pussy is this, Tashima?" Dom Dom barked.

Yours and Dyon's, I thought as I whined, "Yours!"

"Let that nigga know that shit!" he growled while hitting corners within me that still had cobwebs on it.

"Fucck! I love youuuuu!" I passionately voiced as I clung to my first love with everything in me.

Removing himself from me, Dom Dom barked, "Bend over."

Oh no! Oh no! He finna get some shit out of me that I ain't willing to sign up for, I thought as I did what he demanded.

That motherfucking nigga licked and sucked on my asshole so damn great that I almost fell on the ground. I hadn't had a tongue swerve there since the last time he did it. Dom Dom made love to my asshole so wonderfully that he outdid his previous times. I cried and nutted. That was all a sister could do. Like my pussy, my face was soaking wet when he entered me.

"Put that perfect arch in yo' back, baby," he sexily growled, popping my left ass cheek.

Upon doing what he told me, Dom Dom fucked the shit out of me as I held onto the door panel for dear life. I was in heaven as my juices slipped out of me onto his dick. I was in utter disbelief that I went without all of his excellent loving for twenty-one years, and now I was receiving it outside of a home that I purchased for us.

Lifting my butt, Dom Dom hit my G-Spot, and I fucking lost it. I really lost it!

"I'mma leave him alone, Dominick Rodgers! I don't want him. I need you, Dominick! I need a family with you, baby. It was you that I thought of when I was with him. I motherfucking love you. I never stopped. I promise I never stopped loving youuu!" I whined as my body became hotter than a volcano, hotter than a car without a thermostat, and hotter than a bullet slamming into someone's head.

"Now, I know shit real. You better let me see this shit come into fruition, an' trust time is windin' down before I step in an' stop that nigga from breathin'," he voiced as he drilled me for everything that I had.

"Ohh Goddd! Dominniicckk!" I sensually hollered as I thought about what I said and what was about to go down—trials and tribulations with two hood niggas that I loved with every fiber in me.

CHAPTER TWO

Dominick "Dom Dom" Rodgers

"Jessusss, Dom Dom!" my baby sexily moaned while my face was buried inside of her pussy.

From round one until now, which was round six, I wouldn't let her breathe good enough before I began touching, licking, and sucking on her body. My dick had no manners when it came to Tashima; not to mention my celibacy of twenty-one years. I was making up for old and new; a nigga was putting in work. All of the birthdays, holidays, and just because sex took place since we arrived at the decked-out home. I fucked her on every piece of furniture in every room within the house.

With shaky limbs, Tashima shook her head vigorously from side to side as she whined, "Dom Dommm."

I didn't remove my mouth from her sweet pussy as I said, "Yes, baby?"

"You are driving me insane," she breathlessly voiced while poorly rubbing the back of my head.

"Good," I chuckled before shaking my head and lifting her bottom; I wanted my face to disappear in her pretty, hairless pussy.

I needed her to know that I was home, that she wasn't dreaming, and that we would be good for life. The situation she had with Dyon had to be done; I wasn't going to have it any other way. Like I told her, he had her for twenty-one years, and that was too long.

It was apparent he didn't cater to her body like I did. Tashima was tight as fuck with sensitive spots all over her body. That nigga wasn't doing shit in the bedroom; if he were that pussy wouldn't have been desperately begging for me to claw it open. By Dyon not doing the job right, it was all good in my eyes because the previous time he had gotten between Tashima's legs was the fucking last time.

"Make love to me, Dominick," she voiced lowly while looking at me.

I wasn't ready to make love to her because I was still hungry. However, whatever she wanted when she wanted, she would always get it. After several slow, long flickers of my tongue from her pussy opening to her clit, I slid my tongue upwards, causing Tashima to whimper my name all the while wiggling her thick, chocolate body.

"You know I love you, right?" I asked after kissing the base of her neck.

Nodding her head, she replied, "Yes, I know."

"No matter what, don't you ever forget that."

"I won't," she spoke erratically.

My dick was at her opening, throbbing and eager to slide inside of her perfectly-sized, hot and wet oven. For the sixth time, I entered Tashima as if it was the first time, nice and slow. She gasped before whimpering. I loved the sounds she made while holding me.

Slowly, we began to enter into a world that neither of us would want to leave. Every corner inside of her gushy insides, I hit with such passion that tears slipped down her face. I kissed them away before we glared into each other's eyes. There was nothing that we could say that we hadn't already said.

The love was in our eyes as if it was the first time we were around each other. The passion and heartfelt chemistry were there. My need for her was at an all-time high as I was sure that her demand for me was just as high. There was no doubt that I was going to spend the rest of my life with Tashima. It had been on my mind when I was seventeen years old.

"I'm cummin'!" she moaned as she thrust faster on my wet tool.

"Then, bust on me baby, bust on a real nigga's dick," I growled as I pinned her legs beside her head and passionately yet savagely dug in her core.

I didn't have any plans of nutting along with Tashima, but I be damned if her pussy muscles didn't clench super tight and sucked my white boys up out of me and deep into the tunnel of her pink walls. Even though, I came that didn't stop me from thrusting my hard dick inside of her. I didn't stop grinding, sliding, and swerving inside of Tashima until she told me that she was exhausted. I had to make my dick go down, and that was one hell of a process.

"Tub time?" I asked as I rolled over with her in my arms.

"Yes, please," she giggled, looking into my eyes.

"I told you it was going to be a long flight with me fo' the next couple of days," I replied while rubbing the small of her back.

"And I see no lies that you told either, sir," she voiced while slowly gliding her shaky hand up and down my chest and abdomen regions.

"Can we lay here fo' a minute before I carry you to the bathroom an' bathe you?" I sincerely asked.

"Yes," she cooed.

I became quiet as I thought about the years that I had spent away from her. She had wanted to come and see me, but I wouldn't allow it. We wrote and talked to each other faithfully. I had okay days as I had horrible days. The only person that got me through those awful days were the thoughts of holding her in my arms. The loving kisses we were going to put on each other's lips held a nigga down more than her sweet letters. I physically missed her birthdays and holidays, but I had many pictures of her, Momma, and Desaree on those special occasions.

I had someone draft a ring for her twenty-first birthday, and Momma found a jeweler in Savannah, Georgia to make it. The beautiful gold ring sat on her left ring finger as she massaged the side of my neck. On her twenty-fifth birthday, I had Momma pay for a trip for three to Hawaii. Tashima took Desaree and Dyon; I knew that she would. It wasn't like Tashima had any friends; hell, they were her friends. A part of me was pissed off that Dyon went, but I had to realize that she had been dealing with that nigga since I had been locked down, which, I had granted. Her dirty thirty, I paid for a trip of three to Dubai. I knew she was going to take that nigga Dyon; to my surprise when I learned that she didn't take him; she took Momma instead. There was a lot of strife between her and that character because Tashima decided to take my mother instead of him.

I had to make many illegal moves behind bars to get a smartphone for that trip. All those moves that I made were worth it; it was the first time, in a long time, that I had seen Tashima's fat, juicy pussy as she slid two fingers around her little ocean. She thumbed her clit just right. She performed a sexual dance that had my dick brick hard within seconds. Within minutes of seeing her pussy upside down while she was pussy popping on her head, I badly wanted to feel her in that position. After the visuals she gave me, my dick stayed in my hand.

"What are you thinking about, sir?" she softly asked, looking at me.

"All of the precious moments I physically missed concernin' you."

"Oh. Well, you won't miss anymore, baby. We are finally together," she sincerely spoke as my cellphone rang.

Reaching towards the nightstand, Tashima yawned. I looked at her and said, "Yo' ass finna baze before you crash out."

"A'ight," she giggled, closing her eyes.

With my phone in my hand, I saw my mother's name on the screen. Quickly, I answered the phone with a happy, "What's up, lovely woman?"

"Hey, Son. Your ass been out for quite some time and hadn't called me. I wonder why is that?" she laughed.

"Wellll, you know who I had to get to an' why," I chuckled as I laid on my back as Tashima snuggled closer to me.

"My plane will be landing in Atlanta in ten hours. I expect you and Tashima to be waiting in the airport lobby. Understood?" she spoke in a bossy tone.

"Yes, ma'am."

"I'll see y'all then."

"Alright," I voiced before we ended the call on a loving note.

Tashima began to snore softly; it drove my dick to wake up. I knew she was exhausted, and her pussy was sore, but I had to have some more of her. Gently, I placed my baby on her back and sucked on her neck while telling her how I much loved her and why.

With her eyes closed, Tashima moaned while wrapping her legs around my waist.

Slowly, she opened her eyes and sexily asked, "You gonna wear my ass out, huh?"

"Somethin' like that." I smiled while sliding my dick inside of her nutty kitty.

ΩΩΩ

"So, did y'all have a great time, rekindling?" Momma snickered before shoving a forkful of Cobb Salad into her mouth.

Being the foolishness nigga that I had always been, I sinisterly looked at her and smiled before saying, "An' you know we did."

"Oh my God, Dom Dom, really?" Tashima loudly spoke as she shoved me, almost falling out of her chair.

"Momma ain't crazy. She knew what was up. She will always know what is up," I voiced while looking at the most beautiful woman that had a nigga's heart and soul wrapped around her chocolate fingers.

Silence overcame us as my mother cleared her throat and seriously glared at us. Instantly, she had our undivided attention. It was business time; that was the second reason she had traveled back to the States. Momma didn't say a word as she studied me before observing Tashima. Whatever she was thinking, had me intrigued.

"Momma, what's up?" I voiced as I placed the fork and knife on the napkin.

"Are you really ready to hop back in the streets?"

"Yep. I haven't been in it, but my hands was still tied into a lot of shit."

"Tashima, are you ready to give Dom Dom the reigns back?"

Sighing sharply, she shook her head and said, "Not really. I prefer us to be partners. I have the Russians on lock. I have a meeting next with a connect from Ecuador, and this particular one only deals with females. So, I want to keep the communication between us so that we are getting the best deals."

With bucked, bright eyes, Momma glared at Tashima. Placing her hands over her mouth, my mother shook her head several times before saying, "Holy shit, you got a meeting with *the* Catalina?"

"Yes," Tashima smiled.

Entirely out of the loop, I asked, "Who is Catalina?"

"One of the best, young and motivated coca leaf growers since The Don passed away," Tashima stated.

"Is she related to The Don?" I inquired, rubbing my beard.

"She's his great-granddaughter," Tashima voiced before taking a sip of her drink.

"Is she fair priced like him? What are her requirements and fees for her goods? What makes her the best in the business?" I questioned, looking between my mother and Tashima.

"To some, she isn't fairly priced, but for me, she is. Her requirement is simple: don't mention her name if anything goes sideways. She's giving me a fifteen percent discount off eight-hundred pounds of leaves, per. What makes her the best in the business? Catalina doesn't fuck with anyone just because they have money. She's very meticulous about who she conducts business with. The lands the coca leaves are grown on have the best fertilizer to produce quality, potent leaves, and the bitch knows exactly how to get the dope in without the police knowing, unlike her great-grandfather."

As I took in the information presented to me, I thought about The Don and his ways of handling business. He would never give a discount for any reason, regardless of how much he liked you or how much you've purchased. He had a set price for everyone.

He had the prettiest coca leaves that I had ever seen; thus, the dope was terrific to the fiends.

"What happened to coca suppliers that came from that line before her?" I inquired.

"Wasn't producing good shit. Their competition was at the top of the dope industry. The Don's sons lost massive money by trying to continue their father's legacy. While they lost money and battled over what could've been done better at a lower price, Catalina began to undo the fuck up from the two brothers. With the help from those that made a living off picking coca leaves, Catalina catered to the dying acres of land. Once the product began looking healthy like it used to when The Don was on top, Catalina knocked the competition back down."

"Well, it sounds like it's a go wit' the Catalina chick," I spoke before clearing my throat.

"How do you really feel about what I said, baby?" Tashima asked, eyeing me.

Grabbing her hand, I kissed it and sincerely said, "I'm good wit' it. Tell me what you need me to do."

"What you've always done. This is your organization, baby, I was just taking over until you returned. The Russians and Catalina are the only ones I want to deal with. Everyone else was your plugs. I think they will prefer dealing with you versus to me," she chuckled.

"So, they've told me, but I like how you handled their asses. I'm stickin' to the routine an' the prices that you set. I loved how you paid attention to the overpricin' of products. You did shit in a smart way, an' I love that. I just want to make the business aspect of our lives just as successful as our personal life."

"Is there anything specific you want me to do?" Tashima asked, gazing into my eyes.

"Introduce me to everyone. After you meet wit' Catalina next week, I need you to relax an' enjoy six months without havin' to deal wit' any type of dope talk. I need yo' mind an' body ready fo' these babies I'm finna pop in yo' ass," I replied earnestly, causing Momma to spit drink on the half eaten food on the ceramic, expensive plate in front of her.

"Sonica, by now, you should know that you shouldn't eat or drink anything when Dom Dom is present," Tashima snickered.

My mother nodded her head and said, "True."

"How's the real estate, web designing and company marketing doing?" I asked Tashima.

With a smile on her face, she replied, "Very well. Of course, you know the real estate is doing well and there's no need to discuss it. What we need to discuss is me being more involved with web designing and company marketing. Those companies pay top-notch dollars for my suggestions."

"What do you need to do to become more involved with that?" I inquired.

"I want more companies to work with. I need you to make sure you leave me enough energy to focus on our legal monies," she smiled warmly while touching my hand.

"Say no mo'," I chuckled before continuing, "If you think of anything else, just let me know."

"Okay," she replied as we glared at each other.

While we didn't take our eyes off one another, I thought of how much she had grown. Even though she dabbled in the street life, Tashima excelled in marketing and web designing for five Fortune 500 companies. Three and a half years into my prison bid, I told Tashima that she needed to find a career that would have her bank account sitting nice and lovely. With all the illegal shit that we had going on, we needed another business to clean the money through. Sonica's business and the few homes that we rented out wasn't enough.

Tashima took several career tests before deciding that she would lean towards becoming a marketing agent for Fortune 500 companies and a web designer. At first, I was worried that they wouldn't hire her. Honestly, I thought she would've picked a profession that would be easier to obtain that came with a handsome salaried package.

To my surprise, five years into my bid, Tashima happily told me that she had taken an internship job for a small company in the city, thanks to Sonica's connections. The internship wasn't a paid gig, but she accrued the knowledge that made her one of the most highly sought after business consultant and web designer. I had to admit that her Bachelor's degree in Computer Science was the perfect fit for her.

As far as the marketing side of things, Tashima didn't need any schooling for that. She sold massive quantities of dope with a smile on her face. Her talk game was good as fuck, which made companies eager to pay her under the table for legal and illegal activities. I advised Tashima to stay on the straight path. It was best to keep things nice and simple; she was already up to her neck in drug dealing, and I wasn't due to be released for years to come. The last thing I wanted was for her to get jammed in a blue-collar crime.

Over the years, Tashima became one expensive ass female. No matter the price, her clients always paid what she asked for and praised my girl for doing an outstanding job.

"Why are you looking at me like that?" Tashima blushed.

"Just thankful for you. You are one of the smartest and beautiful women that I know besides Momma. A nigga lucky to have you in his life," I replied as her phone rang.

While looking at her phone, my baby's face and mood changed. Sonica noticed the change as well and asked Tashima was everything okay. She nodded her head without looking at my mother or me; therefore, I knew she was lying. The fuck nigga had to be calling her. I didn't take my eyes off her as she ignored the call. Instantly, I was angry. I thought I made myself clear when I told her that she needed to end things with Dyon, expeditiously.

Growling, I glared at her. She refused to look at me; so, I lowly barked, "Look at me."

Upon doing so, I calmly yet nastily asked, "Why in the fuck didn't you answer the phone? I thought I made myself clear in what I need you to do wit' that damn situation."

"You did, Dominick, but I need more time than that. Shit is chaotic. Dyon's hands are tied into the plug from Texas. I need to wing him off Julio before I dismantle his and my relationship," she voiced in a shaky tone.

With the knowledge of that fuck nigga dealing with my connect from Texas, I growled and shoved back the chair I was sitting in. With a stern facial expression, I asked, "What's the number one rule between us, Tashima?"

"Always be honest with one another."

"So, why in the fuck haven't you been honest wit' me 'bout who took over my Texas connect?"

"I knew it would cause issues."

"How long has that nigga been over that?"

"For eight years."

Placing my eyes on my mother, I asked, "Did you know 'bout this shit?"

Sighing sharply, she nodded her head and said, "Yes."

Shaking my head, I looked at them and said, "Y'all know damn well that I would never give anyone that damn connection. Julio is personal fo' me. He is the reason I stay in the know of a lot of shit. I would've preferred fo' one of y'all too had taken it over. What in the fuck was y'all thinkin' 'bout givin' that motherfuckin' nigga my primary gotdamn plug?"

Before they could open their mouths, I hastily said, "Don't worry 'bout fuckin' respondin'. Don't even worry 'bout me ridin' up outta Atlanta wit' y'all asses. I'll make my damn way back to Alabama."

As I walked off, Tashima loudly called my name. I ignored her while I retrieved my phone to contact Julio. It was time to take my organization back in full throttle. I didn't give a damn who Tashima had her hands on. She did some shit she had no business doing. I was going to fix that shit before I exited the grounds of the expensive restaurant.

Julio Mateo and I were not ordinary working partners. I realized that the very first night that Sonica introduced him to me when I was twelve years old. By my appearance, he knew that I didn't want to be in the game. That night, I opened up to him like I had never done with anyone. While I vented, Julio sat back and listened. When it was his turn to talk, I learned a lot about the five-foot-eleven, fair-skinned, mixed with Black and Mexican blood, exquisitely dressed meth supplier. He never wanted to be in the game as well, but the love he had for his mother was the reason why he decided to step up to the plate and fill his father's shoes. From that night until now, Julio wasn't just my supplier; he was a good friend. From my personal to business life, Julio was there, guiding me in the right direction until I was able to stand on my feet.

There was no way in hell I was going to lose one person that helped me through the hard times for a fuck nigga that wanted my spot. Dyon had to go and fast, and I didn't give a fuck who didn't like it!

They really got me fucked up. They doing som' cross shit. Before a motherfucka cross me out, I'mma X their asses all the way out, I thought as Julio answered the phone.

"I've touched down, an' we need to talk, my man," I breathed in the phone as I tightened my jaws.

CHAPTER THREE

Dyon

"Her phone ringin', but she ain't answerin' it," I told Desaree as I heard Nixon in the background asking her what she wanted to eat.

"Maybe that's a good thing. Hopefully, she's somewhere reflecting on her behavior," Desaree spoke in a hopeful tone.

Shaking my head as I walked through the front door of Tashima and my crib, I said, "Nawl, she ain't reflectin' on her behavior. She on som' mo' shit. Just be careful. I'm finna try to reach out to her again."

"Okay," she replied before we ended the call.

As I opened the refrigerator's door, my cell phone chimed. The chime was familiar; it was specifically set for Julio, one of the sternest connects that Tashima put me on.

Quickly, I answered the phone.

"Dyon, I'm calling to inform you that I will no longer be working with you anymore," his deep voice spoke.

My soul left me as I found myself asking, "Why? What is the problem?"

"Just prefer to deal with Tashima."

With an angry facial expression, I nastily spat, "Yeah."

After I ended the call, a slur of explicit words left my mouth as I dialed her number. I knew damn well that she wasn't that upset with me over my brother's actions that she would cross me the fuck out. I just knew that she wouldn't do any type of hoe shit like that.

As her phone rang, I angrily said, "Answer this fuckin' phone, Tashima!"

She didn't answer, which resulted in me spending half of the night calling her before I decided to send her a lengthy text. I was pissed and hurt. I would've never crossed her out; I didn't see myself doing anything of that nature to her. For her to hit up Julio and make herself number one with him was not the thing to do. What she failed to realize was that we were forever partners in the dope game. I became greedy, and I was used to living with power and money. She was not going to take the bond that I built with Julio; she knew that I was not going for that fuck shit!

Around midnight, I received a call from her.

"So, that's how we playin' now? You just gonna snatch Julio out of my grasp like that?" I asked nastily before tugging on a tightly rolled blunt.

"Dyon, I didn't have a say so in the matter. You know I would never cross you out like that. It wasn't up to me. It was Julio's choice," she replied before sighing.

"What reasons did he say?" I inquired, skeptical of what she was speaking about.

"He didn't give me a reason either. He kept saying that he only wanted to deal with me."

"I bet he did," I quickly replied as I moved my neck from side-to-side before continuing, "Where are you?"

"In Atlanta."

"What are you doing up there?"

"I needed to get far away from my sister and your brother before I did something I had no business doing," she calmly replied.

I called bullshit! Tashima was not a rational thinking female when it came down to Desaree. Thus, I knew that she was up to something.

"You do know that I know you better than that right? So, be one-hunnid wit' me ... what are you up to?" I asked, sitting upright on the sofa.

"I'm drinking and thinking. I have a lot of shit in play right now that need all of my attention," she exhaled.

Not believing her, I asked, "Since Julio dropped me. Who do you have in mind to connect me wit'?"

The line went silent as I overheard crickets and other bugs creating an annoying symphony. Angrily, I shouted, "Tashima, what other connections do you have in mind fo' me?"

"At the moment, I don't. That's why I'm thinking who can I get underneath my thumb so that you can handle your thing."

"Bullshit! You have enough plugs to give me one of them. You have too much on yo' damn plate anyways. Sonica got you runnin' 'round this bitch like you are a damn queenpin. I know you have scoped out som' shit fo' yo'self. Therefore, I know you have scoped out others to place someone else in their path. You have grown into a beautiful, smart hustler. It's time to start crossin' out Sonica an' her bitch ass son. You've earned them enough money. You've grown his organization before turnin' it into yours. Them niggas love, listen, an' respect you. They ain't gonna do that shit fo' him, an' you know it."

"Dyon, I'm not crossing anyone. You know that is not how I roll," she spoke in an agitated tone.

Every time I say something about crossing out Sonica and her son, Tashima turns into a bitch.

"Look, I'm tired of coming second to a nigga that's locked up. You gonna make a fuckin' decision. Either it's me, or it's him. You will not have both," I told her as my heart raced.

I knew that I was doing too much by giving her an ultimatum like that. When she and Desaree had no one, they had Sonica and

Dom Dom. They put her on; they were the reason that she had accomplished so much wealth and respect. Regardless of what they had done for her, it was time for her to let the past be the past.

"I will talk to you when I come home," she spoke coldly.

"An' when will that be?" I asked nastily.

"Whenever I have things figured out," she softly replied in a frustrated timbre.

Pissed, I ended the call. Something had drastically changed. Why it changed? I didn't know, but I knew that I wasn't going to stand for it. She didn't have to make a decision between Dom Dom and me. I was going to make that decision for her. The man in her life was going to be me, and this time, I would not fail in killing the nigga.

With my phone in my hand, I dialed my brother's number. He didn't answer the first call, but the second call he answered in an annoyed timbre. Instantly, I knew what he was doing.

"Damn nigga, most folks wouldn't call back a second time if someone doesn't answer their phone. What in the fuck do you want nih, Dyon?" Nixon spat as I heard the headboard knocking lightly against the wall.

With my eyes locked on a picture of Tashima dressed in an all-black bodysuit, I spat, "I won't keep you long, nigga. I need you to put a ticket over Dom Dom's head. Make sure this time, you don't get a pussy ass nigga to wipe him off the map. I need that nigga to die wit' a dick in his mouth. ASAP."

"A'ight," he replied before saying, "Don't call me back no mo' unless som' shit really 'bout to go down."

"Bet," I confirmed before ending the call.

Placing a pre-rolled blunt to my black lips, I mischievously spat, "That nigga gotta go. Him an' his damn mother got too much power over my guh. Once he's down, then Sonica will be next. That's the only way my baby an' me will have a happily ever after."

CHAPTER FOUR

Tashima

After Dyon rudely ended the call, I didn't see the need to call him back. He was upset, and he had every right to be. Without a doubt, I knew Dom Dom had something to do with Julio wanting to deal with me only. My first love was fucking with shit he had no business doing. I knew Dom Dom felt that I betrayed him by allowing Dyon to take the lead with Julio, but the truth of the matter was, Julio was ready to pull away from Dom Dom's organization. I couldn't allow that to happen. Therefore, I had to have a slick talker on board to keep Julio satisfied and happy. Dyon was the best person to take on Julio. He sold meth quicker than anyone I'd ever had the pleasure of working with.

A set of headlights crept into the driveway, causing me to cease my thoughts. Not worrying about who it was, because I knew exactly who it was, I sat back and waited for the tall, fine bastard to step into my presence. I had some questions for his ass.

Dom Dom took his time getting out of the car. When he finally opened the car door, a trail of thick, white smoke exited behind him. He held his head high as he tugged on the blunt; I focused on the red flame at the end of the blunt.

When he stepped on the porch, he didn't look at me. He was pissed, just like I was. The second Dom Dom placed his hand on the handle of the screen door, I shot out of the comfortable chair, sternly shouting his name.

Not looking at me, he growled, "Don't you ever call my fuckin' name like that. Do you understand me?"

"Fuck that! I will call your name how I see fit. You will not walk in that damn house like you ain't gonna tell me what in the hell you did and why."

Laughing, he slowly turned around, dramatically, glared into my face and said, "I don't have to tell you shit that you already know. I'm sure that you spoke to Julio or at least to Dyon. Julio was supposed to have been under yo' fuckin' control not that fuck nigga Dyon."

"He was going to pull away, Dominick. I had too much on my plate to deal with Julio. The best person I knew that could handle him was Dyon. You were adamant on me being the one to deal with Julio and that product. Well, baby, I couldn't. It took me two weeks just to get rid of it. Whereas, Dyon moved that shit within two days. He was constantly re-upping the order."

"Well, since you couldn't do the one thing I really needed you to handle ... I think it's time fo' you to rest up. Like I said before,

I'm home an' I'mma take the reins in full throttle. Playtime over wit'. Time to get this illegal money," he spoke coldly before stepping into the house, leaving me outside feeling lonely and sad.

Plopping my ass in the chair, I shook my head and thought of the ways that I could've done things differently. After thirty minutes of critically thinking, I didn't see any way that things could've happened. Dom Dom wanted Julio to stay on his team; I did that, but I had to have Dyon to take over. Dom Dom wanted me to grow his organization; I did that. He wanted me to buy land and commercial buildings in different states; I did that shit without any problems. Everything I did, I did it because I loved him, and I wanted what he wanted, minus him cutting off Dyon. I didn't like that shit one bit, and I had to let him know that.

Before I left the porch, I dialed Desaree's number. I prayed that she answered. I really needed her advice. After the way I acted towards her about Nixon being her unborn child's father, I wouldn't be surprised if she didn't answer my call.

When the automated voicemail talked in my ear, I ended the call and shook my head and thought, *Now, I don't have anyone to talk to about this damn triangle I'm in. What the fuck!*

Sighing sharply, I stood and said, "Let me go poke the damn hornet's nest."

As I sashayed in the house, I heard Reggae music playing from the back porch as Dom Dom lit four of the Tiki torches that were a few inches away from the back porch's foundation. I was not a fan of Reggae music; however, I liked the beat and flow of the unknown artist creativity. When I stepped onto the porch, Dom Dom briefly looked at me before looking away and tugging on the blunt that sat in between his thick, juicy lips.

"So, you ain't got nothing to say to me?" I asked, walking towards him.

"Come suck and fuck me, I might say something to you then," he nastily replied, taking a seat in the black lounge chair.

Taken aback at his attitude, I was aroused, upset, and confused. As I glared at the fucker, I had to evaluate my mental. There shouldn't have been a reason I was turned on by his nasty tone. The way he spoke to me was as if I was a hoe. Shaking my head, I chuckled at the thought of putting a gun to his head and cursing him the fuck out. That shit would equal a disaster; one that I wasn't up for—one that would forever fuck us up. Since I couldn't shoot him; I decided that I was going to Mortal Kombat his dick with my mouth, first. I wasn't going to leave an inch of it not sucked or licked on. It was going to be my pleasure to finish his ass off with my delightful, fat, and wet pussy that sat in between my thick thighs.

One way or another, that bastard was going to watch his gotdamn mouth when he talked to me. I demanded respect from everyone else, and Dominick Rodgers was no fucking different.

"So, that's what you want, huh?" I spoke while nodding my head as I seductively walked towards his fine, ugly self.

"Straight like that," he voiced while eyeing me.

He had no idea that I was going to rock his fucking world and then take my ass back to Montgomery, Alabama to the nigga that held me down for twenty-one damn years. I was not going to put up with Dom Dom's nasty attitude over a simple choice that I knew was best for his illegal business. He had the wrong one fucked up that was for sure!

Standing in front of him, I eyed his great smelling behind as I slowly descended. Nibbling on my bottom lip, I aggressively pulled his stiff dick out of his white gym shorts. His freshly washed body and cologne had me in love with the scent rising off him. While I stroked his dick, we glared into each other's eyes; it was clear what we were feeling. We were angry and horny. We were in love but frustrated.

In need of relieving those negative emotions from our mental and establishing trust again, I looked into his eyes while slowly licking up and down on the head of his mushroom-shaped head before making circles around the small hole on his dick head. His body relaxed as the blunt, which was pressed tightly between his thumb and forefinger, fell on the ground. I giggled, causing him to groan and slid further down the lounge chair. Dom Dom's eyes fluttered at the soft licks that I placed upon his tool. He raised his hands to my face, I knocked them away and slid his dick down the dark tunnel of my throat.

"Fuccckk," he moaned as his legs tensed.

He wanted me to suck and fuck him. Bitch show him who really running shit, I thought as I allowed my wet, hot mouth to destroy the bastard that sat in the chair squirming like a little bitch.

"Baby, shiiii," he moaned as he thrust his dick into my mouth.

All for giving sloppy head, I removed my mouth from his tool, spit on that motherfucker, and gobbled that dick up while fondling his balls. I repeated the nasty actions until I had him acting like I was when he first blessed me with his tongue.

"Oh, my fuckin' God! Why you so damn nasty wit' it?" he loudly groaned.

With his dick in my mouth, I growled, "Shut the fuck up, nigga."

"Oooh shit. It's finna be a ... oohh my Goddd, Tashima," he moaned while pumping into my throat.

With my petite hands wrapped around his tool, I dirt bike the dick; shortly afterward, I began to suck and hum on his sensitive head. He lost it when I slid my mouth from the head towards his balls. One sack and then another was in my mouth. While I jacked his dick, I continued loving on his hairless balls.

"Mane, get the fuck off them thangs like that," he whined, like a pussy bitch.

Sternly looking at him, I shook my head and continued pleasing the rude fucker.

"Tashima, baby, please stop. Shittt, stop," he groaned while trying to move my head and hands from his private area.

"Nawl, boo, you wanted me to suck and fuck you, remember? That was the only way that you were going to talk to me, right?" I nastily spat before spitting on his balls and inhaling them in my mouth.

"Oooh, my motherfuckin' father! On my life, I'mma do som' shit to yo' ass! You can't just be eatin' the dick up like that an—"

His statement was cut short because I quickly and sexily deep throated his tool. I was sick of hearing him talk. I no longer wanted him to speak to me, civilly. I wanted to see his ass at his weakest point, and I had him right where I needed his no manners ass to be—in the palms of my hands, shaking, and teary-eyed.

The second a tear slipped down his face, he spat, "Don't make no fuckin' sense how you on the soles of yo' feet showin' out like this. Got a tear slidin' down my motherfuckin' face, an' I can't gather enough energy to wipe that motherfucka off."

The moment I felt his dick throbbing, I removed my mouth and hands. I glared into his handsome face as his mouth opened and quickly closed. There was nothing that he could say to me at that point. Standing with my head held high, I pulled off the little skimpy, floral dress, and seductively dropped it on the ground. As I moved away from Dom Dom, he weakly asked where I was going. I didn't respond as I took a seat in a lounge chair inches away from him.

With my eyes on the fucker, I slowly placed my feet on the seat of the chair and barked, "Come eat my motherfucking pussy before you stick your tongue in my asshole, nigga."

With bucked eyes, he looked at me as if he was going to say something smart. He never did, which was good on his part. I was going to give him a run for his money. As he ascended from the chair, he glared at me in the sexiest way that had my pussy starving to feel his fingers, mouth, and dick.

Dom Dom and I toyed with each other. When he gave me energy that I didn't like; I inhaled it and spat it back at his ass. If he wanted to play games with me, then I would put the damn controller on two players. I was the best at playing games; hell, I did for twenty-one fucking years!

As he took his time walking towards me, I placed my right leg behind my head, slowly moved my hand towards my pretty, shaved pussy and played in it. He groaned; I giggled. Intrigued by how he was going to react to me playing with myself in person, I toyed with my left titty all the while exploring my hot fortress. It wasn't long before my juices were heard as I lightly cooed and nibbled on my bottom lip.

"Damn, baby, that pussy super wet," he moaned, climbing out of his white T-shirt, boxers, and gym shorts.

My body became hot as I thumbed my clit and fucked my fingers. If Dom Dom thought I was pressed about him taking his time, he was a motherfucking lie. There were plenty of nights that I had to indulge in self-pleasure; I didn't mind getting myself off before the main course of dick took me out of the game, momentarily.

In front of me, Dom Dom dropped to his knees. Before he sucked my fingers away from my pussy, he blew me a kiss and mouthed that he loved me. I didn't reciprocate that energy. I wanted him to feel a little fucked up inside. With my fingers in his mouth, Dom Dom took his time sucking off my sweet juices. He didn't mind groaning as he swallowed my goodness.

One flicker from his tongue and I placed my other leg behind my head. With a devilish look upon his face, Dom Dom smirked before burying his face in between my wet thighs.

I'm sorry. I love you were the words that he wrote on my clit before dipping his tongue in and out of my jewel box, slowly and passionately.

"Dominiiicckk," I whined as I slowly rode his face while my hands traveled towards his strong, bulky shoulders.

As lightning bugs danced around our backyard, so did stars above my head. I was in Dom Dom's Pleasureland, and I didn't want to leave, but I had to. I had to teach him a lesson about talking to me as if I was a nothing ass female. It would be his last time doing it; I could promise myself that. I allowed him to give my body the ultimate pleasure before I shoved his head away from my pussy. A sloppy, nasty tongue kiss ensued as he picked me up and slipped his manhood into my fortress.

"Tashima," he groaned while wrapping his hands around my back.

"Dominick," I moaned as I wrapped my hands around his neck.

Our beautiful, sexual dance had started. It was slow and sweet. How we felt about each other was felt through our love organs and kissing. He didn't miss a spot within my honey pot as my juices didn't miss an inch of his dick and balls. We rocked each other's world as I howled out his name while tears streamed down my face at the same time my pussy exploded on his dick, causing a massive flood to appear on our abdomen regions. He had me wet and shaking like I was in an earthquake.

"I love you, Dominick," I voiced as I gripped the back of his neck.

"I love you the most, Tashima."

He brought my head towards him; I sucked his bottom lip into my mouth. Slowly and with perfect precision, I sucked and licked it. He groaned when I did the same actions to his top lip. Dom Dom was deep inside of me, knocking on a corner that was foreign to me. Instantly, I stuttered his name. A huge grin appeared on his face as he bent to the ground and wore that damn spot out!

"Shitttt! Oh, my Goddd! What ... fuck that, beat this pussy up right now, Dominick Rodgers!"

Laughing, he did just that. My body went limp as I breathlessly called out his entire name, again. The type of dick that he delivered while squatting had me not wanting to teach him a lesson. I wanted to curl up in the bed alongside him as I placed my thumb in my mouth. He was on the verge of knocking my pink walls loose. I had to get my shit together. He didn't breed me to be a weak bitch for nobody; thus, I dug deep inside of me and reciprocated that same energy.

It took me a minute to regain control, but when I did, it was a wrap. He was lying on the concrete porch with his hands behind his head as I rode his beautiful, wet stick. From the top to the bottom of Dom Dom's dick, I swerved my pussy; I went in for the kill the second I began sucking on his neck, which I didn't do for long. Dom Dom didn't like having his neck sucked on.

While riding him cowgirl style, I bounced my ass while popping my pussy on him. I loved the doggy-style position; therefore, I placed my face on the concrete and repeatedly slammed my pussy on his dick all the while clenching and unclenching my pretty kitty. I zoned out and fucked him just like he wanted me too. I didn't know how long I was in the zone, but the second I felt pinches on my ass I looked at Dom Dom whom had a painful expression on his face.

"Guh, get yo' thick ass up!" he loudly spoke, popping my booty cheeks.

With a smirk on my face, I stopped moving.

"Shit! Tashima, hell nawl! Shitt, nawl! You was ridin' the fuck out of yo' dick, but my ass an' back ridin' the shit out of this concrete. Mane, we gotta go in the house. My motherfuckin' body burnin'. All my damn skin on this concrete."

"I'm sorry," I laughed as I slowly lifted off him.

For the life of me, I couldn't stop laughing. I poorly told him to turn around so that I could check out his body. As I glared at his naked behind, I had a smile on my face while admiring Dom Dom's lower back and the top part of ass, which had several scratches not far from the skinless areas.

"Come on so I can put some ointment on it," I laughed as I grabbed his hand.

"You ain't gettin' on me no damn mo'! On my momma, I ain't askin' you to get on me!" he voiced as he shook his head.

Tears streamed down my face as I laughed at Dom Dom's dramatic antics. He fussed from the time we left the back porch until he laid on the bed as I applied antibiotic ointment on the wounded areas.

"I told you to fuck me not rape me. What the fuck was you thinkin' 'bout, Tashima?" he asked as his face was stuffed in a pillow.

"Fucking you," I laughed.

"Mane, that was not fuckin'. I had been tappin' on yo' ass an' sayin' stop repeatedly like a lil' bitch ass nigga. You kept going an' going. I ain't gon' lie like that pussy wasn't bitin' an' feelin' good but gotdamn it that concrete bit harder," he fussed as I rolled over and howled out in laughter.

Ring. Ring. Ring.

His phone rang, and he poorly reached to grab it.

"So, we done?"

"Hell nawl, we ain't done, but you ain't gettin' on me no fuckin' mo. I mean that shit, Tashima," he stated before answering his phone, which he placed on speaker.

"I'm surprised y'all answer. Thought y'all would be making up by now," Sonica chuckled.

I was still laughing as Dom Dom ignorant ass said, "Hell nawl, had to cut that shit off. Damn guh done fucked the skin off my back an' ass."

"What? How? You know what, I don't even want to know. Y'all have a goodnight. Call me in the morning," Sonica hysterically laughed before ending the call.

Dom Dom rolled over and glared into my face. I didn't want to continue laughing at him, so my face and his dick had a meeting. I needed to put us back on the road of Pleasureland. While he laid on his side, I took his dick on a lovely, wet roller coaster ride. It wasn't long before he was deep inside of my pretty kitty. My feet were on his shoulders, and my mouth was drier than a severely dehydrated person's lips. Soft kisses graced every inch of my face and neck as Dom Dom sweetly made love to me.

Rubbing his head, I whispered, "I never meant to undermine you. I would never go against your wishes, but as the head honcho, at that time, of your organization, I had to make a business call that would benefit us. Everything I did, it was for us. Forgive me for not having another person to handle Julio."

Looking into my eyes, he softly replied, "I forgive you, baby. I 'preciate everythang you did fo' me ... us. You conquered shit at an early age. Half of the time, you pushed me to do better, be better. I can't hold a grudge or be angry wit' you fo' makin' a boss decision. But I can be pissed at the fact that you ain't broke shit off wit' that nigga yet."

Here we go wit' this shit, again, I thought as Dom Dom pinned my legs behind my head and wore my coochie out while damn near biting off my neck.

Angrily, I said, "Now gotdamn it, Dominick, suck on my neck don't bite the bitch off!"

"Keep testin' me like I don't want you all to myself, an' I'mma do somethin' way worse to yo' ass," he growled in my ear while placing his hand around my neck.

"Ooou," I cooed as my pussy became wetter than a public pool.

"I love you, an' I'll go to the extreme to make sure that you belong to me an' only me. Understand?" he spoke while sensually clawing my pretty kitty.

"Yesss," I whined as he tightened the grip around my neck while evilly gazing into my eyes.

"You an' me were meant to be the thugs of the streets … not you an' that nigga. Do you know how I felt when motherfuckas told me how you an' him were doing it up in the streets? Them bitches had the nerves to pronounce you an' him Mr. an' Mrs. Thug. That fuckin' title was supposed to have been fo' me an' you. An' you an' me only," he angrily growled in my ear while delivering me the devil dick.

My air supply was getting a little too short for my likening. Immediately, my pussy went dry. I was no longer turned on; I was fucking scared. I tried to remain calm, but a sister couldn't breathe. Frantically, I began to remove his hand from around my neck. I wasn't successful. As he fucked the dear life out of me, Dom Dom spoke the very words that I was afraid he was going to say.

"I want you to kill that nigga. Let me know its motherfuckin' real."

When he removed his hands from around my neck, I gasped for air and shoved him off me. I hopped out of bed and ran towards the back porch. I had to get away from him; he had lost his damn mind. There was no way in hell I was going to stay in that house with him after what he did and said to me. I would've been a fool.

Busting through the screen door, I was shaking as I retrieved my dress and quickly placed it over my head. When I turned around a naked, terrifying Dom Dom was leaning against the door while aggressively biting on his bottom lip. Rapidly, I moved out of his way without looking at him.

"Where in the fuck are you going? We ain't done," he spoke as I tried to step inside of the house.

Right then, I knew that he was beyond upset. He was furious, and I was not going to be subjected to his shit for the rest of the night.

"To handle what you commanded of me," I weakly spoke as he forced me to look at him.

"You ain't gon' do shit because you in love wit' that nigga," he shot back, shoving me against the door.

I remained silent as my body shook from fear.

"See no lies I told, huh?" he questioned seductively licking his lips.

"No," I heard myself say as I watched his hands.

"Do you even love me? Or you just love the way I fuck an' eat you?" he questioned, balling his mouth.

"Dominick, you know I love you. You've been known this shit. I hadn't had you in between my legs in twenty-one years. So, you know it's pure, unconditionally love that I have for you," I honestly voiced while glaring into his emotionless eyes.

"How in the hell can you love me an' that nigga?" he questioned with a puzzled expression on his face.

"Easily," I quickly replied before continuing, "You were my very first love. The one that taught me a lot about the streets. Took me in when I didn't trust a soul. Hell, I barely trusted you. I fell for a hustler that gave zero fucks about other's feelings. I fell for the nigga that would break his damn neck, making it back to me when he had to pick up money. I fell for the nigga that shaved my hairy pussy without a care in the world. I fell for the nigga that loved my sister as if she was his little sister. I fell for the nigga that had my back when I felt like crawling into a dark hole. I would never lose my love for you no matter what nigga came in and stepped into shoes that he could never fill like that motherfucker the took my virginity, soul, heart, mind, and never had any intentions of giving it back. I fell for Dyon because he was a business partner with good working ethics. I fell for his genuine touch when I was sad about you not being free. I fell for his sincere words when he told me that everything would be okay, and he had no damn idea that the reason I was crying myself to sleep or wanted to be alone was because I missed the hell out of you. I fell for the nigga that held me tightly when I feared that something would happen to you while you were in prison. I'm sorry, Dominick, but the truth of the matter, I love y'all in ways you could never imagine. Y'all have different qualities that make me love y'all differently. You get all of me; whereas, he doesn't. I don't love him more than you. Obviously, because I'm here with you. You can't ask me to kill someone that I love and think that I will do it. I'm sorry, Dominick, I can't kill him because I love him too much."

    The snarl that escaped his mouth frightened me so badly that I didn't stop shaking, nor did I take my eyes off him.

"If he demanded that you kill me, what would your response be?" he asked.

"The same thing I just told you," I voiced in a shaky timbre.

Sighing heavily, Dom Dom looked at me, shook his head, and said, "Mane, I'mma release you. I ain't wit' that back an' forth shit, an' I sure as hell ain't wit' that sharin' shit. Not wit' my main dame. Gone back to Alabama an' be wit' that nigga. You ain't gotta worry 'bout me callin' an' textin' you no mo'. Don't touch no money out of our joint bank accounts. I'll have yo' name removed off it an' give you half of the bread that's in it. As far as the buildings that you got in yo' name, whatever you see fit to do … then do that shit. The connects that you accrued, whatever you wanna do … do that shit. If you decide to keep movin' illegally, just know that yo' name won't be tied to my organization. Get yo' own. If you ever get in a jam an' need my help, call Momma. She'll reach out to me, an' I'll help you out that jam through her. No need in me sayin' the words you are used to hearin'. You know how I feel 'bout you."

Dom Dom left me at that damn screen door feeling lost and weak as several tears escaped my eyes. My soul was gone. My head was heavy. My shoulders were low to the ground as I held my head high. I couldn't undo his words and the pain that soared through my body. I didn't know what to say to make him recant his words; I didn't give a fuck about the properties or the money in our joint accounts. All I cared about was losing the main motherfucker that I loved with every fiber in me.

When I finally moved inside of the house, my heart dropped to my ass the second I saw him fully dressed with keys and phone in his hand. I wanted to call out his name, but my voice box didn't work. I tried to move from the oval, glass kitchen table, but my damn legs wouldn't budge. My nerves were shot; they weren't working at all. The moment he opened the door, I held my breath.

He lowered his head and slightly turned it to the right and said, "I needed you to be my wife. The mother of my kids. I needed you to be by my side like you'd always been. Most importantly, I needed to be wit' you because I made a promise to myself that I was never going to miss a single fuckin' day of being in yo' presence 'til the day the Lord took me from this earth."

After he turned the lock on the door, Dom Dom walked out. A hellish, hurtful yell escaped my throat as I tore up the kitchen. Glass, dishes, the oven door, you name it was everywhere as pain rippled through my body something awful. Dropping to the floor, I cried and cried and cried until my stomach started to hurt.

My baby can't be done with me. He just can't be, I thought as I stared at the front door, hoping that he would run back inside, pick me up off the floor, and tell me that he was never leaving me like he had promised years ago that he would never do.

When I heard the engine of the car start followed by loud music playing, I laid on the floor as tears slid down my pretty, brown face. Dom Dom was done with me.

CHAPTER FIVE

Dom Dom

Next Day

As I sat in the comfortable seat of the airplane, my mind replayed the scene from last night between Tashima and me. I hated her for telling me the truth about her feelings for Dyon. Truthfully, I rather her lie to me. I didn't want to fathom her loving him; didn't care that her feelings for him were not on the same scale as her feelings for me. I wanted her to love me and me only. It broke my soul to call it quits with her; I made a choice for her since she couldn't do it. That was the last thing that I ever thought that I would do. I loved her with every ounce of blood that flowed through my body. Tashima was a nigga's heartbeat. That woman was the soles to my feet. My baby was the bones of my ribcage. She was my everything, but I refused to share her any longer. I did that shit long enough because I had no choice.

When I closed the door last night, I stood on the porch and listened to her tear up the house as she loudly wailed. She was hurt, badly. I wanted to walk into the house and tell her that I loved her. I wanted to hold her and tell her that I was sorry for calling it quits, but I couldn't. My legs wouldn't allow me to turn around. I was stuck, on that damn porch, hearing her cry her little heart out.

I was angry for putting her in a position to love two men and not being able to let off-brand nigga go. I had already done the worse to her while I was deep inside of her. I didn't mean to choke her until she couldn't breathe. I didn't mean to scare her to the point she hopped out of bed, trembling. I didn't mean to walk behind her and put fear in her heart, further pushing her into Dyon's arms.

Sighing sharply, I wondered what she was doing and thinking. Grabbing my phone off the holster, I unlocked my phone and opened the text message box. After I pressed her phone number into the recipient box, I shook my head and glared at her name. Disappointed, I dropped my phone on my lap. I wasn't going to send her a text. I was going to be firm with my decision of leaving her alone unless she sought after me that she had ended things with Dyon.

I had to get my mind right; I had a five o'clock p.m. meeting with Julio before I was due in Alabama for a meeting with my crew. I gave Momma a specific task of informing those that there would be a meeting at my home at midnight. Of course, she asked several questions as to why Tashima was not hosting the meeting. There had never been any secrets between us, so I told her. I thought she would've felt why I did what I did, but instead, she was furious for me breaking things off with Tashima.

Even though she said the same thing Tashima said, I wasn't hearing that mess. If the situation were reversed, there wouldn't have been any way another bitch would have my heart like that. The broad would've been a fuck thing; she would've moved my dope or whatever I told her to do but my heart, soul, and mind would've been on Tashima, simply put! I guess that was the difference between men and women. Women get caught up in feelings and shit; while men didn't.

"We will be arriving at our destination within fifteen minutes," the flight attendant spoke through the intercom.

Pleased, I was eager to rest before I had to talk with Julio and look at an industrial building that I had seen online for sale. If the meeting with Julio went well, I would be looking into bringing some type of company into his city all the while cleaning my illegal money through the business.

Ding. Ding.

Tapping the screen on my phone, I saw that I had a text message from Julio. Quickly, I opened the text. Within a few seconds, I nodded my head and replied accordingly. He stated that he had engagements that he must attend during our original meeting time and that he had sent two of his men to retrieve me from the airport. I was okay with that; the quicker we handled business, the sooner I was able to move on to other business matters.

Exiting the airplane and claiming my luggage went in a blur; Tashima was on my mind. I wished she was by my side as I dealt with Julio. I would've done some nasty things to her in the airport's bathroom before we made our way to the hotel room. At the thought of doing something naughty in a public place, I had to chuckle to myself. The first time I ate her pussy in the park, it was in the middle of the day, and she damn near lost it. She was looking around nervously and stuttered constantly. It wasn't long before she loved doing grown folks shit in public.

"Long time no see. Welcome back to the free world," Julio's main man, Chiiko, stated from behind me while wiping has hands on a brown napkin.

As we dapped each other up, I replied, ""Thanks, man. It feels good to be back."

"I know it does. How does it feel to place the crown back on your head, man?" he inquired as a group of excited people zipped passed up.

While walking towards the entrance/exit doors, I sighed deeply, briefly looked at Chiiko, and said, "Truth be told, I'm ready, but then again I ain't."

"You'll be back to your normal thuggish self before you know it," he voiced as he pointed towards an all-white, new model Jeep Wrangler.

"No doubt," I voiced as Meno, Julio's second main man, grabbed my luggage.

In a matter of seconds, I was sitting in the front seat as Chiiko and Meno informed me of the latest bullshit that was going on in the dope game. They mentioned some crews that I had dealt with; while the others I didn't know who they were. Apparently, they had some flaw shit going on with the drugs. Of course, snitches were involved. I made sure to pay attention to the main niggas names that they called, Fred Minx and Drano Rock. They were into some shit that had the Feds looking at them and everyone else they were associated with.

When we arrived at Julio's large estate on the northern side of Baytown, he stood in between two large, beautiful pitbulls. Chiiko stopped the truck inches away from Julio; I hopped out with a genuine smile on my face. Within proximity of an old friend, we embraced in a manly hug before dapping. Nothing had changed about Julio other than his somewhat aging face and several streaks of gray hairs that were in the front of his head.

"Damn, Julio, you gettin' old on me, ain't it?" I joked as we ascended the stairs to his large home.

"Hell yeah. These damn kids will do it," he replied, laughing.

"How many do you have now?"

"Ten."

"Gotdamn. No wonder you got gray hair," I replied as I shook my head. There was no damn way I would have ten kids. Shit, three was enough for me.

"And we have a set of twins on the way," he voiced as we stepped across the threshold of the elegant home.

"Dude, when are you going to stop pumpin' babies in Angel's ass?" I asked with a raised eyebrow.

Shaking his head and removing stray hair out of his long, oval-shaped face, he thoughtfully replied, "Hell, it isn't me. She's the one that wants to pop them out left and damn right. I want to have a vasectomy, but she doesn't want to hear that shit."

"Well, hello there, stranger," Angel spoke softly as she waddled into the foyer, holding her swollen belly.

"Hey there, woman. There's no need in me askin' how you've been. Obviously, great," I stated as we embraced in a friendly hug.

"Indeed. Where's Tashima?" she sweetly asked.

"She's in 'Bama."

"Tell her I said hello, and she must be present for the birth of her goddaughters," she smiled while rubbing her belly.

With a shocked facial expression, I said, "Wait a minute. She didn't tell me that y'all decided to make her a godparent."

"She doesn't know. Hell, we decided the second you called me last night. I knew that you guys would be perfect for our daughters," Julio spoke while glaring into my face.

"Wow, now that's an honor, but you do know I don't change diapers, right?" I laughed.

"And neither do I, my friend," Julio chuckled.

"You two are awful," Angel stated before continuing, "Honey, Marina, will bring the drinks shortly."

"Okay," Julio said while popping his wife on her behind.

Moving into the business room, which still looked the same, Julio and I sat down. Before we started discussing the heavy shit, Marina brought the alcohol. Once she closed the door, business was in session. The meeting went well until Julio brought up Dyon. I had a nice amount of liquor in me so I couldn't hide my true feelings for the character.

"He brought in so much money. Why don't you like him?"

"Tashima."

With a frown on his face, he said, "Explain."

I gave him the rundown. As I talked, his body language had me intrigued. There was something that he knew that I didn't, and I was dying to know.

Standing, Julio asked, "Do you want to know some real shit?"

"Always," I replied before gulping down the rest of the clear liquor in the small, crystal glass.

"She doesn't love him like she loves you. When you first introduced Tashima to me, I saw the adoration, love, and admiration in her eyes for you. The way she held your hand, kissed the back of it and kept her eyes on you told me enough about her character and how she felt about and for you. When she introduced me to Dyon, she didn't have those feelings in her eyes for him. She didn't react to him the same way she did to you when Chiiko and Meno took him outside to talk. It was as if she cared but not really. I pulled her to the side and asked her what was between him and her; she told me the truth. She told me that she loved him, but not the way that she loved you. She even went as far as to say that she didn't want Dyon working with me, but he was the best one to sell my product. She had a tough call in making that decision, Dom Dom, but she did it because she knew that you wanted to keep me on the team. You can't fault her for loving someone while deeply in love with you, handling your organization, and being in an illegal game when all hell could break loose, and she would have to take the hit. Loosen the reigns on her neck and understand where she is coming from. You were gone for twenty-one years, man. What you thought she wasn't going to fall for someone that you told her it was cool for her to deal with from the beginning? If you thought that she wasn't going to fall for him, then you must've been using my product."

After hearing what he had to say, I dropped my head and lowly replied, "I called it quits between her an' me."

"What?" he sounded off in a shocked timbre.

Nodding my head, I replied, "Yep. I told her to choose. She couldn't so I made the choice fo' her."

Shaking his head, he seriously said, "That was a stupid ass thing to do. Now, she's free to be in his arm's because you shoved her there. Don't get mad when you see a ring on her finger from him. Remember, you called it off. Remember, you asked for another man to take what *rightfully* belongs to you."

"Julio, I choked her 'til she could barely breathe. I shoved her up against the screen door because I was furious an' angry wit' her. I had never treated her that way. I knew I had to call it quits or something terrible was going to happen, an' that's what I didn't want."

"My brother, my friend, fix that and fast. She's your queen, and you are her king. Tashima knows where home is. Trust, my brother, she knows where home is," Julio spoke sincerely as I nodded my head. Too bad that I didn't know where home was for her.

As I stood, Julio extended his hand and I placed mine into his. While we shook hands, which were an indication that our meeting was over, I asked about the industrial building not far from his home.

"It's up for grabs. I was looking into it, but it's too much work that needs to be done. Damn people want $640,000 for that building. In my eyes, it's going to take more than that to get it up and running."

"Previous owners in severe debt?" I inquired as we walked to the door.

"Yes."

"I think I'll be able to talk them down. I'm going by to look at it. Hopefully, it's what I need."

"What will you turn it into?"

"If I can get the right automobile makers on my team, it will be a manufacturing company," I smiled wickedly.

With huge eyes, Julio said, "In that case, my friend, we might need to look into that building together. Sounds like a great way to clean our money."

"Exactly," I replied before we embraced in another hug and dapped each other up.

"I'll be in touch within four days with directions for the shipment," he stated as four children happily called his name.

"Time to get in daddy mode," he chuckled.

"A'ight. It was nice seein' you, an' have fun wit' the fam."

"Always," he replied as I descended the steps with Chiiko and Meno in front of me.

Once inside of the car, I asked the fellas, "Aye, y'all remember that dude Dyon?"

"Yeah," they replied in unison and in an unpleasant manner.

"Why did y'all say 'yeah' like that?" I chuckled.

"Don't too much care for him. Glad Julio decided to toss him out of his circle," Meno spoke as Chiiko drove off the estate.

"What was wrong wit' him?"

"He seems sneaky. To overprotective over Tashima. Tried to step on her toes by coming out to Texas without her knowing," Meno spoke calmly.

"I didn't like the way he walked or held his head," Chiiko chimed in.

"Meno, what did Tashima do when she found out that he tried to step on her toes?" I inquired curiously. He was telling me something that I didn't know.

"It took everything in her power not to shoot him in his kneecaps. Julio had to stop her from doing it. After she calmed down, which Dyon was excused from the room by that time, Julio told her the best way to punish him was to demote him for three months. She really wanted him out of the loop for good."

"Was that 'round the summertime of last year?" I asked curiously.

"Yep," they replied in unison while nodding their head.

Ah, that's why the money was not at an all-time high.

"You got a solid one on your team, mane. She's just like Angel. A rider. A go-getter. You *need* to put a ring on her finger. So, I can finally say to y'all ... *I Now Pronounce You, Mr. and Mrs. Thug.*

The first time Chiiko and Meno laid their eyes on a timid Tashima, they fell in love with her immediately. The same night, Angel, fell in love with her as well. Angel was pregnant with her fifth child and was having a horrible time with the pregnancy, morning sickness, backaches, etc. Tashima was the one that told her about relaxing remedies and the sound of rain while enjoying a hot, bubble bath. Every night, Julio would call and thank Tashima for the advice. Angel was able to sleep better than she had before. My baby brought peace and warmth to Julio and those close to him. They didn't mind telling me that she was the one for me, which I already knew that.

Chiiko and Meno took me to the abandoned building. As Julio had said, there would be more money tired into bringing the building to life. Not only did the building needed work so did the parking lot and the areas torn up cement behind the building. The light posts and security guard stand needed severe building structure.

While I glared at the property, I envisioned it being a successful manufacturing company. The land that the building sat on was massive. If I wanted, I could add more to the company. There was no doubt in my mind that I was going to purchase it. However, I didn't want it in my name. The only person that could buy property without a problem was Tashima, and I wasn't going to involve her. The next best person was my mother.

When I arrived at the hotel and had gotten comfortable, I received a text message from Tashima. With a racing and pleading heart along with sweaty palms, I opened her text message. I was disappointed in what I read; to the point, I had to reread it again.

I have spoken with Ivan and Catalina. They are eager to meet you. I have attached their numbers to this message. Call them at your earliest convenience.

Her message was clear-cut; she was done with the streets. I felt some type of way. She was supposed to have been my queen while I was the king of the streets. How was I supposed to respond to her statement? Simple. I sent her a 'okay' text. It was apparent that I wasn't who she wanted; regardless if I broke things off.

In need of seeing my mother soon as I touched down in Alabama, I called her. On the fourth ring, she answered the phone.

"Hey Captain Asshole, what do you want?" she asked smartly.

Ignoring her tone and greeting, I said, "I need you to pick me up from the airport in Montgomery at ten."

"Okay. Anything else?"

"Yeah, but I'll talk to you 'bout it when I get wit' you."

"Okay," she quickly stated.

With a raised eyebrow, I asked, "Why are you tryin' to get me off the phone?"

"Because I'm partaking in grown folks business and you are messing that up, Son."

"Who you doing the nasty wit', Momma?" I laughed.

That woman hung up the phone, causing me to burst out laughing. It was short-lived as Tashima was on my mind.

Hopping away from the bed, with my phone in my hand, I dialed her number. I had so much that I wanted to say to her, but my pride got the best of me. By the first ring, I ended the call and powered off my phone.

"Shit, I said all that I needed to say. If she wants me like she say she do, then she will have to make the first move," I voiced as I stripped out of my clothes.

CHAPTER SIX

Tashima

While I sadly sat at my sister's kitchen table, I decided that it was best for me to leave the dope game. The only problem I was going to be telling Dyon that I was no longer moving illegally. He was going to be pissed, but if he did what his sneaky ass tried to do with Julio last year, he had a few ducks in his back pocket.

Within a matter of seconds, I reached out to Catalina and Ivan; I spoke highly of Dom Dom, and they welcomed him warmly. Shortly afterward, I informed Dom Dom about Catalina and Ivan. A part of me hoped that the would recant his words from last night, but another part knew that he wouldn't.

As I stared at the 'okay' text from Dom Dom, my heart ached, and I didn't know what to do other than place my phone down and talk to Desaree about my feelings.

"So, what are you going to do?" Desaree inquired after I spilled my soul to her.

"I have no idea, but you know how I feel about Dom Dom. Those feelings I can't get rid of," I sighed as I placed my head on her tan and beige marbled, square table.

"Do you even want to get rid of those feelings for him?" she probed, biting her turkey bacon sandwich all the while glaring into my eyes.

"Desaree, even if I wanted too they wouldn't budge. That man has my heart like none other."

TN Jones

"Well, you can't have both. They hate each other with a passion because they want you to themselves. Dom Dom called it quits between the two of you, so you are free to be with Dyon."

"That's the damn problem. I don't want to be free of either of them. I want to be with whomever, whenever, and wherever. I don't want to be tied down to just one of them. They kept me going. I need them as I'd always had them, but of course with Dom Dom free," I whined as if I was a little girl.

Laughing, she asked, "And you came here hoping that I was going to tell you how you were going to have them without an issue, successfully?"

"Yesss," I spoke, not looking at her.

"Well, sis, I can't help you there. You know I'm in love with one person and one person only. My baby zaddy," she squealed, causing me to look at her.

"Um about that, I'm sorry for blowing up and causing you to panic. Will you forgive me?" I sincerely said.

"Of course. So, that means Nixon and I can be in public together without you killing him?" she asked, earnestly.

Nodding my head, I replied, "Yeah."

"So, you finally came to your senses?"

"Not really. It only took for my mind to become boggled with men shit for me not to be giving a damn about you and Nixon. At this point, my situation is bigger than yours. Just don't come whining and crying to me when you find out what he's capable of."

Rolling her medium-beaded, brown eyes, she sighed and said, "He will never do any of those things to me."

"Okay," I replied as her phone and doorbell chimed.

"I'll get the door," I voiced as she answered her phone.

As she chatted on the phone, I sauntered towards the door with my mind in a million places. When I opened the front door, I wasn't expecting to stare into Dyon's fine ass face while Nixon stood behind him, awkwardly glaring at me. Stepping to the side, I couldn't take my eyes off Dyon. So many emotions flooded me until it wasn't funny.

The second Nixon waltzed in between Dyon and me, I grabbed his wrist and said, "I'm sorry for overreacting. Just please do right by my sister and y'all's baby. If you don't, then there will be hell to pay."

With a huge grin on his face, he said, "You ain't gotta tell me that, sis. I got mine over here."

Nodding my head with a pleasant facial expression, I spat, "You better."

As Dyon and I watched Nixon walk into the kitchen with a yapping Desaree, he pulled me close to him and wrapped his arms around my waist while placing a kiss on my forehead. Breathing deeply, I inhaled his masculine scent mixed in with his signature cologne. The smell of him, me being in his arms, and his steady breaths against my forehead caused me to purr after I deeply exhaled.

"You enjoyed yo' time to yo'self?" he inquired, looking down at me.

Nodding my head, I had to lie. "Yeah. Got a lot of thinking done."

"Have you squared away the issue wit' Julio? Or do you have another connect in mind?"

"I don't want any dealings with the illegal world anymore. I'm going to put all of my focus on creating websites and marketing strategies for my clients. Also, I'll dibble and dabble in real estate," I softly replied as I gazed into his eyes.

Dyon's eyes narrowed as his jaws tightened. He was pissed; he was eager for the streets to be under his control. He loved the little power that he had; he wanted to be the best damn thug that the city and surrounding cities had ever seen. He wanted to be the man.

"Why are you done all of a sudden?"

"I don't want this lifestyle anymore. Hell, I never did. I did what I had to do because Dom Dom asked me to take over while he was locked up."

"So, who takin' over now? Sonica?" Dyon inquired with piercing eyes, damn near planting a hole in my face.

"Dom Dom's taking it over."

"How?" he asked growling.

"He's out."

"How long have you known he's been out?" he spoke through clenched teeth.

"Since he touched down, which ain't long," I heard myself say as Dyon sighed sharply before shaking his head.

"You been wit' the nigga?" he voiced angrily.

Looking into his dark, cold eyes, I asked, "What do you mean, been with him?"

Through clenched teeth, he replied, "You know exactly what the fuck I mean, Tashima. Did you fuck the nigga?"

I didn't open my mouth as I glared into Dyon's face.

"Answer me, damn it!" he yelled, gently pushing me against the wall.

"Some of the time we fucked, the others we made love, and then some of the time we sexed," I replied as I didn't take my eyes off him as my heart rapidly beat.

"Wit' or without a condom?"

"Without."

"Was you in Atlanta by yo'self, or was you up there wit' him?"

"With him and Sonica."

"So you being in a room by yo'self was a lie?"

"Not necessarily."

"Explain that shit."

I couldn't start at the middle of the bullshit, but I sure as hell wasn't going to start with Dom Dom showing up at our home; thus, I lied and said that he had called me and told me that he was out and took the story from there. I kept out the part where Dom Dom wanted me to break things off with Dyon and commanded that I kill Dyon. The less I said on that matter; the better things would be for them.

"Tashima, you going to choose. It's either me or it's him. You will not have both of us," Dyon sounded off.

"I'm not choosing, Dyon. Dom Dom broke things off because I told him the same thing you are demanding me to do."

There wasn't a sound that escaped his mouth as he gazed into my eyes. I knew a thousand things were flowing through his mind; if I were him, thoughts would be flowing through mine as well. After an eerie silence between us, Dyon walked towards the front door.

"Dyon," I called out, weakly.

"What?" he stated, not turning around to look at me.

"Talk to me. Tell me how you are feeling."

"I'm feelin' fucked up inside, Tashima. If he hadn't cut things off between y'all, you would be right underneath the nigga before crawlin' to me. I love yo' ass. I have always loved you, but I ain't finna come second to another nigga. Before you come back to our home, you need to make sure that nigga is out of yo' system. Understood?"

He didn't give me time to respond before he walked out of the door. Slumping against the wall, I couldn't believe how things were turning out for me. The two niggas that I loved with all of my heart had me at a crossroads that I never thought I would have to walk across, so soon that was. While I was against the wall, in utter disbelief, Nixon and Desaree called my name.

"Huh?" I replied weakly as I looked at them.

"You alright?" Desaree asked, walking towards me.

"Um, not really, but I'm going to head up outta here. Call me if you need me," I told her as I didn't look into her eyes.

In need of grabbing my purse and keys, I bypassed my sister and Nixon. Desaree exhaled sharply before saying, "Things will work itself out. You know this. Try not to dwell on the situation."

"Okay," I lied as we hugged each other.

After I waltzed out of my sister's home, I felt myself melting. I was a mess through and through. I needed my niggas, and I needed them now. The way I felt I couldn't be with one and not yearn for the other. Oh, how I wished that they would get on board with me needing and loving on them. Why did I have to be the oddball that fell in love with two niggas that would move Heaven and Hell for me as I for them? Why I had to be the one to feel great pain by the situation I was placed in?

As I sat in the front seat of my car, thinking about Dom Dom and Dyon, my cell phone rang. Staring at the screen, I wondered what Julio wanted. Quickly, I answered the phone. After the pleasantries kicked off, Julio jumped straight into why he called.

"Dom Dom was out here briefly. He's disturbed, Tashima. He misses you. I don't know how y'all are going to fix y'all relationship, but it needs to be fixed," he spoke in sincerely.

"Things are out of my control at this point. I said what I had to say, and I'm sticking to how I feel Julio. I'm not complete without them … together."

"You can't have your cake and eat it too."

"I know, but some kind of way I have too. I'm not complete unless I have both of them on one accord like before."

"Now, you know that shit isn't going to go that way."

As I placed the key in the ignition, I rolled my eyes and spat, "If niggas can have two females on one accord, I know like hell I can. It's all about patience and the right timing to have everyone on board."

When the last comment left my mouth, a smile spread across my face. I knew exactly how I was going to have them on my team without anyone saying a damn thing about the other. I was going to make them niggas miss me. Let them see me on my G-shit, doing lovely, and not sweating under pressure; that was sure to bring them to one accord. After all, those niggas loved the way I moved in the streets. That was the only way I was going to have them. It was stupid of me to make an irrational decision like that to begin with. Knowing that I had to fix my fuck up, I had to end the call between Julio and me.

"Is it okay if I call you back?" I asked, interrupting Julio.

"Make sure you do so. Angel and I have some wonderful news to tell you. It's apparent that Dom Dom didn't tell you."

Not giving a damn about the news that Angel and he had to tell me, I rapidly replied, "I will most definitely call y'all back. Muah."

Quickly, I dialed Catalina's number. On the third ring, she answered the phone. I gave her a pathetic lie as to why I wanted out, but needed to be back in the game. Without any problems, she welcomed me back on board. After I got off the phone with her, I ringed Ivan's line. I thought my conversation with him would be easy; it was not. That old Russian bastard gave me great hell before saying that he would allow me back into his circle. Grateful, I thanked him several times before our call was over.

With the most important calls made, I dialed Dom Dom's number. To set shit in motion, I had to tell him one thing that would get his juices pumping.

"Hello," he sexily answered.

"I recant what I said about not wanting the illegal life. I still want in if you are willing to have me on your team," I told him as I reversed my whip.

"I never wanted you to stop doing you. So, you know it's no problem fo' you hustlin' wit' me," he breathed in the phone as if he was smoking.

"Okay. That's all that I wanted to say," I rushed into the phone while driving away from my sister's home.

"Tashima," he said.

"Yes."

He didn't say anything right away; thus, I repeated myself.

"Nevermind," he sighed sharply.

"Are you sure you don't have anything to tell me?"

"Nawl, I don't. I'm sure you will give me the rundown on how you want to hustle. So, I'll be waitin' on that phone call or visit."

"All right." I wanted to stay on the phone and talk to him; matter of fact, I wanted to pull up on his ass, but I didn't know where he was. Plus, I had to play a role of not missing either of their asses.

After I cleared my throat, I politely and professionally ended the call. The next phone call was going to take a lot of energy from me. I was sure that Dyon was going to bitch and gripe about me having sex with Dom Dom, and I had one safe way to play it.

When I called his phone, he didn't answer. Therefore, I called again, which he answered. In the background, I heard some noises that piqued my interest and had my heart racing while I gripped the steering wheel.

"Yeah," he voiced in the phone as a broad moaned.

"What in the fuck are you doing?" I asked, trying not to get mad.

"What you think I'm doing, Tashima? I'm gettin' my dick sucked before I fuck," he nastily spoke before laughing.

It took everything in me not to go the fuck off. I had to put myself in his shoes before replying, "Make sure the bitch jiggle them balls like I do. Make sure the bitch suck on the head slow while looking into your eyes like I do. Oh, and please make sure the bitch hold your nuts like I do when you about to nut, nigga. And one more motherfucking thing, the bitch can't have your damn soul because I been took that before we turned seventeen. Have fun, love."

Ending that call, I growled as I felt all types of emotions flood me. I didn't want either of them fucking with anyone but me. However, I was going to allow them to have their little fun, but I was going to bring some hell their way every time they fucking saw me, and that was on my life! There wasn't going to be a bitch in the city that thought they were happily going to have Dom Dom or Dyon without feeling the pressure that I applied!

As I hopped on the interstate, aiming for an apartment that neither of the fellas knew about, I zoomed past cars all the while optimistically saying, "These niggas think I'm playing with their asses. Within three months, they going to be on board with me loving on both of their asses. Within a damn year, we all going to be living in one gotdamn house! Ain't no more fucking playing, hiding and seeking, or none of that shit! I said what I said. I feel the way I feel, and nobody going to tell me what I should, could, or ain't going to do. I'mma have Dominick Rodgers and Dyon Jackson all to my motherfucking self, and they gonna love me even harder, together!"

CHAPTER SEVEN

Dyon

It broke my heart to be with a skeezer that didn't mean me any good. A trick that wasn't shit compared to Tashima; however, I had to step inside of some new pussy and mouth and do me for a while. Tashima's mind was not where I thought it would be after twenty-one years of us being together.

I was super pissed that Dom Dom was out on the streets and had laid with my woman. She blatantly cheated on me with a nigga that she hadn't touched in years. Yeah, I had to show her how it felt for someone that she loved and cared about to give her that same treatment.

So, I didn't mind telling her what I had going on. What I didn't expect was her response. I wanted her to be angry and go off, but instead, she welcomed the shit with slick facts. When I ended the call, I had to laugh because I saw no lies told when Tashima said that she had already taken my soul.

"Is everything okay?" Knoxxy inquired as she removed her mouth off my dick.

"Yeah, bend over," I demanded as I placed a condom on my hardened tool.

After she did what I commanded, I didn't waste any time sticking my dick inside of her wet hole. While I beat her back loose, I was thinking about Tashima and the things that she probably did with Dom Dom. Immediately, I took my frustrations out on Knoxxy's tight, little pussy all because of Tashima's antics with Dom Dom.

As she squeezed the red bed covers, Knoxxy had a poor arch in her back, painfully moaned, and constantly ran from my dick. Those were clear indications that she wasn't being pleased but hurting. Yet, the broad didn't say shit. Little chick had a thing for me, which was dumb on her behalf.

The entire time I fucked Knoxxy, Tashima was on my mind. I hated her for having me behind a bitch, pulling her hair, and dogging her pussy out as if she was a regular thot ass bitch in the streets. Feeling sick at my actions, I rushed my nut out of balls into the condom. As I removed myself from Knoxxy, I shook my head at the ditzy broad and myself before skipping into the bathroom.

She was on my heels, asking me what was wrong. I didn't answer her because she knew exactly what was wrong with me.

Closing the door in her face, I didn't feel any type of way, and I didn't give a damn if she did. I made myself clear years ago that I wasn't stun no other female, and I meant what I said.

After I cleaned my dick, I walked out of the bathroom. On the bed, Knoxxy was sad as she looked at the ground and toyed with her fingernails.

"Aye, I'm finna go," I said nonchalantly.

"Okay."

Walking off, I shook my head at the broad. Before I made it to her front door, she yelled, "Tashima will never love you like I do, Dyon!"

"Because she loves me mo' than you do," I shot back, opening the door.

"If that's so, then why were you up in me?" she asked, stomping out of her room.

"Because I needed to make her mad," I replied before walking out of the door.

"Mark my words, you gonna regret how you just did me," she sobbed.

"Mark my words, ask me do I give a fuck?" I laughed as I unlocked the doors on my car.

Once I hopped in my whip, my cellphone started to ring. I hoped that it was Tashima. I needed to hear her curse me out for what she heard when I answered my phone. When I looked at my screen, I was disappointed. It was Nixon. Quickly, I answered the call.

"What up?" I asked, placing the keys in the ignition.

"Mane, that nigga Dom Dom been out."

"I know."

"How?" he inquired as I reversed out of Knoxxy's driveway.

"Tashima told me."

An eerie silence overcame the phone before my brother said, "Is he the reason that she ain't stun 'bout me an' Desaree?"

"Yep."

"Did she say that?"

"Nope, but you an' I know how crazy Tashima is 'bout Desaree. The only person that could deter her mind like that is that nigga."

"You don't sound right. Are you an' Tashima good?" he probed while I made a right turn out of Knoxxy's quiet, majority White-persons neighborhood.

"I don't know. I know one thing Julio ain't the plug on the Ice tip no mo'. I gotta find another one that has excellent product an' the price isn't too steep."

"What happened wit' Julio?" Nixon inquired curiously.

"The nigga said he didn't want to work wit' me no mo'. So, I'm assumin' that nigga Dom Dom cut me out. I know Tashima wouldn't do that since I was the best one to sell that shit within two to four days."

"Mane, what's really going on?"

"Honestly, Nixon, I have no idea, but I ain't finna lose my guh to a nigga that been locked down fo' a long time. Ain't no way she finna be laid up wit' that nigga after I helped her solidify his organization. I'm finna take that nigga shit an' his life. I got used to the lifestyle an' I'mma continue it. We got a whole Momma that needs our care."

"Speakin' of Momma, we need to go check on her an' Auntie Mesha."

"A'ight. We can make moves today. I wanna talk to her doctor anyways."

Four years ago, Momma and Auntie Mesha were in a horrible accident. Six people died that day. Auntie Mesha walked away with a few scratches, a couple of broken ribs, a fractured leg and arm. Whereas, Momma barely made it; when they finally stabilized her, the doctors told us that she was paralyzed from the neck down.

"Nawl, not today. I was thinkin' mo' like within the next two days. Desaree will be off vacation by then. I'm trynna grease the shit out of our baby's non-existent scalp." He laughed.

With a smile on my face, I replied, "Boy, you so stupid. On the real, I don't know if I have told you or not, but congratulations.

I'm ready to be an uncle. Shid, truth be told, when I'm done being mad at Tashima, I'mma ask her to come off them birth control pills. I'm ready to start a family wit' her ass."

"Do you think she going to come off them?"

"Since that nigga out an' I know she gon' end up fuckin' him again, I highly doubt it."

"Wait! Run that shit back, bruh!" Nixon yelled in a shocked timbre.

"You heard me. Why you think I left Desaree's crib without sayin' goodbye? Tashima had a lot of shit to say, an' I promise you I wanted to knock her damn head off."

"Mane, she told you that she slept wit' dude?"

"Yep."

"An' you didn't tear the top off her head?"

"Hell nawl. We probably would've killed each other."

"That is a deadly situation, Dyon. You really gonna go up against Dom Dom 'bout Tashima? Mane, they got history. Y'all got history too, but y'all's are different than theirs."

"I love Tashima. I have always loved her. Like I told you before, I confessed my feelin's to Tashima when we were younger. Way before she started fuckin' 'round wit' Dom Dom."

"Bruh, I don't want to see you fucked up behind a female. Don't get me wrong, I love Tashima to death, but is she really worth that type of battle?"

Clearing my throat, I nodded my head and said, "Hell yeah, she worth the battle. I know that nigga want to deaden me. If he asked or commanded fo' her to leave me alone, I promise you she told him no just like she told me no 'bout cuttin' him loose."

"Now, wait a gotdamn minute. You told her to cut dude loose an' she told you no?" he questioned, not sure if he heard me correctly.

"Yep," I replied, nodding my head as if he could see me.

"Bruhh, you need to gon' head an' leave her alone. This shit finna be trippy an' chaotic. She gonna be fuckin' wit' you an' that nigga at the same time."

"Fo' a lil' while she probably will be, but I'm finna get that nigga off the streets into a casket real soon."

"An' you think she will be cool wit' that shit? If you do that an' she suspects or finds out that you did it, then you really ain't gon' have her," my brother stated calmly.

"It's only two niggas that got her heart. If one of us is dead, she will be wit' the other. Now, that's known facts."

"Bruh, where you at? I need to talk som' sense into you ASAP."

"I'm finna pull up at the house," I told him as I turned onto the street that I lived on.

"I'mma be there in thirty minutes. I really gotta make you see what type of road you finna go down 'bout a female that has made it clear that she wants both of y'all. So many people will get hurt behind that shit. It may be the one person that both of y'all want, Tashima."

Hearing what my brother had to say didn't move me. There was no way in hell Tashima would get hurt, physically, by me blowing Dom Dom's head off like he did Knox's. Tashima was going to be safe. When I dropped them bullets off in Dom Dom, I was going to make sure that she was in the bed sleep.

"Tashima will be fine, but as far as Dom Dom ... he won't be. I can promise you that," I stated as I saw Tashima's car in the yard.

My heart skipped a beat as I sighed heavily. I thought she wouldn't be at the crib. Rapidly, I told Nixon that I was calm and that he didn't have to come over. He insisted, but I sternly told him that I was okay because Tashima was home. Not liking what I said, Nixon didn't waste time telling me that he needed to re-up. I knew that he was lying, but I told him to come over. My foolish brother knew I couldn't tell him 'no' about coming over to get more drugs.

Pulling into the driveway, I ended the call with my brother and shoved my phone into the sturdy, black holster. Without a moment's hesitation, I shut off the engine before removing the key from the ignition. Even though I was eager to get into the house, I took my time as I held my head high with a sneaky look on my face. I was ready for her to pop off at the mouth so that I could have a reason to go off. I wanted her to see how badly she hurt me by telling me that she fucked the nigga and that she wasn't going to stop dealing with him.

From the door, I heard the radio blasting Lil' Jon & the East Side Boyz song *Nothins Free*. Shaking my head, a smile spread across my face. Tashima was in one of her moods, so I was going to be well entertained as she tried to keep calm. She would play certain songs; throwing out hints that she was upset.

Falling in sync with the beat, I bobbed my head as I stuck the key into the doorknob. As I opened the door, the aroma of bell peppers, onions, and seasonings from the kitchen smelled heavenly. Instantly, my stomach growled. Between Sonica, my momma, and those damn cooking channels, Tashima could throw down in the kitchen. She would put some old school grandmothers to shame. Every holiday, Tashima was over the meals. She was a goddess in the kitchen; like she was in the bedroom and the streets.

As I strolled into the exquisitely designed eating area, my eyes caught a sight that astounded me. Tashima was wearing a purple, snap in the seat, lingerie outfit and purple open-toe heels. In her ears were gold hoop earrings. A gold, swivel-like ring was secured in the middle of her right nostril. A custom 'Queen T,' gold, diamond-encrusted necklace was around her neck as the matching bracelet was on her left ankle. Her sexy ass was oiled up to perfection. Her chocolaty, smooth skin glossed as the bright wattage light bulb from the short chandelier shined down on her as if she was an angel.

Her back was facing me; she had no idea that I was watching her. While she cut the onions into long, thin slivers, Tashima seductively moved her body. Pulling out the barstool, I placed my gun and keys on the table and continued watching the woman who was going to bear my children and take my last name. As I watched Tashima do her thing in the kitchen, my dick began to brick up. I wanted to bend her ass over and destroy the one place that I loved being in.

Grabbing the remote control for the radio, Tashima pressed the down button for the volume. Not turning around to look at me, she asked, "How long have you been here?"

"Not long," I replied.

"Oh," she voiced as she turned to look at me.

"What's up?" I inquired, glaring into her beautiful brown eyes.

"You enjoyed your time out with your little friend?" she asked with a blank facial expression.

Lying, I replied, "Yeah."

Nodding her head with a fake smile on her face, said, "That's good."

Apparently, I was seeking an argument because my stupid ass asked, "Did you enjoy yo' time wit' that nigga?"

With a wicked smile on her face, she nodded her head and voiced, "I sure the fuck did."

Immediately, I hopped away from the table as she turned the volume up on the radio. I was beyond pissed because I knew that she wasn't telling a lie. That was one thing that I hated about Tashima, that bitch didn't see the need in lying.

"I don't give a fuck nigga, I don't give a fuck hoe!" she mouthed as Lil Jon's voiced boomed from the speakers as *Get Crunk* played.

By the time I was in proximity of Tashima, she was super crunk. Her facial expression and attitude had a lot to say about how she was really feeling. Snatching the remote control to the radio, I turned down the volume. Roughly turning her to face me, I glared into her eyes as she did the same to me. A sneaky smile spread across her face before she turned around and finished preparing dinner. I didn't know what to do. Therefore, I stared at her while shaking my head. Not liking how I was feeling or that I couldn't react to knowing that she had slept with Dom Dom, I shoved her ass against the rectangular table; I didn't give a damn that she had a hand filled with cut onions and bell peppers.

"You think you gonna play wit' my fuckin' emotions?" I nastily asked as I unsnapped the lingerie outfit.

"Dude, move away from my freshly cleaned pussy. I don't know where yo' hands been," she smartly replied, laughing.

Not in the mood to play with her, I shoved two fingers inside of her juicy, hot pussy; I made sure to aim for her G-Spot. The second I made my fingers tap dance on the walnut-sized sensitive spot, the onions and bell peppers slipped out of her hand, onto the floor.

"Dyoonnn," she cooed as her body began to shake as her legs gave out.

To the floor, we went. With my left hand cradled behind her head, Tashima had the cutest, sexual expression plastered on her face as she spat, "Nigga, suck on my pretty pussy."

"You must think I'm that nigga how you talkin' to me."

"I know exactly who I'm talking to," she whined as she began to fuck my fingers.

Applying pressure to her neck and pussy, I shot back, "Oh, you wanna play those games?"

Licking her lips, she slowly shook her head, "Nope, I wanna play my game."

For a hot ass minute, she had me stuck with choices of words. Refusing to say anything, I barked, "You gon' learn a lot of shit 'bout me today. On my momma, you gon' learn 'bout me. I been sparin' yo' ass because you ain't like them other bitches that try to come on to me. You got a nigga's heart, but today, this very moment ... I see I gotta knock you down a few inches, an' show you who the fuck I really can be wit' yo' ass."

Placing my hand underneath her thick thighs, I slid her up the side of the kitchen table. I barked for her to put her legs on my shoulders. The moment she placed one of her legs on my shoulders, my face met her oiled pussy with such passion and force that it scared me. I ate her out like I never did before. I tongue kissed, finger fucked, and groaned on that twat of hers. My tongue moved faster than my fingers, and that shit drove her insane.

"Ohh my Godddd!" she screamed as she gripped the back of my head and began riding my face.

I gave her ass a run for her money. Her pussy sounded like moist macaroni and cheese being stirred. I didn't stop; I kept going. I wanted her to explode on my face so that I could tell her to look at me while I sucked every drop of her juices.

"I'm finna cum, baby," she sounded off while rapidly rotating the lower region of her body.

"Mmm," I groaned as I gazed at her.

The expression on her face informed me that she was shocked and pleased. I wasn't the aggressive type when eating pussy. I liked to take my time and taste every piece of her pretty pussy. I never fingered her while I was sucking and licking on her.

After I had my first taste of her juices, I placed her on the table before getting naked. While glaring at me, Tashima tried to stop her body from shaking. She couldn't, and I loved that shit. I was eager to piss her off, so I pulled a condom out of my jean pocket.

When she saw me opening it, an eyebrow raised as she asked, "What in the fuck you putting that on for?"

"Honestly, a nigga righteously don't know who he dealin' wit' … so, I think I need to be safe," I chuckled as I put the condom on my dick.

Sinisterly laughing, Tashima gently but firmly kicked me towards the counter, bent low, and snatched the condom off. Before I could say anything, she roughly grabbed my dick, sniffed it, and said, "Hmph, at least you had the common sense to wash the dick off. She didn't suck on these balls because they smell like the soap that we use."

"Mane…"

That damn woman shut me up without a moment's hesitation with that beautiful, warm, and wet mouth of hers. Twisting her head from left to right, Tashima did the damn thing. My knees buckled at the same time a low howl escaped. The passionate yet savage way she talked to my dick and balls had me like an emotional ass female. I had to snap out the zone, but the way she was toting my dick down her throat all the while fondling my balls had my mind on relax mode.

"Fuckkk," I groaned as I poorly pumped in and out of her mouth.

If I thought that heifer was doing the damn thing, I was sadly mistaken the moment Lil Baby and Moneybagg Yo song *All of a Sudden* blasted from the radio, that fine ass bitch started pussy popping and turning up on the dick. I mean nasty, sexy dick sucking and ball gripping took place. After she deep throated my man a few times, that nasty heifer removed her mouth and spit on my shit only to shove it down her mouth.

"Oohh milawd!" I hollered as I damn near shoved her away from me.

Every limb on my body tingled as she took my dick on a roller coaster ride. Slow then fast, this turn then that turn, fast then slow were the motions of her mouth and hands. I was one weak nigga by the time she gazed into my eyes with a wicked smile on her face. She knew she had me when I started acting like a little bitch; I cooed her damn name and rubbed the sides of her face!

By the time the introduction to *Stop Fuckin' With Me* by Lil Jon & the East Side Boyz sounded off, I wanted to dissolve into a damn puddle. I knew that Tashima was going to perform a combination move on me that was going to have me a weak ass nigga for damn near two months. She was going to get away with whatever she wanted to within that period. I knew this because whenever that song played, she had a nigga crying and begging her to marry me the next day.

Removing her mouth from my dick, she sneakily smiled and mouthed, "Why you fuckin' wit' me?"

After that, my dick was no longer mine! That black, long, fat bitch was all Tashima's! The second Lil Jon came in with his hook, I was one pussy pie ass nigga. I was squirming, moaning, groaning, running from her mouth, and all that shit. I couldn't handle the pressure that she was applying to me. While she did her thing, the sexy bitch was on the floor rocking back and forth along with the beat while making her ass cheeks do tricks. I didn't think my dick could get harder, but it did, and she devoured me.

Moving her head slowly from left to right while showing my head extra attention, I felt my boys marching from my nuts. Usually, I would tell her when I was close to busting, but I couldn't say shit. My body was shaking like hers when I brought her to ultimate pleasure. I was astounded at the posture of my damn body against the hard counter; I was stuck! My eyes rolled in the back of my head, and my mouth hadn't closed since the beginning of the song. I had severe cottonmouth; I knew the corners of my mouth were white as hell!

Tashima placed her petite, soft hands around my dick, dirt biked that motherfucker along with sucking on the head. Within a short amount of time, she moved her hand and began sucking my dick faster and sloppier. My dick throbbed in her mouth. She knew I was about to explode, but that heifer kept sucking while reaching for the radio's remote control. The volume on the radio was lowering as I whimpered her name.

With a pleased expression on her face, she sexily deep throated my man, tightened her lips and slowly dragged her mouth down my dick. The sensation that I felt was like none other. When I realized why I looked at her with bucked eyes. That damn sexy ass bitch was carefully and correctly dragging her damn teeth on my fucking dick!

Before I knew it, I cooed, "Why you doing me like this?"

I knew she wanted to laugh; hell, if I were her I would have. I sounded like a straight-up bitch.

Instead of responding to me, that fine broad kept destroying me.

"Gotdamn, you Mortal Kombatin' my dick. Baby, you know how I feel 'bout you. That guh from today don't mean shit to me. You all that I want. You all that I need. Tashima, you own me, mane, you own me!" I groaned as she sucked my soldiers out of me.

As she swallowed, she sucked on the head gently as she jiggled my nuts. I was drained; she took every damn little thing that I had in me. Hell, I was trying to figure out how was she able to pull that drop out of me since I had emptied my shit in the condom after fucking Knoxxy. My dick was super sensitive but in a good way, and that damn woman was still trying to get more out of me.

"What you lookin' fa? You got 'em all, baby, you got 'em all," I breathlessly squealed, once again like a little bitch.

Smacking her mouth as she stood, she glared into my face with a raised eyebrow, she said, "I was making sure that I got them all. I was real thirsty."

I tried to move, but I was unsuccessful. My dumb ass was poorly standing against the counter, damn near about to fall as I replied, "Mane, I love you."

"How much?" she asked with a conquered smile on her face.

"A whole fuckin' lot."

"Is that so?"

"Hell fuck yes, you know this."

"Let me know it's real then," she laughed before she walked off, ass and titties bouncing.

"Where in the fuck are you going?" I poorly asked.

"Going to run you some bath water. Round two in the shower," she spoke, turning around to look at me.

"What the fuck you mean round two?" I yawned.

"Just what the fuck I said."

"Tashima, I ain't got it in me. You just took every lil' piece of energy I had."

"Ask me, do I give a fuck. Whatever you gotta do to get that dick back up ... you motherfuckin' better. Like I said, round fucking two once I get this bath water ready. Cut that stove off."

When I heard her heels clinking against the stairs, I looked at the ceiling and shook my head. After I cut off the stove, I found the will to leave the kitchen. The moment I placed my right foot on the first step, Tashima yelled my name.

"Yeah?" I replied as I moved up the stairs, shaking my head.

"Bring your ass on, boo," she stated in a mischievous tone.

"I'm comin', woman," I announced as I landed on the last stair, afraid to go in the room.

Placing my eyes on the bed, I wanted to fucking cry. It was going to be a long evening in our household, and Tashima was going to be the leader. Tashima had rose petals, handcuffs, and blindfolds lying in the middle of the bed. Several, tall candles were sitting on the nightstand, ready to be lit.

Naked in all her damn glory, Tashima appeared and said, "Are you ready to be relaxed before getting the best and most exquisite pussy you'll ever have in your life, Dyon?"

"Mannnnee..."

"What?" she laughed, pointing towards the bathroom.

"Bruh, why you doing all of this?" I asked while walking towards the bathroom, head low to the ground.

"Because you need to understand who you really belong to. You need to understand that I love you, and no one and I fucking mean *no one* will love and cater to you like I have and will continue to do," she stated, pushing me against the frame of the door before passionately making love to my mouth with her perfect-sized, juicy lips and tongue.

No, no, no. Dick don't you get hard. She finna destroy us! She finna take us down through there! I thought as my dick knocked against her hairless pussy.

With a smile on her face, she looked at my dick with an evil expression and asked, "Well, hello, there, are you ready for your best friend to cum on you while she's slowly riding you? I hope so because she misses you."

Whenever that damn woman talked to my dick like that, I knew she was going to make my tool act as if it needed a disability check!

CHAPTER EIGHT

Dom Dom

A Week Later

    My mind hadn't been right since I broke things off with Tashima. Every decision that I made concerning my organization, I wanted to reach out to her. I needed to make sure that I was making the right choices in promoting and demoting motherfuckers along with covering more territory within the county. Also, I needed to know who was the best people to move meth like Dyon did. The amount that I received from Julio was a four-persons job.

    Since I couldn't talk to Tashima, I had to call Momma. She didn't help me out like I thought she would. That woman had a listening ear before telling me to reach out to my imprisoned father. I wasn't going to do that shit, and she knew it. I had nothing to say to that man. I prayed that in due time, my mind would be where I needed it to be. I wasn't up for seeking advice about my organization for too much longer.

    Let's get this shit over wit', I thought as I walked towards the entrance of Club Déjà Wu.

Earlier today, Tashima informed me that Catalina wanted to sit down with us in a neutral environment. Knowing that it was going to be about business before shit became personal between Tashima and me, I didn't waste any time telling her that I would be present. I had plans of having Tashima's ass in my bed before midnight. I was tired of not having her in my arms after a long day of hustling and organizing.

"What's up, nigga?" my cousin, Tello, stated as I approached the doors of the club.

As we dapped, I replied, "Shit. Came to breathe fo' a minute."

"Dad told me that you touched down," he voiced, glaring at me as his cell phone rang.

"Word?" I replied as Tello silenced his phone.

"Yeah," he quickly replied before continuing, "I need to holla at cha fo' a minute."

"A'ight," I announced as I stepped onto the freshly cut grass, out of earshot of the nosey security guards.

"What's up?" I stated, briefly eyeing the crowd.

"Dad told me that he and Uncle Marc will be released soon."

With a raised eyebrow, I asked, "How soon?"

"Like two months or som' shit like that."

"And?" I inquired, knowing it was more to the chitchat.

"They want us to merge our organizations together. They want a strong, family-oriented dynasty," he voiced as several females hollered our names.

We ignored the broads as I shook my head at my cousin's statement before replying, "A'ight. What roles are they tryin' to play?"

"Now that I don't know."

Tello was lying through the big gap that sat in between his big, front teeth. Yet, I didn't call him out on his shit.

"One thing, I ain't dealin' wit' is those motherfuckas tryin' to come an' take over. They been gone too damn long to fuck wit' anything that we built. Marc Jack fucked up my chances of me playin' ball. So, he fucked up wit' tryin' to run som' shit," I snarled as I retrieved the blunt from behind my ear.

Nodding his head, Tello asked, "Are you ready fo' the real reason I wanted to holla at you?"

Exhaling heavily, I nodded my head, all the while firing up the blunt.

Sighing sharply, Tello husky-voiced behind spoke, "Dad don't like yo' guh runnin' things. He says a woman's place is to be behind the scene, not in front. When he touch down, he will be an issue fo' her. Just need you to be up on game."

Chuckling, I spat, "Thanks fo' lookin' out, but I gotta ask you. How do you feel 'bout Tashima being in the forefront?"

"On som' real nigga shit, I have a love-hate feelin' 'bout her being at the forefront. One thing I do know, she ain't no snitch. I must admit that she stepped on my toes wit' that Russian motherfucka, Ivan, an' that broad Catalina, who are in town," he stated, glaring into my eyes.

Watch his ass, I thought while studying cousin's body language and chief'ed on my good good.

I liked the fact that he told me the truth about his feelings for Tashima being on the limelight. However, I was going to keep a close eye on the nigga.

"If Uncle Bo Jack asks you to go up against Tashima, will you?" I questioned.

The nigga was hesitant to answer my question; therefore, I said, "You might not want to agree to everything that Unc say. That shit might bring bad blood between the two of us, Tello."

"An' that's the last thing I want. We are fam. The same fam that's out here gettin' this fuckin' money," he spat, profoundly exhaling.

"Well, cousin, it looks like you will have a lot to think 'bout within the next two weeks. We will speak mo' on that topic."

"Why two weeks?" he probed, glaring at me quizzically.

"Because I'm sure there will be a meetin' wit' all of us involved in 'round that time frame, an' guess who will be right by my side?" I voiced with a smile on my face as I put out my blunt.

"A'ight."

"Please don't disappoint me, Tello," I stated in a boss-like tone.

"I'mma try not to. You know I'm loyal to Dad."

"I know," I replied as we dapped.

I didn't move until he walked away. Some shit was about to get ugly, and I had to prepare Tashima for the storm she was going to weather all because of a nigga that couldn't accept the fact that a woman ran the dope game better than he ever could. I never like Uncle Bo Jack. That six-foot, dark-skinned bastard was always up to something. In my opinion, he was jealous of the nigga that helped Sonica create me. From the stories old heads told me, I wouldn't be surprised if Uncle Bo Jack did shit just to be neck and neck with Marc Jack.

While slipping into deep thought, I strolled towards the young and tall security guards. Within a matter of seconds, I waltzed through the loud, heavily smoked out, upscale, and diverse place. As I scanned the front area of the club, I paid attention to the types of people inside. There were goons in the club, but those niggas were dressed in casual wear. Some females wore skin-tight dresses as some wore business casual clothing. There were no chicken head, half-ass naked broads scurrying about. Pleased with the environment, I strolled towards the bar. After I ordered six shots of Patron and downed them, I moved towards the location I was supposed to have met Tashima.

When I arrived in the V.I.P. section, my breath was taken away as I glared at the smiling beauty that swayed her hips beside a laughing Catalina. Before I could make my way towards the women, I was stopped by three big, tanned guys. Knowing what time it was, I outstretched my arms as I glared into their faces. Not one pleasant word escaped our mouths; there wasn't shit that needed to be said. They were just the muscle as I was just the buyer. Once I was cleared, I sauntered towards the ladies. The second I was beside Tashima's fine ass, I grabbed her wrist and placed a kiss on it. At that moment, I needed her badly.

"Hey," she seductively voiced.

"You look absolutely amazin'." I praised as Catalina and I shook hands.

"I supposed we should get the business talk over with, huh?" Catalina stated while looking between Tashima and me.

After we nodded our heads, Catalina led the way towards a small, circular table far away from her bodyguards. While taking a seat, Catalina grabbed a bottle of vodka, dropped two cubes of ice in a cup, and invited us to anything on the table. Tashima asked me if I wanted her to make me a drink, and I happily said yes. My baby was still doing things for me even though I acted a fool, which I needed to apologize.

"So, where do we begin?" Catalina questioned as Tashima handed me a drink.

"With the date of havin' product," I stated before taking a sip of the concoction that my baby made.

"Tonight," Catalina stated.

With a raised eyebrow, I asked, "Where would you like to meet fo' the even swap?"

"The money has already been paid. All you two have to do is walk out of this club with me, and I'll have my other men meet us."

With a smile on my face, I looked at Tashima. She was the G.O.A.T., and I loved it. Uncle Bo Jack didn't know what a valuable asset Tashima was to the dope game, but he was going to learn quickly.

Placing my eyes on Catalina, I said, "Within two months or so, there may be an expansion within my organization. Another group will be joining mine, making my organization huge. The products will be doubled."

"Who is over the other organization?" she inquired as Tashima glared at me with a curious facial expression.

"Tello Jack's crew."

"Um, Bo Jack's son?" Catalina asked with a raised eyebrow as she placed the clear, plastic cup on the table before sitting upright in the chair.

Nodding my head, I replied, "Yep."

Shaking her head, she said, "No go. I will not be affiliated with them at all. Matter of fact, Tashima, I will be returning the money that you spent on the product, tonight."

As I was astonished at her tone, Tashima calmly asked, "Why is that?"

"Bo Jack and his people are snitches. They have ratted on many people within the past two years. I would assume that's why he and his brother are getting out of prison within two months or so," Catalina spoke.

"Just because they told on people doesn't mean that you should stop working with Dom Dom and me. In that case, there will be no merging of any kind. You are the best supplier for what we need. I will not allow any foolery to stop us from working together, making great money," Tashima stated confidently while looking at me with squinty eyes. She was pissed.

"Catalina, can you provide evidence to support what you sayin'?" I asked, not believing a word that she spoke.

One thing I knew, my folks were grimy motherfuckers, but being a snitch was not their thing. I had to see proof of what she claimed. The Jackson's been in the dope game far too long to be snitches and still thriving.

"Yes, I can," she stated as she gazed into my eyes.

"I'm all eyes and ears," I told her as I sat upright.

Retrieving her phone, she fumbled with it as I whispered in Tashima's ear, "I doubt this shit is true. My people don't do no snitchin', period. It has to be a bigger reason why she doesn't fuck wit' them."

Placing the phone in front of me, Catalina breathed, "Read every single word on these fifteen pages."

Tashima leaned over my shoulder and read along with me. The confidential papers read shit that had my head spinning. In black lettering, I read shit that had me in pure disbelief. I saw the head honchos names that ran with Tello. Of course, Uncle Bo Jack's name was on the list. A name I had never heard before was on the list—Nickolas "Nick Jack" Jackson. On the paper, he was referenced as Uncle Bo Jack's brother. Not on one piece of the document did I see my father's name.

As I read, I tugged on my beard. Frederick "Minx" Broadnax and Emmanuel "Drano Rock" Lewis names were on every document as well; those two niggas were Uncle Bo Jack's sons, according to the report.

I wonder is this the shit that Chiiko and Meno was talkin' 'bout, I thought as I continued reading.

When I finished, I looked at Tashima and shook my head. Shit was all fucked up, and it was because of Uncle Bo Jack. Every nigga that was on that report told on top-notch distributors.

Slumping backward, I exhaled heavily while Catalina glared into my face. I didn't have a fucking thing to say. What was there to say? My family was a rat. I didn't want to be associated with those niggas. My momma groomed me never to snitch no matter the number of years I received. By looking at those Federal documents, I had one question for Catalina.

"How did you obtain these papers?"

"My great-grandfather made sure that our family members were equally spread out in Corporate America and anywhere in the world. Ten family members of mine are in high places for reasons of this nature," she stated before continuing, "So, now you see why I will not be working with you two. My livelihood and those back home depend on me in ways you couldn't imagine. I hope you understand."

"Fuck!" I spat as I hit the table.

"Calm down," Tashima said before speaking to Catalina. "How can we ensure that you nor your family will not be in harm's way?"

Before Catalina could open her mouth, I said to Tashima, "You can't. Tello knows and dislikes that you and Catalina were working together. It's best to pull away. I don't need him tryin' to throw you under the bus. Shit too sticky. I received an unclear vibe from that motherfucka before I came inside of the club. As of now, Tashima, we will let Catalina go. I need to figure out what in the fuck is really going on wit' Uncle Bo Jack an' his people."

"Wait, Bo Jack is your uncle ... then who is your father, Dom Dom?" Catalina inquired.

"Marc Jack," I replied.

With a huge smile on her face, she said, "You know what, I've had the pleasure of hearing about your father's loyalty from my grandfather. I will give you two a month to iron out shit within your family Dom Dom. You provide me evidence that things are right with your father and the rest of your crew, and I will supply you with the product. However, I will not work with the other side of your family. I will be giving your money back to you tonight. Okay?"

"Okay," I replied as I extended my hand to Catalina.

Shortly after I shook her hand, Tashima and Catalina firmly shook hands. The meeting was over, and I was highly disappointed and confused as to what had been going on with Uncle Bo Jack. The only way I was going to get some answers was to chop it up with the one motherfucker I hadn't spoken to in a long time, Marc Jack. A lot of shit didn't add up, and I had to get to the bottom of it.

Pulling me towards her, Tashima whispered in my ear, "Let's chill and have fun. All we can do is investigate shit thoroughly.

We still have Ivan under wraps. I have product from him. At least we didn't lose him tonight."

"Shit is bigger than you know, Tashima. Uncle Bo Jack doesn't like how you have the game on lock. He feels like a woman has no business being in the limelight of a man's game. Things finna get out of control, an' I need to make sure that you are safe at all times," I told her as I saw Tello and his crew eyeing us.

"I'm not worried 'bout none of those pussy ass niggas, Dom Dom," she laughed, rubbing the sides of my face.

"Baby, Momma an' I trained you fo' a lot of shit, but what we are up against … we didn't teach you fo' that. I need you to lay low fo' a while 'til I get a handle on things. Please?" I voiced as I glared into her beautiful face.

"If you say so, Boss," she spoke in a sassy tone.

Not in the mood for her attitude, I dropped down on her ass. "Look, I don't have time fo' no smart ass comment from you, woman. Yo' life might be in danger. This is not the time to defy me. Just trust me. Okay."

Rolling her eyes, she quickly replied, "Okay."

Bad and Bougee by Migos played, and the ladies went crazy as the niggas bobbed their heads. Tashima was on one as well. Vibing and rapping along with the song, she pulled me towards the dance floor, not far from Tello and his crew. With the information that I knew, I had to watch those niggas extra hard. I knew that I wasn't going to be able to enjoy Tashima having fun because I had to keep a lookout for the fuckery that could pop off.

Turning around to face the sneaky bastards, I lit a cigarette and glared into their faces. There were a couple of niggas that mean mugged me, but a nigga like me did what I did best—I flashed my gold teeth and shook my head. What they didn't know was that I was on top of their bullshit.

I pulled Tashima close to me, dropped my mouth to her right ear, and said, "Don't be obvious when you are lookin', nor do you nod or move your lips to respond to me. You see that group of niggas in the white pants? They are family or family affiliated. The one in the purple shirt is Tello. That's Uncle Bo Jack's son. Everybody over there is suspicious as fuck. Stay from 'round them. When I drop my hand from around yo' waist, bend over an' shake that ass to let me know that you understand?"

Two seconds after I removed my hand, Tashima sexily bent and clapped that ass so wonderfully that my dick was hard in no time. Ready to head out of the club with Tashima, my eyes landed on Munk. Instantly, I started growling. I had some fucked up emotions towards the nigga that went cold on me when I was in prison. This was the same nigga whose back I had ever since his mother tried to sell him for a crack rock. I didn't understand why he felt the need to kick me to the curb. Yet, I wasn't pressed to find the answer. He fucked up when he became a fuck nigga.

My thoughts ceased about Munk only to be placed on Tashima. A nigga badly wanted to be alone with her fine self. Quickly, I let it be known that it was time for us to go. Seductively licking her glossy lips, Tashima nodded her head as I grabbed her wrist. As we made our way towards the exit, I made sure to leave my cousin with warm and safe wishes before we departed. The best way to keep flaw ass motherfuckers by your side was to continue to affiliate with them. I prayed that Catalina wasn't watching and got the wrong impression.

Once outside, Munk called my name. Ignoring the nigga like he did me, I waltzed on about my business as Tashima told me to see what he wanted.

"What in the fuck do I look like to you? A pussy? Fuck that nigga, mane," I stated as I glared into her face.

"Tashima, tell that nigga Dom Dom to stop!" Munk hollered, a few inches away from us.

"Continue to ignore me like you did when I was prison nigga," I spat, not turning around to look the character in his face.

"Mane, I need to apologize fo' that. There shouldn't be a reason why I stopped bangin' wit' you. I had a nigga in my ear 'bout how disloyal you was to us, an' the nigga fed us good," Munk spoke, causing me to stop.

The only person that came to my mind was Dyon. Briefly, I looked at Tashima before placing my eyes on Munk. I didn't have to tell him to speak his mind because he didn't waste any time telling me what Dyon said and did. Right then, I saw some flaw shit. Munk wasn't the snitching type. If he had an issue with a nigga, he would deaden the shit right then. At that moment, I knew that Munk was under Dyon's control. Shaking my head, I laughed at the character.

"I'mma tell you like this, keep that same attitude you had wit' me when I was behind bars. I don't need anymo' snakes 'round me."

"I'm tryin' to make things right between us, Dom Dom," he replied.

"Well, just know we gucci unless you cross me again. The best thing you can do is move the fuck 'round when you see me. Now, we are done talkin'," I nastily spat while eyeing the fuck nigga.

Nodding his head, he looked at Tashima and asked, "Where is Dyon?"

Clearing her throat, she spat, "You got his number. Why don't you call him and see where he's at."

That nigga Munk was on some funny shit, but I was going to be the last one to have the last laugh—for life!

As she walked off, shaking her head, Tashima's mind was in another place, and I was going to find out exactly where it was.

Before I got the chance to call her name, Dyon's fuck ass stepped to her. Her body language changed the second he wrapped his arms around her before he placed a kiss on her neck. Instantly, my blood boiled. However, I had to check my damn emotions because Tashima and I weren't together.

Clearing my throat, I started walking towards the parking lot. In the proximity of Tashima and Dyon, I said, "Aye, baby, you know where you need to be. Make that shit happen."

The nigga mean-mugged me as I gave him that same energy. With a smirk on my face, Dyon growled while clenching and unclenching his fists. I was ready for whatever he was ready for. I didn't mind getting dirty; it wouldn't have been the first time I beat a nigga to sleep at the club.

"She ain't finna go nowhere wit' yo' ass," Dyon finally spoke.

"I'm not finna go back an' forth wit' you 'bout Tashima. You know where her heart really lies, my nigga. Wit' that being said, if you wanna throw down … shid, let's do this," I calmly spoke as Tashima slowly slid in front of Dyon, putting distance between us.

"Dyon, I'm going to need you to go inside the club. Dom Dom, I need you to head to your vehicle," Tashima calmly said as I walked closer to her.

Within a matter of seconds, we sandwiched her, ready for a battle. Quickly, she placed a hand on our chests. The stares we gave each other was real, and she knew it.

"Tashima, get the fuck out of the way," Dyon and I stated at the same time.

"Hell no. I said what the fuck I said. There will be no fighting, gunplay, or back and forth arguing, period. Go outside of what I say, and both of you will fucking lose me. Once I'm gone, not a soul will have plenty of money in their pockets because I will take all that shit and the plugs with me. Think I'm playing … go against me, and see how dusty you motherfuckers will be without me," she stated firmly before walking off.

Her words rung loud and clear in my ears as Dyon and I watched her walk away. I knew when to test Tashima, and when not too. Apparently, Dyon did as well because that motherfucker didn't look at me when he walked off, heading for the entrance of the club. One thing the fuck nigga had better know was that come hell or high water, I was going to serve his ass a gourmet dish that no restaurant could provide, and there wasn't a bitch ass thing that Tashima was going to say about it.

Walking towards my whip, I replayed everything that Catalina showed us, what Munk said, and his and Tashima's body language, when the nigga stepped to me. There were questions that I had to ask, concerning Munk; I needed answers before I left the club's ground. The only person that could provide me those answers was Tashima.

When I approached her car, she rolled down the window and looked at me. Licking my lips, I said, "What do you know 'bout the shit that Munk said?"

Sighing sharply while shaking her head, she said, "A lot."

Glaring into her face, I probed, "What did you do when you learned of the information?"

"Checked Dyon and the other niggas that believed the fuck shit."

"You didn't see the need to get them niggas out of the way? Out of my organization," I loudly stated.

Not looking at me, she shook her head.

Through clenched teeth, I barked, "Fuckin' look at me when I'm talkin' to you. Who is you really fo' Tashima? That nigga or me?"

"Both of y'all," she blatantly spoke.

Before I knew it, I snatched her ass out of the car through the damn window before pinning her against the idling vehicle. "You really are fuckin' wit' a gotdamn mental patient. Do you not know that? You think I won't burn yo' ass, Tashima? If you think I won't, then you are fuckin' sadly mistaken. I can't trust you. As bad as I want to, I can't trust you. You gotta get the fuck from 'round me, an' stay the fuck from 'round me. Understood? Come get all of yo' shit out of my motherfuckin' house."

After releasing her, I wanted to break her fucking nose. Instead, I walked away because I knew once I hit her, I wasn't going to stop. The walk to my whip was a horrible one as my night's plans of having Tashima in my bed didn't go the way I had hoped.

Without a moment's hesitation, I dialed my mother's number. On the third ring, she answered the phone.

"He finally rings after being M.I.A. all damn day," she chuckled as I hit the unlock button on my key fob.

Not in a joking mood, I said, "I need you to tell that nigga, Marc Jack, I need him to be callin' my line first thing in the mornin'. We got som' shit to discuss immediately. Oh, you better talk to that bitch, Tashima, before I kill her motherfuckin' ass."

CHAPTER NINE

Tashima

My night didn't go according to plan, especially the causal meeting with Catalina. There were a lot of things that I had to figure out and solve within two weeks. I wasn't going to let Dom Dom's stupid ass family be the reason why we couldn't work with Catalina. I didn't know what he had up his sleeves, but I knew he was going to get to the bottom of things. When and how he was going to handle the situation, I had no idea.

After Dom Dom aggressively snatched me out of my car, I was sure that we were not on speaking terms. If Munk would've never reached out to Dom Dom, there wouldn't have been a reason he was super upset with me. He would've never found out how Dyon stepped on his toes or how I handled those niggas, which wasn't how he would have wanted me to handle them.

Truthfully, it seemed as if Munk was up to some shit. Typically, when I felt that way about someone, they were up to no good. It was my duty to see what his ass was up too, and I guaranteed that Dyon was behind it. There would be no saving the nigga this time because I meant what the fuck I said about my loves not harming each other.

After I left the club, following suit behind Dom Dom, I called Catalina to let her know that I was ready to retrieve the duffel bag of money. Within twenty minutes, we met at a fully capacitated Waffle House on the Boulevard. Within a few seconds of having the money in my hand, Dom Dom and I gracefully walked towards our vehicles without saying two words to each other. I felt extremely salty about that. I tried making conversation with him, but he ignored me.

As I shook my head, I hopped in my whip and peeled away. In need of thinking clearly, I didn't want to be in the house. Therefore, I rode around the city. My thoughts were everywhere. I was nowhere close to having Dyon and Dom Dom by my side, and that infuriated me. It seemed like they were never going to get on board with what I wanted. Was I selfish? Yes, but I didn't give a damn. I wanted what I wanted, and they had to submit to me.

Ring. Ring. Ring.

Sighing heavily, I retrieved my phone and glared at the screen. It was Dyon. I took my time answering the phone because I wasn't in the mood to deal with him.

"Hello," I spoke as I turned down the volume on the radio.

"I guess you wit' that nigga, huh?" he nastily spat.

"Dyon, don't start that shit. To answer your question, no, I'm not with Dom Dom. I'm riding around town. I need to clear my mind."

"I bet you do," he hissed nastily.

"Like I said, don't start that shit," I aggressively spoke.

"You can't have both of us, Tashima, and I'm going to make damn sure that you choose wisely," he coldly spoke, sending chills down my spine.

Sitting upright in the seat, I asked, "What are you up to, Dyon?"

Evilly laughing, he replied, "Nothin'."

Knowing that he was lying, I said, "Dyon, whatever you and Munk have up y'all's sleeves ... I would advise y'all to bite down on that shit. The last thing you, him, or anyone else want to do is piss me the fuck off."

"Like I motherfuckin' said, I'm going to make sure that you choose wisely," he spat before ending the call.

Not wasting my time calling him back, I dialed Dom Dom's number. My call was forwarded to the voicemail. Therefore, I called again. In between me calling Dom Dom, Sonica buzzed into my line. I ignored her calls as I feared that Dyon was going to harm Dom Dom. Not able to get through to Dom Dom, I stopped calling his phone and dialed Sonica's number. On the fourth ring, she answered.

"What is going on between you and Dom Dom?" she asked curiously.

"Before I answer that question, I need to know ... when the last time you talked to him?" I quickly rushed into the phone.

"About forty minutes ago. Why?"

"I need you to call him and see if he answers for you. If he does, tell him to answer my call immediately."

"Honey, I'm going to be honest with you ... Dom Dom doesn't want to talk to you. You have rubbed him the wrong way with that Dyon character. So, give him some space. Please give him space, or he will hurt you," she softly stated.

"Sonica, I completely understand that, but I need you to call him and deliver my message. I'm a little thrown off, and I need to talk to him," I told her, ensuring that I was careful with my words.

"Okay. I will call him now, and then I will call you back. We need to talk about what he told me."

"Okay," I replied before we ended the call.

Ten seconds later, I received a call from Sonica saying that Dom Dom answered the phone and said that he would call me tomorrow. Becoming angry, I told her okay. While she talked to me, I made my way to his house. I wasn't going to wait until tomorrow to speak to him; I had shit I needed to express.

"What were you thinking about saving Dyon's ass when you knew he was in the wrong?"

Rolling my eyes, I replied, "Sonica, Munk is at fault also. If he was supposed to have been Dom Dom's ace boon coon, there shouldn't have been any way another nigga stepped on Dom Dom's toes."

"Very true, but you didn't answer my question. Why didn't you react accordingly when you found out what Dyon did? Why did you save his ass, Tashima?"

"I … I guess I hoped that he would never make that mistake again. I hoped that he would fly straight by me giving him a stern warning and punishing him for his misdeeds," I replied honestly.

"And now you see that shit didn't work, huh?"

"No, it didn't."

"Sweetheart, you are involved in a love triangle, and those things never end well. You have to sit down and figure out which one of those guys you want to spend the rest of your life with. It's apparent they are not going to be dealing with sharing you."

"Sonica, that's the problem. I can't choose which one. They make me complete. I can't have one without the other. I have always had them in my life, so why should anything change?"

Chuckling, she said, "Sweetheart, you knew damn well what was going to happen the second Dom Dom was released from prison. He had been telling you for years what it was. You are making shit harder for yourself and them. Every time they see each other, words will be spoken. What happens when you are not present? No need to answer that question because you already know."

As I turned into Dom Dom's neighborhood, I zoomed towards his home as Sonica continued to lecture me about the love affair I was involved in. When I pulled into his driveway, I told Sonica that I would call her back. She didn't want to end the call, but she had no choice once I lied about a business caller buzzing in. After I completed the call, I shut off my engine and dialed Dom Dom's number. He sent me to voicemail. Angrily exhaling, I exited my vehicle before making my way towards the front door.

Upon entering the freshly scented home, I locked the door and sauntered towards the kitchen, all the while calling Dom Dom's name. There was no response; therefore, I walked towards the garage to see if his whip was inside. After I saw that it wasn't, I began to blow up his phone. He was going to answer that motherfucker one way or the other. Fifteen minutes of calling his phone without an answer, I had to stop. He was hell-bent on not talking to me.

As I sighed sharply, I snatched the cordless phone off the cradle and dialed Desaree's number. On the fifth ring, she answered the phone.

"Hey. How are you feeling?" I asked, taking a seat at the kitchen table with my cellphone in my hand, texting Dom Dom.

"Lying in bed. Sick as hell."

"Do you have crackers and ginger ale?"

"Yes, Nixon made sure that I had those before he left."

"Oh. Him and Dyon together or he out making rounds?"

"Probably both. I know he got a call from someone concerning Dyon. After he called his brother, it wasn't long before Nixon left the house."

Lord, Dyon, what do you have up your sleeves? I thought as I asked, "I need you to call Nixon on three-way. I need to know exactly where they are."

"What's wrong?" she asked in an alarmed tone.

"Dyon might be up to something concerning Dom Dom. Dom Dom isn't answering any of my calls, and I'm beginning to worry that Dyon has done something he had no business doing."

"Okay. Hold on for a second," she rapidly spoke before the line became silent.

When I heard Nixon's voice, I muted the phone and listened.

"Where are you, baby?" Desaree whined.

"Ridin' 'round wit' this knuckleheaded brother of mine. Trying to talk som' sense into his ass."

"I got sense, nigga. These other pussy ass niggas—"

"There that motherfucka go!" Dyon yelled excitedly.

"Shit, Dyon! Slow the fuck down, nigga. I got a baby and ole lady to get back to," Nixon rapidly spoke, causing me to leap away from the table, aiming for the front door.

My heart pounded as Desaree asked several questions in a panicky tone as Nixon yelled, "Don't do that shit, bro! Let that nigga be! Leave Tashima's ass alone! This shit ain't even worth it. Put that damn gun—"

I knew the call ended because Desaree called Nixon's name several times. I ran as fast as I could to my car. I didn't know exactly where they were, but I had to hit the streets. It was a high possibility that Dom Dom was in the hood, chopping it up with his crew.

"Tashima, what are you going to do?" Desaree asked in a frightened tone.

"I'm going to find Dom Dom!" I yelled in an agitated tone.

Desaree knew that I wasn't going to sit on my ass after hearing what Nixon spoke. She had no idea what I was experiencing with Dom Dom and Dyon.

As I sped away from my other home, my nerves were shot while Desaree asked a thousand questions. Not able to focus, I poorly answered them. My ability to carry a conversation with my sister was inadequate. Thus, I told her that I would call her back. She didn't want to end the call; therefore, I told her to be quiet. After she did as I demanded, I began talking things out, like I usually did.

By the time I made it to the hood, I didn't see anything. It was calm. A few guys were standing outside, shooting the shit. Somewhat relieved, I made my way towards another hood that Dom Dom was over. While driving recklessly, a call from Catalina disturbed my self-talk. Instantly, I pondered what she wanted.

"Desaree, hold on for a second," I quickly said.

"Okay," she responded before I answered Catalina's call.

The background noise was overwhelming, and it irritated me. "Hello."

"Tashima, you need to get to Baptist East instantly. Dom Dom has been shot, and it doesn't look good," she spoke, causing my body to shut down briefly.

Anger and sadness consumed me immediately as I replied, "I'm on my way."

"Okay. My guys and I will fill you in the second you get here."

"Alright," I replied as I ended the call.

I was thankful that Desaree was still waiting on the other line. "Sis, I need you to get to Baptist East, right now."

"Why? What's wrong? Is Nixon hurt?"

Mashing the gas pedal, I replied, "No. It's Dom Dom. He's been shot, and his condition doesn't look good."

"Oh my God, I'm on my way," she shrieked before asking, "Do you think Dyon had something to do with it?"

"Without a doubt, I do." I fumed.

"I'll be there soon as I put on some clothes."

"Alright. By the way, don't call Nixon at all. In due time, you will be able to talk to him. The less said on the phone, the better; however, I need you to call Sonica and let her know what is going on," I ordered.

"Okay," she stated before ending the call.

Letting my phone drop in my lap, I began to pray that Dom Dom would survive. After I finished my prayer, I started thinking savagely. My angry thoughts were for Dyon. He was going to feel the pressure that I was going to apply to his ass! He must've thought that I was playing when I told him to never step to Dom Dom in any way. Seeing that he felt he was the man, I knew that I had to put that nigga in his place and fast.

Since he wanted to go against the grain, he was going to feel something that would haunt his ass for the rest of his days! It was going to be the last time that I told him something, and he disobeyed my command! Dyon Jackson was going to learn that my word meant every-motherfucking-thing!

I Now Pronounce You, Mr. and Mrs. Thug 2

CHAPTER TEN

Dyon

Twenty-one years ago, I knew that some shit would pop off, eventually, between Dom Dom and me, and it would be all because of Tashima. Do I blame her? No. Do I blame Dom Dom for not letting her go? Hell no. He knew what we had. Why? Tashima was a damn good woman, even though she did shit that I didn't agree with. She was the best female to have by your side; she was truly there for you through the thick and thin. Her loyalty was phenomenal. To the point, I tried not being mad at her for loving Dom Dom; yet, my feelings got the best of me, and I took it out on him. I wanted her to be like that fuck ass nigga Munk. He didn't mind switching ships the second I concocted a lie about Dom Dom cheating him and three other niggas out of money.

The moment I saw Tashima walking beside Dom Dom at the club, I wanted to spray his ass with bullets. My anger reached an all-time high. It was one thing for her to tell me that she had lain with him, but it was another thing seeing her smiling, glowing, and strolling along with him. I was eager to whoop his ass, but the queen spoke, and I had to bow down—for the moment that was. I knew I was going to have my time to chop that nigga down at his knees. It was only a matter of time before I pulled out my chopper and let the bullets do their job.

Before I arrived at the club, I chopped it up with Munk. He informed me that Dom Dom was not to be underestimated. He had been saying that for years. Therefore, I told his ass to put on a performance that would have him back in Dom Dom's good graces. I needed that done so that he could cease that nigga from breathing. Upon a text from Munk, I learned that he wasn't successful, which pissed me off. I wanted my hands somewhat clean when Tashima asked me was I behind the nigga's demise.

After I watched Tashima and Dom Dom leave the club—after I saw him snatch her out of her whip—I took it upon myself to take actions into my hands. That nigga had to go! He violated big time by mistreating my love.

While in the club, I received a text from Nixon. Somebody told him that Dom Dom and I had a disagreement. He tried his best to command that I leave Tashima alone, and I let it be known that I wasn't. She was the air that I breathed, along with the main person that I needed in the illegal world that I never wanted to be a part of, to begin with.

Nixon was the reason I left the club's ground; he angered me with his useless chants of why I shouldn't be running behind a woman that was never going to be mine solely. I cursed my baby brother out before he checked me something awful. I didn't see any lies that he told; he said that Tashima would continue to fuck with Dom Dom and me, at the same time. I didn't see a lie told when he said that she would divide her time between the nigga and me and that eventually, she would want us to live in one house. That's when I knew that nigga's, Dom Dom, breathing ability had to cease, and I was going to pull the damn trigger.

As I sat in the front seat of my whip, smoking on a blunt, my brother called, trying to get me to see the bigger picture. Nixon told me to meet him at the most frequented gas station on the Boulevard. While I drove to the desired destination, my brother ranted and raved about the situation I was placed in because of Tashima. I ignored everything that he said. I was going to have everything that I wanted, and it was going to be because I was determined to have it.

When I arrived at the store, I scoped out the scenery. I was looking for Dom Dom's truck. I never saw it. Nixon was still in my ear preaching; I grew tired of hearing him talk. So, I ended the call and dialed Tashima's number. I was sure that she was with Dom Dom since they left at the same time. The thought of them having sex placed my mind on evil mode. The second she answered the phone, I paid attention to the background noise. I didn't hear anything unusual, but a nigga was still skeptical. She said that she was riding around the city to think freely. I didn't know what to believe; all I knew was that Dom Dom had to go. Before I ended the call, I made sure to leave the impression that I was going to knock lover boy's socks off his motherfucking feet!

After Nixon showed face at the gas station, he hopped in my whip. While we rode around the city, he talked about me leaving Tashima alone. He had no idea that I was on the hunt for Dom Dom. I went to all the places Dom Dom could be. I was disappointed when I didn't see him.

Traveling on the north side of town, my eyes landed on his truck. I became excited as I was one step closer to having Tashima all to myself. When I snatched my weapon from underneath the seat, I didn't give a damn that Nixon was with me or that he was on the phone with Desaree. My brother tried his best to talk me out of shooting Dom Dom's truck up. Nixon's words were ignored. I sprayed that pretty motherfucking truck.

As I watched Dom Dom's whip roll into a ditch, I knew my job was done. Looking in the rearview mirror, I saw two SUV'S rapidly pulling behind the nigga's damaged vehicle. With a smile on my face, I pat myself on the back as Nixon angrily hollered at me. I didn't pay him any attention; he would get over what I did, eventually.

In high spirits, I took him back to the gas station to retrieve his car. Before he exited my whip, I made sure to tell him not to say a fucking word to Desaree and to inform her not to mention a word to Tashima. I was sure Desaree was going to ask several questions.

Once I arrived home, I was one happy nigga. I was eager to see R.I.P. Dom Dom on T-shirts. In the mood to celebrate, I kicked off the festivities by waltzing toward the liquor bar and grabbing the unopened bottle of white Hennessy. Chugging half of the contents, I took off my shoes and plopped on the couch. Patiently and happily, I waited for the black goddess to call or come home with news of Dom Dom being shot and that I was at fault. Crazy as it sounded, I was eager to see tears streaming down her face as she pointed her gun at me.

Twenty-five minutes later, I was still on the sofa waiting for Tashima. Anxious to hear her voice, I called her; she didn't answer the phone.

Maybe she hadn't heard the news yet, I thought as my cell phone rang.

Eager for the caller to be Tashima, I quickly snatched my phone out of my pants pocket. When I looked at the screen, I was disappointed to see Munk's name. Thus, I took my time answering the phone.

"Aye, I guess you took matters into yo' hands, huh?" he breathed into the phone as chaos surrounded him.

Not the one to offer any answers to a nigga that I didn't trust, I asked, "What you talkin' 'bout?"

Chuckling, Munk replied, "I caught the drift, but anyways that nigga Dom Dom health ain't looking good, woe," Munk stated.

"Where you at?"

"Baptist East parkin' lot."

"How do you know his health at looking good?" I inquired as I fired up a cigarette.

"Because they shut the hospital down, an' the folks that carried him inside ... told him not to die on them."

"Good. By tomorrow, we will officially be in the streets takin' over. Since Tashima will be grievin' an' shit, I will be out an' 'bout makin' shit happen. I need you to get Chug, Fresh, an' Vano up to speed 'bout what we talked 'bout before appearin' at the club."

"A'ight," he replied before I ended the call.

"God is good!" I hollered as I stood, threw my hands in the air, and jigged.

Ring. Ring. Ring.

Looking at my phone, my attitude changed upon seeing Auntie Mesha's name. With shaky hands, I prayed that she didn't say that something happened to Momma while she was sleeping. Before answering the phone, I took a deep breath.

"Hello," I stated as I took a seat on the sofa.

"Hey, Dyon," Auntie Mesha spoke calmly.

The calmness of her voice prompted me to ask. "Is Momma okay?"

"She's sad and upset that she hadn't seen you or Nixon. Why haven't y'all been down here to spend time with her? Yes, y'all send money, but y'all are not spending quality time with her. That is not right, Dyon, and you know it. She had never left y'all's side even when the odds were against you and Nixon. I must admit that I'm really disappointed in the two of you," my auntie spoke in a disheartened tone.

Hearing what my auntie had to say, I felt low as fuck. I didn't like how I felt, and most importantly, I didn't like knowing that Nixon and I hurt our mother in a way that we had no business. With the streets, Tashima, and Dom Dom present, I knew that I hadn't been the best supportive son lately, and that didn't sit right with me. Auntie Mesha was right, Momma had been there for us through thick and thin. I felt like a guppy for leaving my mother's side and putting her off on Auntie Mesha to care for her. Even though Nixon and I handsomely paid auntie every week, it still wasn't right that we weren't the ones to care for her as she did for us. We made the streets and our women number one priority instead of the woman that gave birth to us.

"She wants to talk to you," Auntie Mesha spoke.

"Okay," I heard myself say in a child-like voice.

Within a few seconds, my sad mother spoke, "Hey, Son."

"Hey, lady. How are you?" I voiced as tears welled in my eyes at the image of her lying on a hospital bed, not able to move anything other than her head.

"I'm not good, Dyon. It's been a real struggle for me. Not only physically but mentally. I haven't seen you or Nixon in three months. I barely get phone calls from you two. I feel as if I did something wrong to y'all. I'm being punished, Son, and it's not a good feeling. My baby sister has looked after me ever since the accident happened, and it's not fair for her to do so since I have two able-bodied children. What did I do to you and Nixon? I thought I gave y'all everything that y'all need … love and support. What did I do for y'all to desert me in this manner? Y'all were the only reasons that I didn't pursue ending my life at the hands of doctors in Switzerland," she cried.

I was at a loss for words as a huge, gray cloud formed over my head. I hated to hear her weep when I was younger, and I sure as hell hated now. I felt like pure shit as tears welled in my eyes before pouring down my face.

"Momma, you didn't do anything to us. We have been selfish with our thinkin' an' time. I'm so sorry for how you are feelin'. I promise you we will do better, startin' tomorrow. We will be there, bright an' early in the mornin'. Okay? I love you, an' you know Nixon loves you also."

Weakly, she spat, "All I need for you and your brother to do is purchase a plane ticket for Switzerland within the next four days and look for hotels to accommodate y'all. Mesha has made the arrangements for me to attend the facility that will be the last sight that I'll ever see."

"Momma, no, don't do this, please," I begged as I began to cry.

I didn't give a fuck how big of a thug I was in the streets I broke down at the thought of burying my mother. The fact that Nixon and I were the main reasons why she had Mesha arrange things further put me in a fucked up headspace.

"The decision is finalized. I want to see my sons before I close my eyes forever. Understand?" she softly wept.

As I cried, I shook my head and said, "Momma, we can do better. We will do better. I will move you into the home Tashima an' I share. I'll hire a caregiver to teach me to care fo' you. I'll leave the streets alone an' get a regular job like you always wanted me to have. Just change yo' mind, please."

"This is not a fucking life for me, Dyon! I didn't want this from the beginning. I didn't want to be anyone's burden, especially not Mesha's. Just accept that things didn't go as planned. Be there for me, this one and final time, Son. By next week, I will not be on this earth."

"I'm sorry, Momma, I'm sorry I wasn't there fo' you like I was supposed to have been. Momma, give me an' Nixon another chance to make things right. Please?" I begged as my body grew weak while I cried to the only woman that saw me at my most vulnerable point.

"Every month, for the past year, I give y'all another chance, and my mind gets weaker and weaker. Looking at my sister, aging, and not living her life, I feel so low and helpless. It's time that I gracefully leave this earth, Son, and that's non-negotiable. Either you will spend my last days with me or not … either way, I will be dead by next week. I love you and Nixon with every fiber in my body. Have a good night, Son," she spoke before she told Mesha to end the call.

Mesha didn't say goodbye or anything, she simply ended the call. With the phone stuck to my ear, I yelled, "Momma, nooo! Don't leave me like this! Please!"

I glared at the wall as I didn't have the will to move or call Auntie Mesha back. I was glued to the sofa, feeling worthless. I cursed out Nixon and myself for not being the sons that Momma raised us to be. I hated the way she felt. Even more, I hated myself for always putting Tashima and the streets first. I couldn't find the will to hate her because she highly begged me to have Momma live with us. All I thought about was having fun freaking all through the house without attending to my mother. I was fucking selfish and soon to be without a mother.

Pissed to the max, I slung the Hennessy bottle across the living room, smashing it against the wall. I couldn't believe the conversation I had with Momma. I didn't understand why she couldn't give us one more chance. That's all that we needed.

Ring. Ring. Ring.

Dropping my head to look at my device, I saw Auntie Mesha's name and quickly said, "Lord, please let this be good news."

Taking another deep breath, I answered the phone.

"Dyon, I'm not calling to discuss your mother's request. I'm calling to pass a message from Bo Jack," she said. I could tell that she had been crying.

"I don't want to hear anythin' that nigga got to say," I angrily spat; I wanted to talk more about the decision that my mother made without Nixon and me present.

"Nephew, you are about to lose your mother forever. You need to get to know the man that has turned over a new leaf. He wants to make things right with you."

Angrily, I said, "The nigga didn't want anythin' to do wit' me then ... he sure as hell ain't finna—"

"Shut your ass up, Dyon! The past is the past, and for the past seven months, Bo Jack has been there for my sister way more than you could imagine. Surely way more than you and Nixon. Yeah, he provided money as well, but at least he brought some peace to her mind. Peace that could've come from you and

Nixon's presence. I am not going to go back and forth with you about Bo Jack. Once I give you his number, either you going to reach out to him or not," she stated with an attitude.

Knowing that I had no dog in the fight I was trying to give my auntie, I sighed deeply and told her to provide me with the nigga's number. After we ended the call, I stared at the ten digits. I fumbled with the decision to reach out.

After exhaling heavily several times, I dialed the nigga's number. On the fourth ring, he answered the phone in a muffled manner.

"You got ten minutes to speak yo' peace," I told the husky-voiced dude.

Chuckling, he spat, "I heard you was a boss ass nigga. You get that from me. While you runnin' 'round these streets, livin' up to yo' last name, you need to know yo' family so you won't be out here fuckin' wit' family an' makin' retarded ass babies. First off, you have a shit load of siblings som' in Alabama an' others spread throughout the United States. Tello Jack is yo' brother, which I'm sure you know. That nigga don't mind reppin' who his daddy is. Angelica Norman is yo' sister, which I'm sure you already know. As far as the rest of yo' siblings, you will meet them Sunday at yo' great-grandma's house, if you decide to show face. Oh, and another thing, Dom Dom is yo' first cousin. His daddy, Marc Jack, is my brother."

"Woe, I know you motherfuckin' lyin'?" I spat in a shocked tone as I thought, *Tashima finna lose her mind behind this shit, or she finna drop me one.*

While I shook my head and sighed Bo Jack spat, "What the fuck I look like lyin' nigga?"

"Don't you think I should've been known who the fuck my family is?" I questioned, in disbelief.

"Yep, but yo' mother was adamant on you not being introduced to them."

"Look, nigga, don't motherfuckin' lie to me. I know that you didn't want me, an' that you wanted her to have an abortion. I don't believe this 'new life turn over' Auntie Mesha speak of ... so, what's the real fuckin' reason you reached out to me?" I angrily replied, not wanting to hear shit about his motherfucking family.

"Smart an' sharp, I like that," he chuckled before continuing, "I need you to keep up the good work. I need you to cease Dom Dom from breathin'; yeah, I heard 'bout how you an' him beefin' over Tashima, which you an' I will have a long talk 'bout. He an' his daddy got me all types of fucked-up. The streets has my name written all over it. Wit' my other seeds an' you doing y'all's thing, it will be success fo' us. I'm sure you understand where I am going wit' this message, right? If not, we will talk in person when I'm released from prison within two weeks."

Out of all the shit he said, I focused on one thing, his ass in prison and talking on a cellphone.

Frowning, I asked, "How in the hell are you talkin' on the phone at this hour of the night?"

"Let's just say that I have mo' power than you think I do. I have so much power that motherfuckas that's against me think I'm gettin' out in two months or so instead of two weeks. Now, to the most critical question of the day ... what side will you choose?"

Nigga, I don't fuck wit' you. I choose my side, fuck nigga, I thought as I said, "Text me the address I supposed to be at Sunday along with the time of my arrival."

"A'ight."

Ruthlessly, I ended the call. I had a lot of shit to think about. The only nigga that I had problems with turned out to be my cousin. Then, I had debated whether I should tell Tashima, which it didn't take me long to arrive at the conclusion that I wouldn't say anything about it. With that thought out of my head, I focused on was it a smart move to play underneath Bo Jack and Tello's crew. The only way to know was to check out his family members and see where their heads were concerning being loyal to their asses. Shortly afterward, my thoughts of Bo Jack's family, Tashima unknowingly fucking cousins, and the streets were no longer on my mind; the conversation that I had with my mother was more important.

Instantly, nothing else mattered to me. I was overwhelmed, sad, and pissed at myself. I didn't know what to do or how to think. So, I called Tashima. She was the only one that could help me sort things out and possibly bring an excellent proposition to my mother.

When Tashima didn't answer the phone, I slapped my head into my hands and sadly spoke, "I need you, baby, please come home soon."

"Shit is all wrong, an' I know it's my fault. Father, God, I'm comin' to you humbly. I did a horrible misdeed tonight, an' I know you are punishin' me fo' it an' will continue to punish me. I have hatred in my heart fo' Dom Dom. I wanted him dead, but after speakin' to my mother I don't any mo'. If you aid my mother in changin' her mind, that hatred fo' him will cease. Basically, I am sincerely prayin' to ask you not to let Dom Dom die in exchange fo' my mother changin' her mind. Nixon an' I will do right by her. I promise we will. Just don't take her away from us. I'll change my ways fo' the better. In the name of Jesus, I pray. Amen," I cried.

CHAPTER ELEVEN

Tashima

It was chaotic in the emergency room. Word circulated fast about Dom Dom's condition and location. Bitches hooted and hollered about Dom Dom as if he was their man. Dick riding ass niggas that knew of Dom Dom was in my face asking questions, and I politely ignored their asses. Munk's bitch ass was beside me, inquiring about Dom Dom's health. Not liking the fake shit that was going on around me, I spazzed out. The rowdy crowd shut the fuck up and began praying. Meanwhile, Desaree rubbed my back as Munk glared into my face.

"What in the fuck are you looking at Munk? First of all, why are you here? You were quick to jump on Dyon's dick after being Dom Dom's friend for so long. Second of all, If you are here because Dyon sent you, I would really advise you to get the fuck out of here before you be in a gotdamn operating room as well," I nastily spat, looking at him.

Not saying a word, Munk moved away from me. His presence was needed, but not for Dom Dom or me. I was very sure that he was here because of Dyon, whom I couldn't wait to get my hands on.

Upon my arrival at the hospital, the on-call surgeon informed me that Dom Dom had to have surgery, and that his condition didn't look good but they were going to try their best to save him. I had never been the type to pray, but while sitting in that damn hospital with Dom Dom on my mind, that's all I did. I prayed until there were no more words left to say.

"Where is my son?" Sonica loudly asked while entering the emergency room.

As I hopped to my feet, the security guard tried talking to her, but she didn't hear a damn thing he said.

While walking towards her, I said, "Sonica, he's in surgery."

"What happened to him?" she voiced, lips quivering.

"He was shot in the neck; as a result, he lost a lot of blood. We need all the prayers we can get," I softly voiced as I grabbed her hands.

Nodding her head, she closed her eyes. Shortly afterward, we began to pray. Once we finished, Catalina asked to speak with me. I told her that I would have a second to talk with her, but I wanted to make sure that Sonica was all right.

As we walked towards the empty seats beside Desaree, Sonica stated to me, "Tashima, go ahead and talk to her. I'll be fine."

"Are you sure?" I asked as Desaree grabbed her hand and placed a kiss on the back of it.

While nodding her head, Sonica replied, "As fine as I can be … for the moment that is."

"Okay," I voiced as I didn't move.

I glared at Sonica and Desaree as my sister softly breathed, "I know this is bad timing, but I feel that you need to have a little hope and faith."

Desaree placed her mouth to Sonica's ear and whispered. Shortly afterward, a small smile appeared on Sonica's face before she looked at Desaree and said, "Oh my goodness. That's going to be a delight. I'm going to be a grandma. Now, all I need is for my son to pull through so that he can give me grandbabies with Tashima."

Clearing my throat, I said, "Dom Dom will pull through. He's a strong man. He's not going to leave me. He'll never leave me as I will never leave him."

Without waiting for a response from Sonica, I sashayed towards the entrance of the emergency room as Catalina and two of her guys were smoking a cigarette. Upon seeing me, Catalina motioned for us to walk off. Since I had arrived at the hospital, I didn't have time to talk with her. I was eager to know why she was at the scene of the shooting.

As we approached the backend of an SUV that she owned, Catalina cleared her throat, glared into my eyes, and softly said my name several times.

"What's up?" I spoke rapidly as my heart raced just as fast as I had talked.

"We saw what color car the shots fired from."

I already know what color car and who is responsible, I thought as I asked, "Were you following him?"

"Not exactly."

With a raised eyebrow, I probed, "What do you mean, not exactly?"

"We have some people we need to surveillance. We were on the same route as Dom Dom."

"Hmm," I sarcastically spoke.

Crossing her arms, she sassily said, "It doesn't seem like you are too caring to know what car was at the scene when Dom Dom's vehicle was shot up."

Laughing, I replied, "Because I know exactly what motherfucker did it, and why. As soon as Dom Dom is stable, I and *I* alone will handle that motherfucker accordingly. Is there anything else that you want to discuss with me?"

Taken aback at my tone, Catalina shook her head before saying, "No, but if you need my help ... I'm just a call away."

"Trust, I won't need your help. Thank you for everything," I graciously replied before shaking each of their hands.

When I returned inside of the emergency room, Sonica told me that Dom Dom was stable. I was beyond thankful and relieved that my baby was going to make it. Instantly, I thanked God for answering our prayers. Even though I knew Dom Dom was okay, there was sure to be more chaotic times when he learned who shot him.

I stayed at the hospital until he was placed in a room. The sight of my boo lying in a hospital bed with that piece of a gown on his well-built body broke my heart and infuriated me at the same time. I sat close to him, kissed the back of his hand, and whispered to him that I was going to handle the situation.

The second I hopped to my feet, Desaree and Sonica asked, "Where are you going?"

"To one of my houses," I voiced as I didn't look at them.

"I want to know who did this to my son, Tashima?" Sonica angrily voiced.

"Stay right here at this hospital and I promise you will know exactly who did it," I stated before I left the room, running.

I couldn't wait to get home because I was going to fuck up Dyon. He had a hard time hearing when I said not to do something. His ass was going to learn tonight what it felt like to disobey me. As I exited the hospital through the emergency room, everyone asked me questions about Dom Dom; I didn't respond. I didn't care what they thought. Truth be told, it wasn't any of their fucking business, to begin with.

After I unlocked my car doors, I didn't worry about placing the seatbelt over my frame. I wasn't planning on doing the speed limit, which wasn't going to allow me to be in the car for long. While I drove like a bat out of hell through the parking lot, Desaree called my phone. I ignored her call. I didn't have time for my sister to try to talk me out of what she knew I was going to do. She should've known by now that Dom Dom and Dyon meant everything to me, and that I didn't kindly to my orders being disobeyed.

Along the way to the house I shared with Dyon, I cursed out myself for how the guys acted towards one another. I didn't like that shit one bit. I hated to see them hurting all because I refused to make a choice. That's something that they needed to understand. Things would be a lot better for all of us if they simply realized that I couldn't leave them alone.

When I arrived home, Nixon's car was parked behind Dyon's vehicle. With an angry facial expression, I shook my head and loudly voiced every curse word that I knew. I let all of my anger out in the car.

While I let loose in the car, I had the entire scene playing out in my head. I was going to act like I didn't know that Dom Dom was shot. I was going to isolate Nixon and Dyon by asking Dyon could we go upstairs to talk privately. The moment we arrived in our room, I was going to let Dyon's ass have it.

As I gracefully exited my vehicle, I locked the doors and sauntered towards the elegantly designed front door. When I opened it, Nixon and Dyon were discussing their mother. It sounded as if something sad had happened or was about to happen to her. At that moment, I didn't give a damn. I had an important business matter to handle with Dyon. Whatever he and Nixon had to discuss would have to wait until it was time for that nigga to go to the hospital.

"Hey, baby," Dyon stated, looking at me with red, saggy eyes.

"Hi," I softly voiced as I looked amongst the brothers while walking into the kitchen.

"What's up, Tashima?" Nixon spoke dryly.

Catching his attitude, I ignored it by sighing heavily while placing my keys and small, black clutch on the kitchen counter before replying, "Exhausted. Frustrated. Confused. You name it. Y'all alright?"

"Nawl got som' fucked up news from Momma," Dyon replied, standing.

"How fucked up?" I inquired, not really wanting to know.

"I really don't want to talk 'bout it right now," he voiced as I wrapped my arms around his neck before placing a kiss on the top of his lips.

"When you are ready to talk, you know I'm here," I sincerely spoke before continuing, "Um, is it possible that we can speak in private?"

Nodding his head, he told Nixon that he would be back shortly. Dyon had no idea that he was going to return downstairs with assistance from his brother. While climbing the stairs to the master room, there wasn't a word that escaped Dyon's or my mouth. His breathing was steady and calm, just the way I needed it to be; as mine was the same.

Upon entering the room, I closed and locked the door. I walked towards my side of the bed, which I had a .45 hidden behind the black nightstand, taking the gun off safety. As Dyon planted his bottom on the bed, he sighed heavily before looking at me. The look in his eyes tore my heart, but it wasn't going to stop me from doing what I had to do.

"What did you do tonight after you got off the phone with me, Dyon?" I questioned as I removed the chrome and purple .45 from behind the nightstand.

"Rode 'round wit' Nixon to clear my head. The news we got 'bout Momma put me on another level. Why, you ask?" he inquired as he sadly looked at my gun and then at me.

Oh, this nigga act game good or his mother's words shook his ass up, I thought as I voiced in agitated tone, "I'm going to ask your ass one more time ... what did you do tonight after you got off the phone with me, Dyon?"

"I already told you what I did," he responded with a raised eyebrow.

Pow.

"Oh shit! What the fuck Tashima?" he painfully screamed in a shocked manner, all the while grabbing his left leg.

"Why fucking lie to me?"

"Ahh. Oh fuck. I told you I was out ridin' 'round wit' Nixon. Whatever happened ... I was not responsible!" he shouted as I slapped his hands away from his leg before sticking my finger in the hole, causing him to grimace.

As I heard Nixon asking questions along with heavy stomping, I placed the gun underneath Dyon's chin as I spoke through clenched teeth, "You see, you lie too much for me. Little did you know, I was on the phone with Desaree when she was talking to Nixon. I know everything that you did and said."

The look on Dyon's face was priceless.

"Let me expla—"

"Open the fuckin' door, Tashima!" Nixon yelled while banging on the object.

"I don't want to hear shit you have to say, Dyon. You have disobeyed me. You brought this bullshit on yourself, and for that, I'm really angry with you," I announced as I removed the gun from underneath his chin, stepped back, and fired two bullets into his body—stomach and shoulder.

"What in the fuck! Open this damn door, now!" Nixon shouted as he banged on the door several times while his brother glared at me through bucked eyes.

"I told you, and I told Dom Dom that y'all were not to touch each other. I meant what the fuck I said. I let you slide too many times by disrespecting him. You will never go against my fucking word. Learn your fucking place as I have learned mine! From this motherfucking night forward, I am both of y'all's niggas woman. If you don't like it, take the same gun that you shot Dom Dom with and put it to your fucking head," I spat as Nixon kicked in the door.

With my gun pointed at him, he held his hands above his head and slowly said, "I had no dog in that fight, Tashima. I told that nigga not to do it. I just want to get my brother to the hospital."

Not dropping my gun, I told him, "I know. Make sure you take him to Baptist East. If I find out he's not there, I will shoot your ass next, and no, I won't flake out."

As Nixon carefully grabbed his brother, blood seeped onto the white, soft poodle-haired carpet. I had to hold my breath from crying and spazzing out in the room. Things were going to change for my loves and me. I had a lot of making up to do towards them. When Nixon and Dyon were out of the house, I broke down. My men were hurt, and it was my fault. I didn't know how much damage was really done until they were well, and I prayed like hell that I wouldn't regret shooting Dyon.

My face was soaked with tears as I stripped off my clothes. I cried for old and new. I sobbed so much that my stomach hurt. A sister was all cried out and ready to begin my next task—ensuring that I was by my men sides.

Looking at the clock, I walked into the bathroom. I didn't have any time to waste; therefore, I took a quick shower, changed clothes, and exited the crime scene, which I was going to catch hell cleaning when I returned home.

Whew, Lord, this has been one trying week. Give me the strength to deal with the aftermath, I thought as I stepped into the thick night's air.

CHAPTER TWELVE

Dom Dom

Two Weeks Later

"Son, how in the fuck did you let a nigga shoot yo' fuckin' whip up like that?" Marc Jack inquired as he glared into my face.

Sighing heavily, I stared at the nigga and spat, "What else was I supposed to have done, Marc Jack? I was fuckin' drivin'."

"You supposed to have someone watchin' yo' six at all times," he continued, shaking his head.

"An' exactly who in the fuck that was supposed to have been? I don't trust anyone like that anymore," I told him as Tashima walked into the front room, holding a cup of juice.

"Well, you need to employee som' niggas to do that job," he fussed as Tashima handed me the cup.

"Mane, look, I don't need to hear all of that. You rolled how you rolled. I'mma roll the way I want. I'm sick of talkin' 'bout this street shit. I'm in recovery, woe. Tashima handlin' shit. So, why don't you feel free to talk to her," I voiced in an agitated tone.

"I don't mean any disrespect, but the organization was mine, which I handed to you. You got jammed up an' handed it to her.

I Now Pronounce You, Mr. and Mrs. Thug 2

Yes, she has done wonderful things, but this street shit is no place fo' a woman," Marc Jack voiced as Tashima took a seat next to me.

Clearing her throat, Tashima politely said, "No disrespect, Marc Jack, I've done shit that you nor any man could've done or half-ass done. So, I earned my right to do whatever the hell I please in this game. I don't see anything negative that I've done. I've increased the products and money flowing through the organization. I have invested illegal money into stocks. I have fed the same community that you and others affected in a major way. Truth be told, I am the reason why you had some power while still locked down. Instead of being like most Black males are towards females, give me my damn props because I earned the hell out of them."

As the front door opened, Momma strolled in humming and waving as sweat dripped down her face while her earbuds were stuck in her ear. As I observed her chipper behavior, we waved back. Momma had been that way since Marc Jack showed face at my front door earlier this morning. I was stunned that he was out early. From what Tello told me, he and Uncle Bo Jack wasn't expected to be out until two months from now. With that knowledge, I wasted no time asking him why he was out so early.

Looking at me confused, Marc Jack asked, "Who told you that I was supposed to have gotten out in two months?"

"Tello," I replied as Momma waltzed into the living room, kicking off her black New Balance shoes before taking a seat a few inches away from me.

Marc Jack said, "I don't know why he would say that."

"I see there is a serious conversation going on. What have I missed?" Momma asked, looking between Tashima, Marc Jack, and me.

Quickly, I responded, "I saw Tello at the club the night I got shot, an' he told me that Marc Jack an Uncle Bo' Jack supposed to be out in two months."

"Oh," Momma replied, folding her legs.

"Som' shit don't smell right, Marc Jack," I voiced as Tashima placed her head on my shoulder.

"What?" my father asked looking at me quizzically.

Immediately, I was placed in investigator mode. After all, Tashima and I had unfinished business with Marc Jack's family and Catalina. Now, was the best time to ask my father about his family members.

"Marc Jack, how well do you know Uncle Bo Jack? I know he's yo' brother an' all, but how well do you really know him?"

"What kind of question is that, Son? If you are insinuating somethin', you better think twice. I trust my brother wit' everythin' in me," Marc Jack stated with a frown on his face.

As I shook my head, I replied, "Well, you shouldn't trust a rat, an' yes, I have evidence to support what I'm sayin'. Tello an' their crew are snitches. Tashima an' I saw supporting details. A supplier refused to work wit' us because of them."

"Wow," Momma replied as she looked at Marc Jack in a shocked manner.

"I don't believe that shit at all an' neither should you. Where did you get that bullshit from?" he asked while chuckling.

"Catalina … The Don's great-granddaughter," I replied.

Instantly, Marc Jack stopped laughing and glared into the eyes of Tashima and mine. The silence in the room was eerie as we didn't stop looking at one another. Finally, Marc Jack stood, slowly walked towards the large window, peered out of it, and shook his head.

Marc Jack faced us and said, "This shit isn't makin' any sense."

"Do you need to see the official paperwork yourself? I'm sure Catalina wouldn't mind showin' you … since the only reason she considered workin' wit' us, after I check out Uncle Bo Jack an' the others, was because of you. The Don told her great things 'bout you."

Sternly my father replied, "Hell yes, I want to see the paperwork. I won't believe anythin' until I examine every document myself. Bo Jack has never been a snitch. We were breed not to be. This shit is surreal to me."

He was in denial, but I sure as hell wasn't. I didn't see the need for Catalina to lie about some shit like that. What would she gain by lying or falsifying documents? She needed clients to purchase her product.

"Marc Jack, do you have a brother by the name of Nick Jack?" I questioned while he walked towards the sofa.

Immediately, sadness appeared on his face. Something wasn't right, and I was going to press the issue to find out why.

"Why are you lookin' like that?" I asked as he took a seat next to me, glaring into my face.

"Nick Jack died when Bo Jack an' I went to prison. A drug deal gon' wrong," he sadly stated.

Tashima rose off my shoulder, glared into my face. The look we gave each other had my parents questioning why we looked at each other in that manner.

Sighing deeply, I said, "Nick Jack ain't dead. He's a snitch as well. He's on the paperwork also. What I find odd is that you were in the Feds fo' the same charges as Uncle Bo Jack, an' yo' name wasn't mentioned, not one time. Now, if yo' mind all fucked up … just wait 'til you read every word on that damn document. I highly believe those niggas are up to somethin' that has a lot to do wit' our demise. I don't trust Tello at all. When I talked to him that night at the club, his body language was off. He made sure to tell me that Uncle Bo Jack didn't like Tashima runnin' the organization, just like you stated."

Exhaling sharply, he said, "Arrange a meetin' wit' Catalina … ASAP. If we gotta go to her, then I'm ready."

"A'ight," I replied as I looked at Tashima and told her to make it happen.

Placing a kiss on my cheek, she whipped out her cellphone and dialed Catalina's number. On the fourth ring, she answered the phone. Tashima didn't waste any time placing the call on speaker.

"Hello, darling. How are you?" Catalina spoke in her thick, native accent.

"I'm fine. How are you?"

"Better, after hearing your voice. How may I help you, sweetheart?" Catalina flirtatiously spoke, causing everyone to glance at Tashima with a raised eyebrow. I found woman flirtation sexy as fuck; yet, I couldn't tease Tashima about that since important business was at the forefront.

"Hopefully, you are still in the States so that we can talk about what you showed Dom Dom and me two weeks ago," my baby voiced as she connected her hand into mine.

"I'm actually in Las Vegas for another hour or so. Once I leave here, I will make a pit stop into Montgomery. Is there anything else that you will need?"

"No, that is all," Tashima stated.

"Did you take care of that problem from two weeks ago?"

With a questionable look upon my face, I glared at Tashima as I wanted to know what Catalina was talking about.

"Yes, I did. I'm very sure I won't have those problems anymore," Tashima professionally yet sternly voiced.

"Very well, then. Like I told you before, if you need my help in that department, I will gladly put my men on it."

"No need," Tashima stated as she hopped away from the sofa, slowly moving her neck from side-to-side.

Once the call ended between the ambitious women, I asked, "What took place two weeks ago? I know I was shot, an' I know that fuck ass nigga Dyon was shot as well."

Turning around to look at me, Tashima replied with a smile on her face, "Nothin' that you need to worry about. Everything has been taking care of."

Repeatedly, Momma cleared her throat while looking at Tashima. My baby refused to look at my mother, which further caused me to think that something happened that neither of them told me.

"I know damn well we ain't keepin' no secrets up in this bitch! What in the fuck is going on, Tashima an' Sonica? One of y'all better spill the beans. Y'all know who shot me? Tashima, you went and shot the nigga that blasted me?"

Neither of the women said a word as Tashima's phone rang. Immediately, she silenced the device. The only time she silenced her phone in a hurry was when Dyon called or texted.

Angrily, I spat, "Answer that nigga's motherfuckin' phone call, guh!"

"Will you calm down, please?" she voiced while walking towards me.

"Tashima, I'm a whole different nigga since I don't know who shot me; yet, I got a feelin' that you an' Sonica know. I'm on pins an' needles 'bout everybody 'round me, especially yo' ass. So, if I didn't make myself clear when I first touched down, I will make myself clear this time," I slowly and sternly spoke while eyeing her.

Dropping in between my legs, Tashima sighed heavily before saying, "I'm the last person you need to look at skeptically. I have always had your best interest at heart. I've always followed your commands until you asked me for one thing. I need you to trust me now more than ever. Can you do that?"

"Do you know who shot me?" I inquired through clenched teeth.

She gazed at me for the longest before I yelled the question at her again.

Slowly, she nodded her head.

"Who?" I barked in her face.

"I took care of it," she said, eyes searching mine.

Still, in her face, I yelled, "If I gotta ask one mo' time, it's really going to be som' fuckin' problems!"

Not backing down, she firmly spat, "I said I fucking took care of it. All I need you to do is rest so that we can focus on the most important task at hand."

Seeing that she wouldn't tell me who shot me, it was a no-brainer who did it. The only persons she would protect with everything in her were Desaree and Dyon. Since Desaree didn't have any issues with me, the only person left was Dyon.

Hysterically laughing, I hastily and angrily spat, "Bitch, you been up in my motherfuckin' face all this motherfuckin' time ... an' you knew that fuck nigga shot me! That nigga was close to takin' my fuckin' life! All because of yo' ass! There shouldn't have been a reason why his ass still breathin' after the fuckin' shit he pulled between Munk an' me. You are one hard-headed, know it all bitch! If you don't get yo' triflin' ass the fuck up outta my house, I know somethin'! You is one disloyal ass black bitch that I don't need 'round me, period!"

"Son, calm down before you say something that you will regret?" Momma stated while rubbing the back of my hand.

"I'm calm. Just sayin' shit fo' what it is," I snarled as my eyes never left Tashima.

As we glared at each other, I felt as if she was testing me. She hadn't budged or said a word, which pissed me off more. Not liking how she was testing my gangster, I grabbed her neck and shoved her on the floor. Marc Jack and Momma grabbed ahold of me as I balled my fist. I was thankful that they were present because I was going to beat her ass to sleep; too much shit has happened, and I hadn't punished her ass for it. Trying to calm down, I knew that I had to cease the relationship between Tashima and me, but not before I killed that nigga Dyon in her face.

"Tashima, you need to leave," Momma spoke sternly as Marc Jack shoved me onto the sofa.

Standing to her feet, Tashima said, "I had already known that Dyon had shot you before Catalina called to tell me. Once you were stable, I left the hospital and went to the house that he and I share. I politely shot his ass three times. He's wearing a colostomy bag for six months because of me. That motherfucker will have intensive physical therapy because I purposely shot him in a particular area in his leg and shoulder. I meant what I said when I told both of y'all asses not to fuck with each other."

"You raggedy, wouldn't have shit if it wasn't fo' me an' my momma, will never amount to shit but being two niggas cum bucket, treacherous, dangerous, good fo' nothin' but a fuck an' gettin' money, black hoe, get the fuck out of my face. I should've left you an' Desaree fo' dead, bitch! Give all keys to Sonica. Don't you or yo' sister show y'all faces 'round me, or I will gun y'all asses down. Don't step foot in any of the hoods that I oversee. You are no longer fuckin' wit' me an' my people. As far as Catalina, it is what it is," I slowly voiced while evilly glaring at her.

"Dominick Rodgers, stop talking right fucking now!" Momma spoke as she slapped the shit out of me.

"Mane, fuck that bitch! On gawd, fuck that bitch! She can die right along wit' Dyon. I'm sure you'll place her by her father's corpse, Sonica," I spoke as my body trembled from anger while Tashima ran towards the front door with a ringing cell phone in her hand.

That bitch got me all types of fucked up, I thought as the front door slammed.

"Son, you better make sure that she doesn't destroy what I've built," Marc Jack stated sternly.

"Dude, get the fuck from 'round me talkin' shit I don't want to hear. You worried 'bout this stupid ass street shit. Nigga, when in the fuck you gon' be worried 'bout me fo' a fuckin' change?" I angrily hollered as I stood, glaring into his face.

Chuckling, he spat, "I'm the wrong nigga to go up against."

"Shid, we'll see 'bout that shit," I spat before continuing, "You can leave now. You have worn out yo' fuckin' welcome, nigga. Momma, I'mma talk to you later. I need som' space."

Marc Jack acted as if he wanted to say something, but Momma nipped it in the bud. Three minutes later, my house was quiet, and I tore that motherfucker up. I was angry, pissed, and confused.

After I destroyed the kitchen, living room, and front room area, I stood in front of the mirror, glared at my physique, and spoke, "As of this day, not one damn bitch matter to me. From here on out, I will show motherfuckas that I am not a fuckin' Fisher-Price toy."

CHAPTER THIRTEEN

Dyon

My life was awkward and filled with sorrow, pain, and confusion. Not only was Tashima and my relationship strained, so was my relationship with my brother. Ever since Tashima shot me, Nixon and I had been arguing about that incident, the shooting of Dom Dom, and us not being there for our mother as she took her last breath in Switzerland while Auntie Mesha was by her side; we did talk to her before the doctors ended her life.

Nixon had accrued hatred for Tashima because he knew that I wasn't on the right path as far as dealing with her and because we didn't say our goodbyes to our mother in person. Nixon wanted to support our mother, but because of the situation I found myself in, he wouldn't leave my side even though I told him to go. I had a lot of making up to do, and it was going to take a while before he forgave me for the things that happened two weeks ago and still ongoing.

Nixon wanted my relationship with Tashima to be over. Of course, I didn't give him what he wanted; I loved the shit out of Tashima. I knew there would be consequences to my actions for shooting Dom Dom. However, I didn't know that shit would've happened the way that it did. I had to wear a colostomy bag for six months before the surgeon did a reversal surgery. In three months, I would be under the care of physical therapist for my shoulder and leg. Tashima hit me in spots that would cause issues for a minute.

With the foolery that I did, I couldn't be mad at her for my condition. I brought it upon myself. That was another reason Nixon was pissed at me; he felt like Tashima should mean nothing to me. My brother refused to leave my personal life alone, which resulted in his own relationship crumbling. He took his frustrations out on Desaree, which caused him to be in the doghouse; damn near shoving me further in there with his ass. It seemed like he wanted Tashima to be on his ass and mine by the way he carried on. It didn't take me long to put my brother in his place, which resulted in a heated argument.

While arguing with Nixon, he didn't waste any time telling me that Tashima was taking care of Dom Dom and me. Apparently, Dom Dom, Tashima, and I were the talk of the town. People didn't mind telling Nixon that they saw Dom Dom and Tashima together before she arrived home to me. I couldn't focus on what Nixon informed me; I had to focus on myself, physically and mentally. The death of my mother weighed heavily on my soul and heart. I was in a vulnerable state, and I wasn't ready to deal with the matters of Tashima's heart, not yet that was.

Nixon thought I was a pussy ass nigga for allowing Tashima to walk over me. I didn't give a fuck what my brother thought. All I cared about was Tashima and when and where Dom Dom and I would have a gun battle. I tried to press Tashima for answers on that matter, but she would always say that shit was gucci. Those few words informed me that Dom Dom had no idea that I shot him. Yet, I still watched my back whenever I stepped out of my home.

"Time to change that bag. You ready?" Nixon dryly spoke while walking in to my bedroom.

talked to me in a dry tone, which I had grown accustomed to, yet I hated.

"I can change it," I replied as I glared into his face.

"Last time you changed that bag, it was not secured, and shit went everywhere," he replied.

Not giving a damn about the colostomy bag, I sighed heavily because it was time to set things right, respectfully with my brother.

Sincerely, I spoke, "Bro, I made a mistake an' didn't think of the consequences of my actions, or it could've been that I never thought Tashima would shoot me. Either way, it's my fault that you are angry. I am sorry, an' I will spend the rest of my life makin' things up to you. I promise," I told him as he grabbed the medical supplies.

"Mane, just stop fuckin' talkin'," he hissed as Tashima walked across the threshold of the bedroom.

"Nixon, I'm responsible for your brother's condition. I will take care of him. Also, I will apologize for my behavior that allowed you to miss the final days of y'all's mother's life. I meant what I said to your brother and Dom Dom. If they would've listened to me … none of this shit would've happened," she softly voiced as she placed her phone and keys on the dresser.

"Mane, look, you are dealin' wit' two street niggas that love yo' motherfuckin' ass. You can't have yo' cake an' ice cream. They ain't havin' theirs, well Dyon ain't. What gives you the damn right to think you can have both? You didn't think that antic wouldn't cause chaos?" Nixon spat, throwing the medical supplies on the bed.

"I knew it would be chaos, but not this chaotic. I … I …," she stammered, glaring between Nixon and me.

"You fuckin' thought they would come 'round to sharin' you. Live in a big ass house. Being one happy family, huh?" he questioned with a smirk on his face.

Lil' do you know brother, Dom Dom an' I are family, I thought as Tashima looked at Nixon and didn't utter a word or move.

"You ain't gotta answer me. I know what you want. Let me tell you somethin', that lil' plan of yours ain't gonna work, an' it never will. You are playin' in a field that will get people, including innocent, killed. Do you not understand that?"

The soft, nice girl act disappeared when she retrieved the medical supplies, kicked off her shoes, and glared into my brother's face before saying, "I'm well aware of shit can get real sticky. So, sticky, that you wouldn't believe. The best thing you can do is leave shit up to me. From this day forward, neither one of them niggas will do anything to the other. That being said, I would advise you to make amends with Desaree. From what she didn't tell me, shit ain't too good on the home front. While you are worried about my love life, you better be worried about yours ... and the way you breathe."

Angrily, Nixon walked into Tashima's face and yelled, "I don't give a fuck 'bout yo' threats! You ain't shit without yo' gun an' that's fact!"

"Bro—"

Before I could finish my sentence, Tashima chopped Nixon in his throat before kicking him in the balls. She kneeled in front of my baby brother and spat, "Fuck ass nigga, I don't need a gotdamn gun to dismantle a stupid motherfucker like you. I'm not myself when I don't have my niggas, Dom Dom and Dyon that is, on one accord with me. I would advise your goofy ass to stir clear of shit that has nothing to do with you. Now, once the pain subsides, get your ass to my sister and apologize for your behavior. She had no control over anything that I did."

I didn't have a dog in the fight; therefore, I didn't say shit. I had been told Nixon to watch how he spoke and looked at Tashima. No, I wouldn't let her harm him with a gun or any other weapon, but he had to respect the woman because she was the head honcho in everything that we did. For her to demand honor and respect was no different from a top-notch nigga gunning for his respect and admiration. Some males didn't like alpha females, but I didn't see a damn thing wrong with a woman handling her business.

In some cases, women were better at a man's job just because they think further than we do. They planned and executed their strategies better than we did. The dope game was just like any other game in society. Men were viewed to be superior, and the respect came quickly as opposed to the women.

The moment Tashima walked towards me, Nixon stood, shook his head, and angrily spat, "Bro, you too damn old to be actin' stupid as hell. Love ain't all that when you arguin' an' shootin' a nigga 'bout a female. Momma ain't raise you to be a damn dummy. When the day comes an' it's mo' drama than you can stomach, I don't want to hear shit."

"Nixon, go to Desaree an' work on yo' relationship. This one here has nothin' to do wit' you," I told my brother as Tashima grabbed the wound cleansing spray and a large gauze pad.

Without saying goodbye, Nixon exited the room, huffing and puffing. Tashima nor I didn't say a word until Nixon yelled that he locked the door behind him. The air in the room became stuffy as I glared at Tashima. There was so much that I wanted to say, but I didn't know where to begin.

"Um, we in one hell of a tangle, huh?" I stated, trying to break the ice.

"Yep," she replied sadly while cleaning my wound.

"What's wrong?"

"Everything."

"Talk to me. At one point, an' time, you used to tell me everythin'. Why you stopped?"

Sighing sharply, she applied the adhesive glue to the circular area of the colostomy bag and placed it on me before looking into my eyes and said, "I created a nasty web, Dyon. I caused two people that I loved the most pain, anguish, and frustration. How in the hell am I supposed to sleep knowing that there's a possibility that y'all will be at each's neck? I don't want to be on pins and needles whenever I step out with the other. I don't want to hide the fact that I'm in love with you and Dom Dom. I don't want shit to get hectic because I *will* not choose between the two of you."

I knew that I shouldn't have been amazed at what Tashima said because Nixon had called it. Yet, my dumb ass said, "So, what Nixon said was true. You do want him an' me at the same time ... being one big happy family, huh?"

"Pretty much."

Tell her you an' Dom Dom are cousins, I thought shaking my head before saying, "Tashima, that shit ain't right. People would look at us crazy as fuck. Our names would never leave folks mouths."

"Ask me do I give a fuck. Nobody on this damn earth can say what we can and can't do. We don't work for anybody. We, the three of us, damn near own the streets. We feed families. Who in the hell would dare to say something to me about our personal lives? Who sliding off in me within the same day or same week, is nobody's gotdamn business but ours."

Guh, yo' ass got cousins in love wit' yo' ass. She needs to know the truth, I thought as she removed the medical supplies and stray papers off the bed.

"If the shoes were on the other foot, how would you take me sayin' the same shit that you are sayin' to me?"

Chuckling, while shaking her head, Tashima voiced, "I would be just like y'all ... not hearing a damn word."

TN Jones

"Right," I responded as I grabbed her hand.

Sighing heavily, Tashima placed her eyes on me and gently voiced, "I really do hate that I had to shoot you. I badly wanted to shoot you in your neck like you did him."

"I know."

"What made you go against me? Why did you have to thicken shit?"

"I guess I knew that you love him mo' than me, an' that shit angered me. I don't want to share you, Tashima. I feel like wit' that nigga out of the way you'll be all mines. Now, I see that you will not, an' truth be told, I feel like a fuckin' fool, yet I need you mo' now."

Fuck tellin' her. May the best cousin win.

"You should be angry with me, Dyon. Why aren't you?" she inquired while lying in the crook of my arm.

"Because I can't be. Even though I didn't get a chance to talk my mother out of leavin' this world, or that I couldn't be there, physically, wit' her durin' her final days, or understand why I can't leave you alone after you shot me an' ordered Nixon to take me to the same hospital as Dom Dom, I can't place hatred on you. I have to target that energy on myself. I am the reason why all of this negative shit started."

Sincerely glaring into my eyes, Tashima bit her bottom lip while placing her hand on my cheek. Slowly, she moved her face towards mine before planting her juicy lips on mine. My once comatose dick was brought to life. The fucker was harder than ever. As bad as I wanted to part Tashima's legs, I wouldn't dare with a shit-bag strapped onto my body. I couldn't see her sucking on my tool as feces dropped in the bag. There was no telling how I would react.

Climbing on top of me, Tashima unbuttoned her bottoms. While she kicked them off, I removed my mouth from hers and said, "Nawl, I don't want to do anythin'."

"Because of the bag?"

Nodding my head, I said, "Yep."

"Fuck that bag. Through the good and the bad, that dick belongs to me. So, whenever I want it … I'mma get it," she sassily spoke while taking off her pink thongs.

"Fuccck," I groaned as my eyes landed on her pretty, fat pussy.

"Are you going to deny me, Dyon?" she purred before biting her bottom lip.

"Never, but I feel uncomfortable as hell tryin' to engage in sex."

"Let me fix that for you," she announced with a wicked smile on her face.

Tashima hopped off the bed and walked to the closet. When she returned, she had weed and a cigarillo pack in her hand.

Gently, she sat on the edge of the bed and did her thing. Lovingly, I watched my beauty as I awaited her thick body to be on mine.

Five minutes later, we were outstretched on the bed and smoking, all the while listening to a mixed CD that was in the stereo system.

Gracious for the weed, my confidence level was restored. My prior thoughts of not having sex until the removal of the colostomy bag were obsolete. I was ready to eat and dick my girl down. With the blunt pressed between my lips, I puffed on it while climbing between her legs. After I inhaled three times, I passed it to Tashima. With one hand behind her head, she took a couple of hits from the blunt before placing it in the ashtray. As she lovingly gazed at me, I took pleasure in sucking on her thighs while squeezing on that juicy ass of hers.

Before I could sniff the pussy good enough to have Tashima squirming, the damn doorbell chimed as my cell phone rang a unique tune that I had assigned for Auntie Mesha. Knowing not to ignore the call, Tashima answered my device.

"Hello," she stated in the phone as I huffed and sat upright.

"Okay. I'll be down to open it," Tashima replied before pressing the end selection on my phone.

As she placed the device on the nightstand, Tashima said, "Mesha's at the door."

"I kinda figured that," I spoke as I handed Tashima her shorts.

"We going to pick up where we left off the second she's gone," my baby voiced as she jumped to put all that ass in her denim shorts.

"We sure as hell are," I loudly spoke, slumping onto the black covers on my bed.

As pleasantries sounded off between Auntie Mesha and Tashima, I wondered why she was in the city. It had been a long time since she had graced Montgomery with her presence. I highly doubt that she wanted to check on me since she was clear about losing respect for me.

"Hey Dyon," she emotionlessly said, stepping across the threshold of the master bedroom door as she held tightly to a small, red, black, and gold box.

"What's up, Auntie Mesha? What brings you by?" I voiced as I sat upright.

"Your mother wanted you and Nixon to have this," she stated, placing the box on the square table beside the door.

"What's inside of it?"

"I don't know," she voiced blankly.

"Auntie Mesha?"

"Yeah."

"Will you an' I ever be okay?"

"Maybe one day, but that day ain't today."

Nodding my head, I replied, "Okay."

"Do you know who shot you?"

Thrown off by her question, I glared at her before shaking my head and saying, "Nawl."

"Are you planning on finding out?"

"Maybe."

Disappointedly, she spat, "You just had to have this lifestyle, huh? You think this shit is cool? I'm hoping one day you and Nixon wake up and see that it's not. Please don't let me have to bury y'all too. Better get out while y'all can. I'm sure y'all have enough money to be and do whatever y'all want. Talk to you whenever."

"Okay," I replied as she exited my bedroom with Tashima on her heels.

Moving off the bed, I aimed for the table that held the exquisite box. The moment I held it firmly in my hands, I sighed heavily. Thoughts of my mother flooded my mind, and I became sad. A part of me wanted to open the box, yet another part wasn't ready to deal with the contents inside.

While I sighed sharply and held the box, Tashima walked into the room, asking, "You okay?"

"I don't think so," I told her as I eyed the box.

"Let's take a seat and look inside together," she softly voiced while grabbing my arm.

While making our way towards the bed, I felt the urge to open the box by myself in case a stream of tears seeped down my face.

"Can I have a minute to myself?" I asked, not looking at her.

"Sure thing," she quickly stated while leaning towards me and planting a kiss on my jaw. "I love you."

"I love you mo'," I replied as she turned, walking towards the door.

After Tashima closed the door behind her, I carefully opened the box. Upon the sight of the contents, tears streamed down my face. There were several pictures of my mother, Nixon, and myself; every major holiday and just because photos were taken. Behind the stack of images were two stationary papers, one with Nixon's name and another with my name on it. Taking a deep breath, I retrieved my letter and sat the box on the bed. As I stared at Auntie Mesha's handwriting, tears steadily seeped down my face.

My Precious Firstborn,

You have no idea how much you've made me happy and complete. I raised you to my best ability, and I know that I didn't fail you. Always remember that what you put in the universe, you'll get it back. I hate that our time was cut short by the accident, but even more, I hate that I had to leave you and Nixon. Do not grieve for me as I am no longer hurting or angry. I am at peace because this isn't a life for a woman who was once independent. Take care of your brother, and never leave his side for anything. When you want to see and talk to me, close your eyes, call my name, and I'll be at your side, listening. Know that I loved you forever and a day, Dyon, and I always will.

Always, Momma.

I reread the letter multiple times in hopes of coping with the fact that she had to do what was best for everyone involved. In the end, I wasn't ready to accept that decision. Blankly, I placed the letter inside the box and glared at it. As I grabbed my phone, I overheard Tashima talking to a nigga with a raspy, deep voice. Without a doubt, I knew who was in my motherfucking house. Growling, I slowly stood and maneuvered towards the bedroom door.

How in the fuck did this nigga get my motherfuckin' address? I thought as I descended the stairs with a raised eyebrow as Bo Jack talked to Tashima in a fake tone. My girl knew when people didn't want to carry a conversation. Thus, she didn't say much to him.

When I landed on the last step, I glared into a long-shaped face, dark-skinned, shiny baldheaded, six-foot-two, muscular nigga. Bo Jack was dressed in the latest clothes and shoes. Gold jewelry was around his neck, wrists, and two rings on his pinky.

"My Son. We finally meet alas," he spoke, gold teeth shining brighter than the lights in the kitchen.

"Who told you where I lived?" I inquired as I stared into his eyes.

"Damn, no hey, or how are you?" Bo Jack asked while walking closer to me.

"Nawl. You are an uninvited guest who don't suppose to be free. So, who told you where I lived?" I spoke with more bass in my voice.

"I'm Bo Jack. Whatever I want to know, I will have within a matter of seconds, Dyon," he stated, inches away from my face before continuing, "Is there somewhere we can talk privately?"

"Yeah, right here," I told him as Tashima walked towards me with a confused expression plastered across her face.

"Good. Men talk is just fo' that men," Bo Jack announced in a tone that I didn't like while looking at Tashima.

Tashima sinisterly chuckled while slowing her pace and eyeing Bo Jack. The man didn't tear his eyes away from my chocolate lady. The look he gave her but me on edge, and I quickly checked him on it.

"Whatever heat you feelin' fo' that one, you better back off Bo Jack. She ain't you or nobody else's lick," I sternly stated as Tashima climbed the stairs.

With his hands in the air, Bo Jack chuckled before saying, "A'ight. Damn, Son, don't tear the top off my head. She's beautiful, mane."

"An' smart as fuck. Real ghetto when she wants to be an' 'bout that life. So please don't get shit twisted. Furthermore, stop callin' me, *Son*. You don't have the right to call me that," I stated as I pointed towards the sofa.

I didn't move from the stairs until Bo Jack walked away from me. I didn't trust the nigga at all; he wasn't going to walk behind me.

As we sat on the sofa, I looked at Bo Jack and asked, "What happened to you gettin' out in two months?"

With a serious look upon his face, he replied, "Oh, that was a lie. You see, you never tell people when you really hit the streets. A lot of motherfuckas don't know the Internet will tell you anything that you want to know. If you were smart, you would've found my location an' found out that three days ago was my release date."

Ring. Ring. Ring.

Tashima's phone rang; I heard it loud and clear. That meant either that she was listening to our conversation from the corner, or she had the bedroom door opened. On the second ring, she answered the phone. Immediately, I wondered who called her.

"To the conversation, we had two weeks ago, Dyon, I want to be powerful than I was before. With you an' Tello doin' y'all's thing, I would be back on top within a week. All I need fo' you to do is bring yo' muscle an' knowledge. You've been workin' wit' Tashima, so I know you know all of Dom Dom's organizational plans. So, tell me somethin' that I don't know?"

As I looked at Bo Jack, I realized what type of nigga that was talking to me. He was a gotdamn cross. He didn't want to get to know me; he wanted to know what I knew about his nephew. Shaking my head, I laughed.

"What's so funny?" Bo Jack asked as Tashima rapidly descended the stairs.

"Excuse me, fellas, I don't mean to interrupt, but um, Dyon, I'm finna make a run. I will be back," she rapidly spoke while gazing into my eyes.

She finna be gone fo' a minute. Guess she finna go take care of that nigga, I thought as I angrily voiced, "A'ight."

"Don't sound like that. I'll bring food from a restaurant. I don't feel like cookin' tonight."

"A'ight," I spoke through clenched teeth as she dropped her head towards mine.

Before I could move my face, Tashima placed her hand on the side of my face and lovingly spat, "I love you, and I always will. Don't you ever forget that."

I didn't acknowledge her; I simply stared into her eyes. They told a story that I wanted to hear. They saw things that I needed to see. As I studied her body language and eyes, Bo Jack made unpleasant noises. He was doing that shit on purpose, and I knew it pissed Tashima off. To the point, she stepped across the sofa, sat in my lip, and parted my lips with her tongue. After we engaged in a kiss that left my dick super hard, she slowly hopped off me but not before dropping my phone in my lap.

As she walked away, she said, "I will be back soon as I can, Dyon."

"A'ight," I replied.

With one thing on my mind, I wished that Bo Jack wasn't in my face. I didn't want Tashima out of my grasp. I didn't want her in the arms of my fucking cousin. I needed her with me; to console me as I thought of my mother and how I mistreated her.

"That girl got you an' that nigga wrapped 'round her pretty, long, black fingers," Bo Jack chuckled, shaking his head.

His comment and laughter ceased the disappointment of Tashima leaving the house.

"Can we wrap up this discussion that we were havin'? I have somewhere to be within thirty minutes," he rapidly spoke as his phone chimed.

"Actually, this conversation been over wit'. You must think I'm som' roody poo ass nigga. Bo Jack, I'm not pressed fo' a father. I never have been. My mother been great to me. You wasted yo' time tryin' to have a street-related relationship wit' me; that's the only reason you sought after me in the first place. You ain't going to use me like you used my mother. I can't help you in anythin' that you got going on. I got my own shit to handle."

As Bo Jack tried to lecture me on how we could take over the dope game, my cell phone chimed. Looking at my phone, I saw that I had a text message from Tashima. Instantly, I opened the message.

My Choco Baby: *Don't trust him. He and several people that run with Tello, including Tello, are snitches and on some cross shit.*

Me: *What do you mean?*

My Choco Baby: *I'll show you everything when I get back. I'm headed to pick up the proof now. There's a lot of shit you don't know about that father of yours. If you don't trust anyone, I need you to trust me. Please.*

Me: *Okay.*

Exhaling slowly, I shoved my phone into my pocket and looked into the man's face that helped my mother create me. I tried to read the nigga, but he had one hell of a poker face. The way he approached me told me that I didn't need to fuck with him on any level.

"Since you ain't tryin' to hear anythin' that I'm sayin' right now. Hopefully, you will hear this, you do know she gon' to be wit' that cousin of yo's, right? You gotta be real careful wit' that one, or she will do yo' ass terrible. Truth be told, you need to get rid of her ass ... once an' fo' all," Bo Jack stated with a raised eyebrow.

If she is, not in the way that you think, I thought as I replied, "Nigga, you ain't in a position to tell me shit 'bout a broad. You didn't do a good job by my momma. So, the best thing you can do is leave my personal business alone," I spat before telling him, "Thanks fo' the insight of how you think shit should go, but I can handle my own. I been handlin' it fine without you. Have a good one, Bo Jack."

Seeing that I wanted him out of my presence, he stood, nodded his head, and spat, "That pussy got y'all niggas actin' stupid. You'll be beggin' fo' my help once she has you in a pile of unnecessary shit."

Chuckling, I spat, "Have a good one, Bo Jack. It was nice talkin' to you. I'll be in touch when I'm ready to meet the family an' shit."

"Yeah," he stated while walking towards the front door.

Hopping to my feet, I was behind that nigga, ensuring that he didn't put any type of spying devices in our home. The text messages that Tashima sent me, I was going to take heed to it. She had never been wrong, and I sure as hell doubt that she would ever be wrong.

Shit, finna get real crazy in these streets. I need to make sure that my body is up fo' the shit that's going to come our way, I thought as I watched Bo Jack hop into the driver's seat of a new model, money green, Yukon SUV.

CHAPTER FOURTEEN

Tashima

Upon seeing a handsome dark-skinned dude at the door, I was puzzled as to whom he was, and what he wanted. When he asked for Dyon, I was intrigued by the mystery guest whom my love didn't inform me was coming over. The man looked and talked to me as if I was a simple-minded bitch. His somewhat polite speaking was fake as hell, and I gave him that same energy back.

To my surprise, I learned that the person in the house that Dyon and I shared was none other than the snitch of all snitches, Bo Jack. I didn't want to leave Dyon alone with the motherfucker since I only knew one thing about him. I didn't want Dyon to say anything that could be used against him.

As I decided to take my pretty ass time walking up the stairs, I thought about outing the fuck nigga that had some smart shit to say to and about me. That was until Dyon told that nigga a loving thing or two about me. Bo Jack had no idea who the fuck I was, even if he heard some unpleasant shit. I would shoot his ass in front of his son and go on about my day with a smile on my face.

I Now Pronounce You, Mr. and Mrs. Thug 2

One thing I didn't expect to learn was that Dyon and Dom Dom were cousins; thanks to Marc Jack and Bo Jack. My damn mind was blown, so blown that I didn't know what I should do about my feelings for them. As I stated a thousand times before, I needed them as much as I needed oxygen. I didn't want people to think I was nasty for dealing with family members, but shit, I had severe feelings for them that wouldn't go away. We had been through a lot.

With the newfound knowledge, about Dom Dom and Dyon, I was at a crossroads. I would have to decide which one I would be with because knowingly fucking cousins was not my thing. My fucking heart ached at the tough decision that I had to make. It wasn't long before my thoughts disappeared, thanks to Catalina calling to inform me of her whereabouts and that I should be at her hotel room within one-and-a-half hour.

In need of getting out of the house to vent about what I learned, I called my sister and told her that I needed to talk. Desaree stated that she needed to vent as well; therefore, we decided to meet at a Vaughn Park.

When I descended the stairs, I prayed that Dyon wouldn't act a fool about me leaving so soon and returning later in the day. The last thing I needed was for him to think that I was going to lay up with Dom Dom. I didn't want to have an argument about someone that talked so nasty to me that I cried on the way home to him.

After I told Dyon that I would be back, I didn't expect for him to be angry without saying more than two words. That damn Bo Jack worked my nerves with the weird noises that he made while evilly looking at me. To let him know that no matter how much he down talked me to Dyon, I wasn't going anywhere. My fucking name held weight in his son's heart and soul. Once I sincerely told my man that I loved him, I sensually and sloppily kissed him. My body was set ablaze as I couldn't wait to get back to him so that we could finish what we had started before Mesha showed face.

When I arrived inside of my car, I knew that I should've told Dyon about Bo Jack. Not going to leave our home until he knew the truth about the handsome, dark-skinned man, I texted him all the while praying that he didn't say a word to Bo Jack about what I knew. After I texted Dyon, I started the engine on my vehicle and left.

Along the way to Vaughn Park, I thought about what happened between Dom Dom and me. My feelings were still hurt, and I was yet to receive an apology from him. Never in a million years would I have thought he would have spoken harsh words to me and shoved me on the ground while talking mad shit. Just because I hurt him by keeping his shooter a secret didn't give him the right to talk to me like I was a piece of trash. If he were a nobody, I would've shot the shit out of him in front of his parents. Our history saved his ass.

With the nasty words that were spoken to me, I still loved him; however, I had to think about us more so than I had to think about Dyon and me. Dom Dom had been doing a lot of spiteful shit lately, and it was starting to be too much for me. I was very sure the second he thought about his behavior, he would be calling and apologizing. Justifying his action, I put myself in his shoes. I would've spazzed out to, maybe not as bad as he did on me, but I would've went crazy. Therefore, I tried not to dwell on his behavior so much.

Arriving at the park, I wasn't surprised to see the number of people visiting the vast acres of land. I was lucky to find a parking spot, one that was beside Desaree's gray crossover vehicle. She was sitting inside with her eyes glued to a parenting magazine. Seeing the word 'parenting' caused me to smile as positive emotions soared through me; I couldn't wait to be an aunt and one day become a mother. Oh, how spoiled our kids would be, and it would be mostly my fault.

As I shut off the engine, Desaree rolled down her window and said, "It's hot. I'm not about to get out of my car. We can vent in privacy in my nicely chilled truck."

"That's fine with me," I said as I hopped out of my whip.

The sun shined brightly as the heat waves didn't mind attacking my body. I hated the summer with a passion. The humid air, bugs, and I didn't go hand in hand. I loved the fact that I could sport my body in shorts and sundresses, but the heat made you want to walk around naked.

By the time I reached the passenger's side of Desaree's vehicle, I had exhaled and wiped a bead of sweat off my forehead.

"Hey, sissy," Desaree spoke as I opened the door.

"Hey. How are you?" I asked as she placed the magazine in her lap.

"Okay, I guess. How about you?"

"Girl, if only I could find the words to describe how I really feel."

"In that case, I will go first. It sounds like you have a heap of shit to get off your chest."

"I do, and you should go first."

Sighing sharply, she said, "Okay, so Nixon and I are having problems. Those problems stem from you shooting Dyon and still caring for him. I must say so myself, I do find that a little weird. Yeah, I know how you feel about Dyon, but look at the situation for what it is. It's an unnecessary, messy web. Things will only get worse, sis. Your issues are spilling into my home, which I hate. Nixon gets angry every time I tell him to mind the business that pays him. Yet, I don't expect him to actually stay out of your and Dyon's business because Dyon is all that he has besides our unborn baby and me. I guess what I'm asking ... is for you to decide who you *need* to be with. I don't want to see any more turmoil brought to Nixon. He's highly pissed that he wasn't in Switzerland with their mother. Even I felt bad about that."

"Nobody kept him in the States. Dyon told him to go. If he feeling ill about things, then that's on him. I told him that I would be caring for Dyon, and that's what I have been doing. I shot Dyon for a reason, and y'all know this shit. Now, as far as me, choosing ... that's surely hard now. Things have gotten a little more sticky than I had ever imagined that it would be. I have history with them, Desaree. I'm taking care of them until they fully recover. I can't stop loving them. Hell, I'm hoping that I hadn't lost Dom Dom. He's super pissed at me. By the way, I need you to stay clear of him. He spazzed out on me today while Sonica and his father were present. If it weren't for them, then Dom Dom and I would be physically hurt."

"Why he spazzed out?" she asked, with a raised eyebrow.

I knew not to have a leaky mouth with Desaree, especially concerning Dyon. She would tell Nixon, then there would be another shootout, and someone was going to die.

Shrugging my shoulders, I replied, "Can't tell you that."

"Whatever," she said as I saw Dom Dom's truck pulled into the park.

Instantly, my heart started to pump fast as my thoughts moved a mile per millisecond. As Desaree talked, I zoned out and focused on one of the niggas that drove me insane. While he parked his whip, I wondered whom he was meeting. Ten seconds of him stepping out of his vehicle, a light-skinned, pretty, average height, big booty broad wearing a short, blue sundress and bronze sandals ambled towards him, smiling with her hands outstretched. When he placed a kiss on her forehead as she kissed the base of his throat, I growled as I balled and un-balled my fists. My soul was hurt, and there wasn't a damn thing that I could do as I watched him grab her hand and connected their hands before they walked towards the green plains of the park.

"Why are you growling?" Desaree asked.

Pointing towards Dom Dom and the chick, I replied, "Because of them."

"Whoa!" she exclaimed, mouth open.

Placing her eyes on me, she questioned, "So, if he is that affectionate with another broad in public, then you know what you have to do; hell, he letting it be known that y'all are done. If he went to this extreme, then that blow up y'all had was severe. Tashima, what really happened between you and Dom Dom today?"

I Now Pronounce You, Mr. and Mrs. Thug 2

Desaree was right; for Dom Dom to be in the public's eye with another female, affectionately, things were not right between us. My eyes became teary at the thought of someone else being his pride while I was nothing to him. Not wanting to talk to my sister nor be around her, I knew that I had to end our time together. I wanted to be myself while I cried and drank. That was the only way I was going to get myself together.

After I told Desaree that I would talk to her later, I exited her vehicle, not scouting the park for Dom Dom. The second I hopped in the driver's seat of my car, my cell phone rang. Retrieving it out of my front pocket, I saw Catalina's name. Quickly, I answered the phone. The same way I answered the phone was the same way we ended the call. Her message was blunt; come to her now for the documents. As I peeled away from the park, I couldn't get the image of Dom Dom being with another woman out of my mind. Tears stung my eyes as my nose flared. My little soul was hurt, and I didn't know what to do with myself.

While driving, my mind was on Dom Dom and the chick before I thought of a question that left me puzzled. Tired of thinking, I was glad when I arrived at the liquor store. Thankfully, the store wasn't filled with people; after all, I had somewhere I needed to be. In no time, I had purchased a bottle of Hennesy and a cup of ice. In a distraught state, I didn't want anything to chase the brown liquor; the type of emotions I housed, I needed the liquid encouragement straight.

In a matter of seconds of sitting in the driver's seat, I filled the cup to the rim and took a healthy gulp of the alcoholic beverage. A chill ran through my body before a warm, bubbly sensation shook my core, which caused me to relax a little. Speeding away from the liquor store, one of the oldie goldie jams, *I Do Love You* by GQ, played on the radio. Thanks to my Dad, I loved that song.

Instantly, I turned up the volume, rocked along to the beat, and sang along. I put my heart and soul into a performance that only drivers would be able to see.

As I grooved to the song, I thought about the men that had a firm hold on my heart. The good moments we had together was at the forefront of my brain. I didn't want to think about the bad; it would only cause me to do or say something stupid.

When I arrived at the hotel, I was glad that Dom Dom nor Dyon was on my mind. I didn't have any more time to think about my love life. It was business time, and I had a grand show to put on for Bo Jack and his fuck ass cronies.

Before I stepped out of my car, I drank the rest of the liquor before checking my hair. Pleased with my appearance, I hopped out of my car quickly; to the point, my head swarmed as I almost kissed the ground. A sister was intoxicated as hell. Loving the drunken feeling, I sashayed my ass towards the entrance of the exquisite hotel that had a spa inside. The workers of the hotel greeted me, and my drunk self enthusiastically waved with a smile on my face. Upon entering the lavish elevator, I pressed the number two button. My fingers lingered a second too long, and I giggled.

I remembered the first time I had gotten drunk with Dyon; we were teenagers. Whew, did I feel great while I was drinking and after we had finished. His fingers, mouth, and dick did a number on me; such a good one that we had gotten drunk, often. The next day, I would have the worse hangover. I didn't like those, so I cut off the heavy drinking. Now, I only drank when my mind was boggled.

Ding. Ding.

The elevator stopped, and I blew out air. The moment the doors opened, I put on my business face and stepped onto the second floor's beautiful red, green, and tan carpets. Retrieving my phone, I dialed Catalina's number. On the second ring, she answered.

"I'm on your floor," I slurred.

"Are you drunk?" she snickered.

"Pretty much," I replied, seeing double.

"Wow. In the middle of the day? You must have something heavy on your mind?"

"Yep and yep," I announced as I stopped in front of her door, which was cracked.

Ending the call, I shoved the phone in my front pocket, greeted her before stepping inside of the chilled, beautifully decorated room. While I looked around the spacious hotel room, Catalina told me to make myself comfortable. Nodding my head, I did just that as I took a seat on the sofa. There was an eerie silence as she looked at me in a way that made me a little suspicious.

"Why are you glaring at me like that, Catalina?" I asked, sitting upright against the soft cushions of the couch.

"Because you are torn up, really. I have never seen you like this. Do you need to vent?" she asked, grabbing two tall wine glasses and an unopened bottle of wine off the counter.

"No, I'll think things through once I have the time to do so."

"Okay," she quickly voiced before taking a seat on the couch. "Now, what are you going to do with this information that you are about to receive?"

"Show it to Marc Jack, Dom Dom, and Dyon, who is one of Bo Jack's illegitimate children that he didn't want a single thing to do with when he was growing up," I blurted out.

"How are you going to show it to Marc Jack?" she inquired with a raised eyebrow.

"He and Bo Jack are free."

"What?" she loudly spat as she placed the wineglass on the carpet.

Nodding my head, I proceeded to tell her how I met the two men. That's when she learned that I was in love with cousins and had been for years. We agreed that Bo Jack was up to something and that we had to find out what it was. I was sure that he was trying to overthrow me as well as get rid of people that he disliked, and Catalina was sure that Bo Jack was going to mastermind his way into purchasing products from her.

For the next forty-five minutes, Catalina and I drank wine while plotting on how we were going to bring Bo Jack and his minions down. It was going to take a lot to infiltrate that man's system, but with the right people in place, we were going to come out on top. Once we stopped discussing business, we chatted about our personal lives. She told me about her upbringing as I did the same. Catalina and I had a totally different childhood, yet, we had the same views on the dope game. We felt that too many men got the big head and tried to outdo one another, causing unwanted stress for low-key drug dealers and their suppliers. Too much sneaky shit took place.

The next topic changed to marriage and having children. Our thoughts on that were different. I wanted to have children and be married, but of course, I wasn't going to be able to marry Dyon and Dom Dom at the same time; whereas, Catalina didn't want any children nor to be married. I was surprised. I thought every woman wanted a loving and doting husband, along with a couple of adorable kids.

"Nope, I will not deal with people and their fuckery. The last thing I want to do is have children involved. Shit will become too risky for me to handle," she stated, drinking the rest of the wine straight out of the bottle.

Ring. Ring. Ring.

Catalina's phone rang. She took her time lifting off the sofa. By her slow movement, I figured she didn't want to be bothered with her ringing device. I couldn't imagine being the 'main' plug. There was no peace. Motherfuckers would regularly call inquiring about picking up dope and etc. Then, some calls had nothing to do with purchasing drugs; those calls, I imagined, dealt with disloyal motherfuckers such as those that were like Bo Jack and Tello, snitches.

Once Catalina answered her phone, I stood and stretched before ambling towards the balcony. Upon opening the sliding door, Catalina talked in her native tongue, aggressively. As I walked towards the black rails on the balcony, I felt a slight breeze graced my body. The liquor in my system had me sweating and feeling as if I was on fire.

Arriving at my destination, I placed my arms on the rails, leaned my head back, closed my eyes, and exhaled sharply.

Zoning out, I focused on the sounds of the busy downtown area; it was soothing. Without a doubt, I knew that it was rewarding to stand on the balcony at night to see and hear the hustle and bustle of people commuting at night. Drinking or not, it was something about the blaring car horns, screeching brakes, loud music that would calm and relax me instantly.

Ah so serene, I thought as a kiss was placed on the sides of my neck while sensual rubs to my stomach and sides caused my eyes to open as my heart raced.

I didn't know what to think, but I knew I loved the way that damn Catalina rubbed and kissed me. My mind told me to pull away from her, but the liquor in my body wouldn't allow me to move, or maybe it was because I didn't want too.

As her soft, pale hands traveled towards the button of my shorts, I held my breath, only for a few seconds. Catalina was close to her target, which had only been touched sensually by Dom Dom and Dyon. The second her thumb arrived at my hot spot, my breathing became erratic as I bit my bottom lip. My calm, erotic reaction scared yet excited me. At that moment, I needed Catalina to take me to a place that I had never been--with another woman that was.

On the balcony, for quite a few people to see if they were looking, I allowed Catalina to suck, lick, and kiss on my neck as she fingered me. My mind was blown at the sexual things that I let another woman do, especially a woman that I was going to work with in the future.

"Mmph," I cooed as two of her slender, long fingers slowly slid in and out of my juicy pussy.

"You like that?" she sexily whispered in my ear.

"Yesss," I whimpered, slowly nodding my head.

"What until you feel my tongue," she stated, provocatively.

The thought of her tasting me had my heart pumping faster as I told myself that I was digging a hole that I wouldn't be able to get out of. For the life of me, I couldn't push Catalina's hand out of my shorts. My ditzy, horny ass began to fuck her fingers while passionately crying out her name.

"Time for us to go inside, Tashima. I've wanted to spread your thick thighs ever since I saw you," she moaned in my ear before nibbling on my ear lobe.

Slowly, I dropped my head. As we walked inside of the chilled room, I had two thoughts on my mind: one, to get the documents that I needed and go, and two, experience a woman between my legs, nut on her fingers and in her mouth, get the papers and go. By the time I reached the table, Catalina had shoved me against the circular object, parted my lips with her tongue, and sexily and slowly took off my thongs. Enjoying the kiss that she blessed upon me, my body involuntarily laid on the table. While her hands roamed my thighs, those motherfuckers opened like a cashier register after the cashier pressed the tender button.

Catalina removed her mouth from mine only to place her soft, petite lips on the front of my neck before licking every inch of it. My little body trembled as her wet tongue made circles on my jugular. A small gasp escaped my mouth as two of her fingers entered my leaky core. That damn cocaine supplier rocked the fuck out of my G-Spot as she sucked and toyed with my titties. I wanted to watch Catalina do her thing, but I felt ashamed for having her in between my legs, in which I wanted her there.

"God, you smell so good, Tashima," Catalina whimpered as she inhaled my hairless kitty.

"Fuckk," I mumbled, anxious to feel her mouth and tongue.

"Look at me while I taste you, Tashima," she seductively spoke, placing her hands underneath my ass.

No, I don't want too. You don't suppose to be in between my damn legs, I thought as I forced myself to look into Catalina's dreamy, hazel-green, almond-shaped eyes.

That damn woman flicked her tongue across my clit, causing my body to relax against the table as I cooed. I thought she was going to be sensual and slow. Fuck no! Catalina turned up with a mouthful of my pretty pussy. If I wanted to tear my eyes from her, I couldn't. She had me locked into what she was doing. I couldn't lie as if her face stuffed in my wet pussy wasn't sexy.

That shit turned me on something awful. I wasn't the timid, shamed being; I turned into the freak that only Dom Dom and Dyon saw.

"Oh my God, Catalina," I whined as I twirled my pussy on her mouth.

Growing bored with the submissive act, I turned into a stern, bossy bitch. I gripped Catalina's hair and rode that bitch's tongue like I did her fingers. She became a savage while indulging in my goodies. Rotating her head from left to right, while spitting on my pussy before savagely sucking on it, drove me insane.

Because of her messy antics, my body trembled as it grew hot. I was beyond aroused and pleased. I was eager to release my clear, sweet juices into her mouth.

"I'm cummin'!" I shouted as she pressed my body closer to her face.

"Let me have all of what your sweet pussy has to offer," Catalina spoke before aggressively humming, sucking, and licking.

"Jesusss," I loudly spoke as I pulled my hair.

Catalina attacked every nerve in my body, and I surely didn't know what to do or say. I was fucking amazed at my body's reaction. The fellas had my body weak, no lie, but Catalina had it on another level of weakness.

"My God, I see why they allow you to do whatever you want," Catalina spoke as her fingers passionately attacked every corner within my hotbox.

"Shiiii!" I yelled as she tapped on my G-Spot, all the while sucking on my clit.

Instantly, I became a wimp. That broad had me running from her mouth and fingers. The intense sensation I wasn't used too. My legs shook uncontrollably as I didn't know what to do with my arms. One minute, they were in the air, and the next, they were dangling off the table.

"Cum for me, Tashima," Catalina sexily spoke.

I didn't want too; her sex skills were too excellent for me to tap out so early. Therefore, I fought my nut. That was until that damn cocaine supplier tapped danced on my G-Spot.

"Aahhoouu," I cried out as my back arched; I exploded.

"Mmm," she groaned as her nose pressed against my sensitive clit—further causing me to moan curse words while twirling my pussy on her mouth.

While my trembling body was slumped against the table with Catalina still sucking and licking on my pretty kitty, I breathlessly said with a smile on my face, "My goodness."

As I came to my senses, Catalina removed her mouth from my pussy, slowly and sexily licked her lips before standing. Sitting upright, I placed my eyes on her. She was in lust with me, and I had to make sure that our little encounter wouldn't affect our working relationship. She had to know that nothing would come of us, and we were never going to do this again.

"Catalina, what just happened between us was cool, and it felt amazing, but this can't happen again. Mixing business with pleasure is never a good thing. I want us to have a working relationship together and nothing else. Can we not let this experience hinder us?" I softly stated as she dropped to her knees and grabbed my feet before sucking on my toes, all the while eye-fucking me.

Satan, I'm not playing with your ass today! This damn woman sucking on my toes! That's my weakness! Why you sic this damn demon on me? I thought as my body grew weak, causing my mouth to form the letter O.

"I know how to separate business from pleasure, Tashima? I suggest you learn how. I have wanted you for so long, and I'm prepared to do whatever I have to just to have your sexy, thick self, legs spread any chance I can get. I don't give a damn that you are in love with Dom Dom and Dyon. I'll be in the background. When they piss you off … I'll fly you out and suck and finger the frustration out of you," she sensually hissed in between sucking my third and fourth toes all the while thumbing my clit.

Fuck me, I thought as I realized that I moved her fingers from my clit and placed them at the opening of my coochie.

"Mmm, you want me to play with Ms. Wet Wet?" she asked after removing her mouth off my third toe.

"Yes," I heard myself say while nodding my head.

"I will gladly do that," she stated as she drove two fingers inside of me, causing my back to arch and my small voice to squeal her name.

"Before I leave the United States, it's my mission to have your juices saturated on every piece of furniture in this hotel room. I want you riding my face while playing with those lovely titties of yours. I want you to do so much shit to you that will have me as your side woman," she aggressively spoke while applying beautiful pressure inside of my dark tunnel.

"Catalliinnaa," I whined as I fucked her fingers.

"You sound so damn beautiful. You have no idea how long I've patiently waited for this day," she softly said while licking and kissing my right thigh.

While I lay on the damn table, feeling great and nutting, I thought, *What in the hell is wrong with me? What in the fuck am I really doing? I'm so fucked right now. I got too much shit going on to be involved with a woman that I need to conduct business with. I have no business allowing and wanting Catalina to touch me in such an intimate manner. Only Dom Dom and Dyon supposed to touch me like this. It was only supposed to have been them and me. This shit is absolutely ridiculous. I'm in love and fucking cousins, I still want to deal with them on that level, and I like how Catalina is making my body feel. I'mma bust hell wide the fuck open!*

CHAPTER FIFTEEN

Dom Dom

Three Days Later

Ever since I kicked Tashima out of my house, I hadn't responded to her texts or calls. I knew that she had some important matters to discuss with me; yet, I refused to talk to her. After learning that she knew about Dyon's actions towards me, I had to make sure that space was between us. If there weren't any, I would be liable to do something to her that I would regret later, such as the way I talked to her. After I had calmed down, I felt terrible about the things that I said to her; however, I couldn't find it in me to reach out and apologize.

I badly needed a distraction to ease my mind from the stressors that were placed in my life. A little fun had never hurt anybody; therefore, I hooked up Janesha Hamilton. I had met her during the last two years of my prison bid. I met the broad through one of the nigga's that purchased products from me. His old lady had a cousin that was looking for a prison pen pal. I was two-sided about the situation. I didn't understand what woman in her right mind would deal with a nigga that was in prison. After ole boy pestered me about the chick, I gave in and decided to hit the chick up. Who knew what she could do for me. I liked being able to have motherfuckers move for me at any time, especially gullible females. After four conversations with her, I could tell that she had her head on her shoulders. She had been single for a while and wanted to chat with someone that she couldn't see—those were her exact words.

The bitch was an okay distraction. She was beasty with her mouth game, but she wasn't shit compared to Tashima's ass. In no form or fashion was Janesha even comparable to Tashima; she was far from it. It wasn't long before I realized that Janesha's head wasn't on her shoulders. The moment she started talking about being my trap queen, I would cease her from talking by pulling out my dick or play in her pussy to keep her from talking about a position she would never fill. I had a trap queen; I was just pissed at her, and I probably wasn't going to be with her on that lovey-dovey tip like that.

Janesha was a thirsty bitch, but one thing I could say that she didn't mind working. She was not the type to sit on her ass and wait on a nigga to do anything for her. That's what I liked the most about her.

I never told her about Tashima; I didn't see the need to since I knew that Tashima wasn't going anywhere. Upon my release from prison, I never thought that I would ring Janesha's line. I didn't have the need to; I would be with my baby, and we would be starting our lives together, just like I had planned. Well, that shit went out the window soon as Tashima withheld information from me.

"What are we going to do today?" Janesha inquired as she stepped into her bedroom with a towel wrapped around her body.

Placing my feet into my shoes, I didn't look at her as I replied, "I don't know what you got going on, but I got som' work I need to do. Maybe later tonight, we can link up an' do somethin'."

"Aww. Well, I understand that you have shit to do, so I'll make sure that I'm free when you are ready to hang out," she replied, slowly walking towards me—licking her lips.

Not in the mood for her, I quickly stood and shoved my shirt over my head before grabbing my pistol and sticking it in the holster. Janesha sexually glared at me, and I ignored her I knew what she was trying and had been trying to do, and it was a big turn off. If she kept up her behavior, she would be demoted quickly to the non-existent bitch zone.

Sighing heavily, I glared into her face and dryly spoke, "I'm finna go."

Pouting, she replied, "Okay. Call me if you need me."

I didn't respond; I walked out of her one-bedroom, stylish, furnished apartment with my mind on one thing, talking to my parents. When I hopped in my whip, I powered on my phone, fired up a cigarette, and started the engine. As I reversed my vehicle, my mother called my phone. On the third ring, I answered the phone.

"Where in the hell have you been, Dominick Rodgers?" Momma questioned in my ear, loudly.

"Chillin'. What's up, Momma? Where you at?" I asked, exiting the secluded, calm apartment complex.

"I'm at your house with your father. We have been trying to contact you for days about some important information. I really do think that you need to see things for yourself," she stated in an agitated tone.

"I'm on the way now."

"Good, because this shit here and your father is about to drive me insane," she sighed.

"Momma, I'll be at the house in fifteen minutes. Okay?" I stated as I slowed for a yellow traffic light.

"Okay," she voiced as I heard my father go off.

"Sonica, I don't think I'm going to be able to wait to drop down on those fuck niggas! How in the fuck can I wait? Mane, a lot of fuck shit going on within my family. These niggas gotta go ASAP!" my father yelled, sternly and angrily.

"What in the hell is really going on? What has happened within these three days I been M.I.A?" I inquired as my father continued ranting.

"Son, just hurry up and get here. I gotta calm this man down before he starts a damn war we aren't prepared to win," she rushed into the phone as I mashed on the gas pedal.

"A'ight," I replied as she loudly asked who was at the door.

Intrigued by someone knocking on my damn door, I stayed on the phone, all the while asking Momma who was at my shit. When she didn't answer me, I pressed the gas pedal further to the ground. The second I heard Tashima's voice, I released the pressure off the gas pedal.

"What in the fuck is she doing at my motherfuckin' house, Momma?" I questioned through clenched teeth as if I didn't know why she was there. It was time to figure out how to take care of the snitches within the Jackson family.

"Just get your ass here! Now!" she shouted before ending the call.

As I drove to my home, angrily, I pondered what I was going to walk in when I stepped across the threshold of my house. I was sure that my father was going to act a fucking fool. Momma was going to calm him down to her best ability. All kinds of promises would be made, and Tashima was going to be the one making those promises. I was sure that was the main reason she was at my house.

Shaking my head, I knew that I had to get home. The quicker we started planning, the faster everyone would leave my damn home, especially Tashima.

With a *Pocket Full of Money* by Alley Boy featuring Young Jeezy playing, I let the song set the mood for me. There was no way in hell that I was going to allow family members to stop my money flow. Hell was going to break loose early fucking with me and mine. Getting myself in the right mind frame, I bobbed my head to the beat and rapped. At the end of the song, I was pulling into my driveway. I couldn't get my whip in the garage, thanks to my parents and Tashima's vehicles.

Sighing heavily, I said, "Work time."

After shutting off the engine, I hopped out of my whip with a stern facial expression. As long as I held that expression, Tashima would stir clear of me unless it was about business. I didn't want to talk to her unless it was about the demise of fuck niggas. She left a sour taste in my mouth, and it was going to stay there until I felt like forgiving her.

When I stepped into my home, I was surprised that my father spoke calmly. Strolling into the kitchen, I loudly gasped and silently said shit at the sight of Tashima. That damn woman was so fucking gorgeous. From chest to toes, she wore in Ralph Lauren: a white collared shirt, black shorts, and white shoes. Her jewelry selection was simple: gold, hooped earrings, a necklace, two rings, and a watch on her right wrist. Her once long hair was cut into a bob. The tips of her hair were dyed blonde. The woman rarely wore makeup; yet, she was sitting at my kitchen table face made up to perfection.

"Damn, Son, say somethin'," my father chuckled as he rubbed his long, salt and pepper beard.

"Um, shit, what's up, y'all?" I stammered as I never took my eyes off Tashima.

"Hey," Tashima softly replied as my parents waved.

Nawl don't fall in that trap. You supposed to be mad at her nigga. Act like it, I thought as I cleared my throat, looked at my parents, and said, "Um, so, fill me in."

As I took a seat across from Tashima, I tried to keep my eyes off her, but that shit didn't work upon me realizing that she had gotten her nose pierced. The ring in her nose fitted her perfectly. It was an excellent addition to her beautiful face.

Jesus, this damn woman, I thought as my father said, "Okay. So, Dom Dom, Tashima provided proof yo' uncle Bo Jack an' som' of his children, mainly Tello, being snitches. Also, Nick Jack is well an' kickin'. I saw him wit' my own eyes. They are up to somethin' big. What that big is? I have no idea. I'm very sure that it does involve me since Bo Jack an' his cronies didn't put me in their paperwork. I'm so lost as to what needs to be done. So, I won't be speakin' much unless I see a flaw in y'all's plan."

"What we do know is that Bo Jack nor you, Marc Jack, don't like the fact that a woman, me, was running your side of the organization. That is enough grounds to know that Bo Jack will make my name sour in the streets, further pushing suppliers and those that work under Dom Dom to not fuck with me, or they could have them try to undermine me or have them spy on us. I propose that we infiltrate Bo Jack's system before they try to get to us," Tashima spoke in a boss manner as she looked amongst us.

With a smile on her face, Momma replied, "What are you thinking, my beautiful daughter?"

Isn't she beautiful, I thought as Tashima replied, "I will be the one to infiltrate. I will leak "false" information. It'll be bait information, of course."

"That plan won't work at all," my father stated, shaking his head.

Chuckling, Tashima nodded her head while saying, "Yes, it will. Everyone in the city has seen Dom Dom with another female as I am nowhere in sight. We are not on "good terms". All I have to do is play as if I want Dom Dom knocked off his throne. I'll make a bunch of promises to Bo Jack just to get him on board with me. It's not like he knows that I'm no longer running things. I've made sure that everyone in the dope game that used to contact me, reach out to Dom Dom. So, as it appears, which is actually true, Dom Dom has cast me to the side and forbade me to work with or underneath him. I'll play the bitter ex-girlfriend through and through all the while playing underneath the very motherfuckers that want to see him dead."

Oh, shit, she saw me with Janesha, and she didn't cut the fuck up. Wow, I thought as I glared at Tashima with a curious facial expression.

"My brother will not believe you at all. He's going to test you."

"And I will pass every damn test with flying colors. That I can promise you, Marc Jack," she stated with a devious smile on her lovely face.

"What if he asks you to kill us in his face?" Marc Jack asked.

"Then, you better wear a bulletproof vest because I have a perfect aim," she voiced, placing her hand underneath her chin.

As her phone rang, she continued, "However, I'm smarter than your brother, sir, I would stir clear of him wanting y'all to be shot. I'll come up with a great lie as to why y'all shouldn't have bullets riddling y'all's body. I have a million reasons why, and he's sure to eat all one million reasons up."

As she retrieved her phone, a smile crept across her face. All eyes were on her as she answered her phone.

"Hello," she spoke shortly after putting the phone to her ear.

"Yeah, I'm almost done. What's up?" she sexily spoke into the phone.

Anger consumed me because I knew she was on the phone with Dyon, a motherfucker that had to see me soon also.

Licking her lips, exposing a silver tongue ring, she provocatively, "Well, in that case, sir, I will be leaving here in about fifteen minutes. Cool?"

Lawd, this bitch don' got her motherfuckin' tongue pierced. So, she suckin' the fuck outta that nigga's dick. She think she finna leave my motherfuckin' house to go suck an' fuck him ... she a motherfuckin' lie! I angrily thought as Tashima sincerely replied, "Me love you too, Dyon."

As I growled, my parents gasped and glared at one another. I wanted to knock Tashima's motherfucking head off. I didn't give a damn if I was pissed off at her; she didn't have a damn right to tell that nigga that she loved him in my presence. She must've thought I was a fuck nigga. She was going to learn that I wasn't.

When she placed her phone on the table, Tashima had one eyebrow raised as she glared into each of our faces while saying, "Are we close to wrapping things up?"

Not a soul said a word as we looked at her. My parents' facial expressions shown how they felt: Momma had a funny expression plastered on her face; whereas, my father was upset. I, on the other hand, was downright angry.

"Guh, you got me all types of fucked up," I spat, pounding on the table.

"And how is that, sir? You are living your best life. You cast me out, remember? I have no choice but to be okay with that. After all, I didn't tell you something that you should've known because I had taken care of the issue. We aren't together. You have the little chick, and I'm … doing me. So, let's not get to wrapped up in the other's personal life. Mkay? No need to be mad about something that you allowed to happen in the first place. Mkay? No need to show your ass because you made shit real motherfucking clear that I ain't shit and that I only was because of you and Sonica. Mkay? With that being said, it's business time as it has always been between us, Dominick," she sassily and sexily replied, gazing into my eyes.

Sonica snickered as Marc Jack glared at Tashima with widened eyes. I sat my ugly ass at that damn table, eyeing Tashima and rubbing on my beard. That damn woman knew how to put me in my place. I didn't see any lies told. There was an eerie silence in the kitchen as everyone looked amongst each other. I had to break the ice.

"Tashima?" I spoke in a deep tone.

"What's up, Dominick?" she sensually spoke, eye-fucking me.

Fuckkk, I love when she call my name like that, I thought as my dick grew hard while I asked, "Did you feel som' type of way when you shot that nigga?"

"Yep."

"In what kind of way?" I inquired as I leaned against the table.

"I was angry, then confused, then sad, and then back angry again. I was disappointed, ashamed, and felt grimy," she replied sincerely.

"Did you shoot him in those places because it would cause him to be in the hospital as well?" I inquired.

Nodding her head, she replied, "Yep. I wanted to shoot him in his neck, but I knew that I would kill him. After all, you and Sonica taught me that if you shoot someone in the neck, they better die."

"Where did you shoot him at? Like location," I questioned.

"In the bedroom ... that we shared," she replied, causing me to growl.

"Who was there?" I probed.

"His brother, Nixon, whom I ordered to take his ass straight to Baptist East and to stay there until I showered, changed clothes, and cleaned up my mess."

"How did Nixon respond to you shooting his brother?"

"He really didn't have much of a response with a gun pointing at his head," she replied with a smirk on her face.

"My God. What have y'all created?" Marc Jack asked in an astonished tone.

"A motherfucking go-getting beast," Tashima sexily spoke, looking at my father.

"An' I fuckin' love it!" my father replied as he clapped, one time.

So do I, Pops. So do I, I thought as I couldn't take my eyes off the bitch that shot a nigga that she loved three times over another nigga, that she also loved.

"Well, since you are cutthroat like that an' Sonica an' my son still has you in their presence … I guess we will go wit' yo' plan, Tashima," Marc Jack spoke before asking, "I have one question. Who in the fuck is this Dyon dude that shot my son?"

Scratching her head with a weird expression plastered across her face, Tashima spat, "One of Bo Jack's illegitimate children."

"Now, wait one gotdamn minute!" Marc Jack shouted.

"What the fuck?" I loudly said.

"Oh my good gotdamn!" my mother replied before placing her hand over her mouth.

"Same shit that I said when I found out … upon him showing up at the home that Dyon and I share. Before y'all get all worked up, let me inform y'all on something. They knew about each other, but neither pressed the issue about being in each other's lives. Dyon and I suspect the only reason Bo Jack has shown his face around him because of the clout he has received due to Dom Dom being imprisoned, and me putting Dyon on. Bo Jack trying to play underneath Dyon to get him what we are falsely going to give him. Yes, Dyon knows. He knows everything … about Dom

Dom and him being cousins all of that shit; however, he doesn't know that I know. Meaning, he didn't tell me. Also, I feel that Bo Jack will try his best to get to Dyon by saying shit that will irritate him … such as the fact that I love Dom Dom. On the contrary, I'm not worried about Dyon doing anything stupid. He knows that I don't play about Dom Dom, and you, Dominick, better understand that I don't play when it comes to Dyon. One thing I can promise everyone at this table, that Dyon is not a threat. He'll have his part in bringing down Bo Jack as well. I will be discussing with him how I want shit to go down between us while we are in public. Dominick, you and I will have an act in public as well. Performance is the key to get me through the door of Bo Jack's crew. I need y'all to really trust me on this one, okay?"

No one said a word. We just glared at her. It took Tashima to clear her throat before anyone said a word, and that damn person was my father.

"So, basically, you fuckin' an' suckin' first cousins, huh?" Marc Jack asked as Sonica slapped his hand.

"What? I'm just askin' just in case she doesn't realize what she said," he stated with bucked eyes.

Sinisterly laughing, Tashima stood and said, "Keep in mind, Marc Jack, I didn't know they were related until Bo Jack was released out of prison. To answer your question, not only have I fucked and sucked first cousins, I took them niggas motherfucking souls. My name holds weight in those niggas hearts, and that's facts. Anywho, I'll be in touch after Dyon, and I solidify our tasks in the demise of Bo Jack and his cronies. Y'all have a wonderful day."

CHAPTER SIXTEEN

Dyon

With a massive grin on his face, Bo Jack showcased his gold grill. I looked at the nigga and shook my head. He was excited to know that I was willing to go up against my cousin and take everything that he thought was rightfully his. Some wicked shit was going to take place, and the best man was going to stand on top with a crown on his motherfucking head. If the streets really knew what was about to happen, motherfuckers would stay in their homes and bow down. Since they didn't know, a lot of fuckery was going to happen, and I was going to be in the center of it all.

"Damn, I gotta pay Tello's ass a stack," Bo Jack happily stated.

With a raised eyebrow, I spat, "Why?"

"Because he bet me a thousand dollars that you wouldn't come on board wit' us because of the fuckin' triangle you in wit' Dom Dom an' Tashima," he replied as the front door opened.

"On my motherfucking life, that nigga gonna hate the damn day he crossed me the fuck out! Who in the fuck does he think he is? I'm the motherfucking reason why that gotdamn organization thriving the way that it is! All hell finna fucking break loose. Fuck nigga going to know exactly what they turned me into!" Tashima angrily spat, slamming the door.

Standing with my pistol in my hand, I hastily said, "What the fuck happened now?"

Stepping into the front room, she cleared her throat and eyed Bo Jack. Clenching and unclenching her jaw, she finally spoke, "I'll talk to you later."

"Hell nawl. You gonna talk to me now," I spoke in a stern tone.

"I don't fuck with your father as he doesn't fuck with me. So, like I said, I will talk to you later," she sassily spoke before walking towards the staircase.

"Tashima, I'm sorry that I rubbed you the wrong way. Will you have a conversation wit' me? I'm sure that we can assist each other," Bo Jack stated in a persuasive tone.

Halting, Tashima glared at Bo Jack, raised an eyebrow and spat, "Oh now, you want to be friendly. Keep that same damn attitude you had when you first meet me, and trust, I'll do the same."

"Baby, just hear him out," I spoke, walking towards her.

"Nawl. I'm good, love. You know I don't need anyone in my face … talking about assisting me in shit. I can handle my own … very well. If he doesn't know that, then he surely will soon enough," she spat.

Clearing his throat, Bo Jack stood and said, "Tashima, I'm no fool to why you are angry. You are pissed at what Dom Dom has done to you. He's discredited you. Paradin' 'round town wit' another bitch. Actin' like you don't exist. I know that shit hurts like hell. Why not help my son an' me bring that motherfucka an' his daddy down? You know all 'bout their organization, an' the moves they will be makin'. Let's hit those motherfuckas where it really hurts."

"Give me one damn good reason why I should team up with you, Bo Jack?" she questioned, placing her hands on her hips.

"Because once I'm back in action full throttle, you an' my son will be my right an' left hands."

"My first impression of you wasn't a pleasant one. Therefore, I don't think we will be a great fit to become working associates. Have a great day," she quickly spoke before ascending the stairs.

Once we heard the bedroom door closed, I turned to look at Bo Jack. The look on his face wasn't pleasant. He was pissed that Tashima turned him down.

Pointing his finger at me, Bo Jack spat, "Once I leave here, you need to fuck an' eat her pussy well. I need that damn guh on my team. Shit will go a lot smoother if she cooperates, Dyon. I'll give her fo' days to come to her senses, or I will force my hand in the matter."

I looked towards the stairs and then placed my eyes on Bo Jack and spat, "You don't need to worry 'bout Tashima. You just handle yo' motherfuckin' end. Keep yo' fuckin' cool. If you don't, you will fuck up a smooth play that will cause a domino effect you don't want to happen. Since you have yo' answer in my involvement in yo' plans, tell me one thing…"

"What?" he questioned as his phone rang.

"Why do you hate yo' brother so much?"

"Because he stole the one bitch that I loved ever since she first moved to this damn city," he spat with an ugly facial expression.

"Sonica?" I asked curiously.

"Yep."

"Damn, Bo Jack, you gonna go against family fo' a bitch?"

"Shid, ain't no different than what you an' Dom Dom doing, ain't it? Don't think just because Tashima ain't fuckin' the nigga, at the moment, that he still doesn't love her ass an' vice versa. Don't forget the history that they shared. He did have her before you … from what the streets sayin' wayyy before you. It was damn near a year or two before she gave you the pussy, right?"

Growing angry, I replied, "If you wasn't a fuck ass, deadbeat ass nigga, I would've known that Dom Dom was my cousin. So, don't get the shit fucked up like I'm you nigga. I would never go against the grain fo' a female. My situation is way mo' complicated than me oglin' a broad that has the hots fo' my brother."

As he growled, I knew he refrained from saying something that would cause us to go at it. Thus, he glared at me in a way that had me chuckling before telling him, "Our conversation is over. If you want me to work wit' you, the best thing you can do is *not* say one fuckin' thing that you think I might not like or this shit over wit' nigga. Understood?"

Sourly, he replied, "Yeah."

"Good," I told him as I pointed towards the entrance of the front door.

Like always, I walked behind him as he exited my home. Upon him opening the door, Bo Jack slightly looked over his shoulder and said, "Make sure she knows that she has fo' days to get her mind right."

"Didn't I tell yo' motherfuckin' ass not to worry 'bout my guh?"

"Yeah."

"Then, please listen to me, nigga. I'm tired of repeatin' myself to you," I nastily spoke, causing him to turn and glare at me evilly.

"You keep forgettin' that I am yo' father."

"An' it seems that you keep forgettin' that I don't respect you. The only reason I am helpin' you is because of the fact that I want that nigga Dom Dom knocked off his throne, fo' life."

"You must want me to apologize to yo' ass fo' not being in yo' life?" he snickered, causing me to become angry.

"Not at all. Momma did a grand job without you, nigga."

"Som' job she did. You are just like me," he laughed.

Taking my gun off safety, I evilly spat, "Strike one, Bo Jack."

Seeing the look in my eyes, he stopped smiling and said, "Sorry. How 'bout I leave before you do somethin' that you will regret?"

"I won't regret shit, but yeah, do that," I replied.

As he walked towards his vehicle, I closed the door. If there wasn't a time that I wanted to shoot that nigga in his face, it was the moment he mentioned that my mother didn't do a good job of raising me. The fact that I knew that he played my momma like a damn piano pissed me off something bad. He didn't know that his days were numbered, and I was going to be the one to pull the trigger on his fuck ass.

As I locked the door, Tashima was behind me, kissing on my neck and saying, "Calm down. Don't let him get you worked up. His damn day is coming. I promise."

"Damn, I hate when you do that shit. Why can't you make a sound when walkin', guh?" I spat as my heart raced.

Chuckling while sticking her hands in my gym shorts, she replied, "You should be used to that by now, sir. It ain't like I just stared walkin' extremely quiet."

"Shid, it's like that?" I asked as my dick grew in her hands.

"Yesss, just like that," she sexily spoke while slowly sliding her petite hands up and down the shaft of my dick before gently squeezing the head.

My knees buckled as I groaned, "Fuck, baby."

"You like that?" she inquired, applying pressure to my tool.

"Mo' than you know. I wish I could feel that mouth of yo's," I voiced as she placed her head on my back.

"You can."

"You can't suck no dick wit' that freshly pierced ass tongue, guh," I chuckled.

"How come I can't? I know that dick ain't been in nobody, nor is it dirty. With that being said, let me talk to him for a minute," she sensually stated while turning me around and shoving me against the door.

"Oh, we on som' boss bitch type of shit, huh?" I groaned, loving how she handled me.

As she pulled out my dick, she didn't say a word while glaring into my face. If I wasn't weak for her ass before, I sure as hell was stuck against the damn door with her crouching. When she flicked out her tongue, I admired the silver tongue ring as it neared my dick. I was so in tuned with Tashima's mouth that I saw the glob of spit in her mouth. Anxious to feel her warm, wet mouth, I held my breath. The second I felt her mouth on the head of my dick, I groaned.

Being cautious, Tashima took her time sucking and licking my man. While my girl was doing her thing, our eyes never left one another. Placing my hand on the back of her newly styled head, I welcomed the wonderful feeling she provided me. Slow sucks and kisses on my dick were a nigga's weaknesses, and she knew it.

Tashima continued the intimate actions for a while before sliding my dick further into her mouth. The moment that broad dropped into her favorite position while sucking dick--sitting on her legs while the bottom of her feet touches her ass--I knew she was going to show out on the dick. That woman of mine made love to my man in a way that had tears streaming down my face. By her actions, I knew she wanted her pussy tore out the frame, and I be damned if I wasn't going to give her the dick just the way she deserved!

"Mane, come up off that dick, guh, Daddy finna give you the dick just like you want it," I groaned with a fistful of her hair.

"I don't want to stop," she spoke with a mouthful of dick.

With a raised eyebrow, I said, "I know damn well you didn't speak wit' my dick in yo' mouth."

TN Jones

"It's not hard to do, sir," she laughed, causing my knees to buckle.

The vibration from her laughing sent a fantastic sensation from my dick throughout my body. I was in awe. I was going to be inside of Tashima all day because I had to feel that sensation until she told me that she wasn't able to take any more dick. Yeah, I was going to sex her all over our damn house.

Removing her mouth off my tool, I snatched Tashima upwards, aggressively yanked off her shirt, unsnapped her bra, followed by unbuttoning her shorts. Seeing that I was going to take over, Tashima became submissive as she purred my name.

"What?" I cockily said while placing my hand around her neck before shoving her against the wall.

"I need you inside of me now," she cooed sexily.

"An' you finna get all of me inside of you, now, an' fo' the rest of the day. Understood?"

"Yes, sir," she cooed, grabbing my hand and placing it on her pussy.

"Tell Daddy what you want him to do to her?" I commanded as I slipped two fingers inside of her hotbox.

"I want you to play with her, and then talk to her, followed by making her cry," she whined, sexing my fingers as I drove them in and out of her.

"Oh, I can do that an' so much mo'," I replied before spreading her lips with my tongue.

Our kiss didn't last long; Tashima removed her mouth from mine as she breathlessly spoke, "Dyonnn, I'm cummin'."

"My girl," I voiced, glaring into her eyes.

"I love you," she whined.

"I love you, mo'," I spoke genuinely as I attacked her pretty kitty and her lips.

Tashima's body began to tremble, causing me to remove my mouth from hers only to place it on her right titty. My mouth wasn't on her breast long before she cried out, "I'm cummin' again, baby."

"My girl," I replied as I nibbled on her nipple the way she had taught me some days ago.

Lately, Tashima had grown fond of her nipples pinched and bitten lightly. Her pussy would be wetter than ever; therefore, I took pleasure in catering to her sexual desires. Honestly, doing that freaky shit had me lit.

Once I took care of her titties, my tongue slowly slid towards her stomach. I drew a heart around her belly button before I kissed the top of her jewelry box. As she spread her legs, she cooed. One stern look at my girl and she placed her left leg over my shoulder, grabbed the back of my head, and threw her pussy on my waiting tongue.

"My Goddd," she whimpered as my tongue swirled and swiveled inside of her sweet-smelling kitty.

As I enveloped my mouth on her love box, all the while passionately attacking it, Tashima's legs shook violently. I knew it was only a matter of time before they gave out. So, I lifted her up the wall as my mouth was still attached to her pussy.

"What you doing to me?" she weakly asked as I shook my head as if I was an angry dog.

The moment the infamous clinking noises sounded from her mouth as she tugged on her hair and ears, I had a smile on my face while eagerly awaiting her delicious juices fill my mouth. Like always, I counted to fifteen.

Before I made it to twelve, Tashima's body shook beautifully as she poorly exclaimed, "Dyonnnn!"

"What?" I asked, sucking on her clit and exploring her pretty kitty with my fingers.

Tashima lowly said, "Baby, I can't move. I can't move."

"I know," I cockily spoke as I lapped her sweet homemade milkshake.

I loved hearing her say that she couldn't move. That was her way of saying that she bowed down, and it was time to bust that pretty pussy of hers wide open and make it cry! Quickly, I removed my mouth and fingers from her leaky core and shoved my dick inside of its home.

"Oouu!" she loudly whimpered, scratching my back.

"You love this shit, don't it?" I growled, pumping faster while swerving my dick from left to right.

"Yes, I dooo," she moaned as she tried to match my thrust; I wouldn't allow her.

I made sure that my dick stopped her from moving. I was doing the fucking, not the other way around. I wanted to feel every inch of her pussy as she would feel every vein running through my big dick. Aggressively, I gripped her head and placed it against the wall. Dancing in the pussy, I gazed into her face.

With my mouth balled tightly, I observed my baby as I drove her insane. Those beautiful titties of her bounced as I slammed my tool in and out of her. Her muscles tightened on my pole as she howled my name, causing me to growl and dig in her core something extreme.

"Dyonnn, what did I do? Tell me what I did," she whimpered breathlessly.

"All the right shit is what you did to get this type of lovin'. Expect this from now on out. Understood?" I harshly spoke while delivering good, steady, and long strokes to the right corner of her leaky kitty.

"I understand, baby, I understtttannddd," she moaned before biting her bottom lip.

Shortly after she came on my man, I pulled out of Tashima and barked, "Touch them motherfuckin' toes, guh."

Looking dazed and ditzy, she stammered, "Waaitt ... what?"

With a raised eyebrow, I laughed while replying, "Touch them motherfuckin' toes, guh. I ain't gotta tell you to make sure that perfect arch in yo' back."

Once she did what I said, I kneeled behind that gorgeous ass of hers and commanded her to shake it. Loving the sight of Tashima's ass jiggling in my face, I smiled and eyed the pretty creature that had the perfect body to be a lingerie model. At that thought, I knew what we were going to do after this sex session; we were going to role-play, and boy, were we going to love it! While my mind slipped into another zone, so did my face. I was eating ass, and Tashima was bumping her damn head on the wall.

"If you don't get yo' no manners mouth off my asshole, I know something, Dyon Jackson!" she sexily yelled as her legs wobbled like a baby deer.

Trying not to laugh at her poor standing, I failed miserably. As bad as I wanted to eat her ass more, I couldn't. My laughing got the best of me. It took her to snap into the dominant role for me to resume normal, well I wouldn't say normal because she had the ups on me and she was still bent over with my dick stuffed deep in her tunnel.

"Shitt nih, baby, you got a nigga feelin' like a bobblehead. Slow that ass down," I groaned as I barely had my hands gripping her behind.

"Good," she voiced giggling.

Tashima was fucking the shit out of me and laughing at my body expressions. A nigga's mouth was open as I tried to say her name. My toes curled in my black socks. My fingers had no power to hold onto her juicy butt; they were twitching. My arms became weak and flopped to my sides. Now, I felt like a shot out bitch.

"Good God. Why you cuttin' up like this, baby? Damn," I groaned while trying to stop my head from moving back and forth rapidly.

"Shut the fuck up and take this pussy the way that I'm delivering it to you. Understand?" she barked, eyeing me.

"Yes, lawd. I motherfuckin' understand," I spoke while finding the strength to relax my toes.

"My boy," she sexily cooed as one of her eyes lowered as the other grew bigger.

"Fuck, yo' facial expression look like Milo off *The Oblongs*! That dick to damn good to yo' ass, huh?" I busted out laughing as I pulled out of her.

"Gotdamn it, Dyon, why can't we be serious for once during sex?" she laughed, standing upright.

"Because God didn't wire me an' you to be serious," I chuckled, pulling her to me.

Wrapping her arms around my waist, she looked up at me and said, "You just ruined my nut. You do know that, right?"

"Nawl, I don't know that. You know I'mma get it bac—"

"Oh my fucking goodness, Dyon!" she loudly yelled as she looked towards her thigh.

Immediately, I started gagging; whereas, Tashima laughed hysterically before screaming, "I done fucked that colostomy bag off yo' ass!"

As I ran towards the staircase, I laughed, "Yo' ass better not tell Desaree 'bout this either! Brang yo' ass on Tashima, I believe I'm shittin' nih."

"I know you fucking lying, Dyon?" she shouted.

"Urgh!" I gagged as I felt warm liquids sliding down my left lower abdomen region.

"Oh fuck nawl! Shit slidin' out this hole. Tashimaaa!" I yelled as I stopped at the opening of our bedroom door.

Stepping on the top stair, that damn woman was in tears laughing and pointing towards our room.

"Mane, come on an' help me wit' this. What in the hell am I supposed to do? You gotta put the bag over it," I spoke rapidly.

"Boy, if you don't get yo' funky ass in the tub. You just letting shit drop everywhere," she laughed, standing.

"I know to take a bath woman, but damn help a nigga out. Grab a towel or somethin' so I can put over this damn thing," I stated, walking into the bedroom.

"Dyon, you have on a whole damn shirt. Place your hand over the stoma. I know that acidic mess is itching," she laughed, causing me to bust out laughing.

"You ain't shit. You know that," I voiced as we entered the bathroom.

"Yep, I know," she giggled as she turned on the water knobs.

Quickly, I took off my clothes and hopped in the shower. Shortly afterward, Tashima was standing in front of me, bathing her King. As she did so, that woman joked, and I laughed. Moments like this were priceless for us. I loved how we joked and laughed with one another regularly. She was home for me, and I would give my life to Tashima. She was all a nigga ever wanted. She was indeed my better half.

After the feces stopped flowing and I was cleaned, I dried us off. Walking into my bedroom, I had the urge to ask, "Baby, you think those birth control pills are still doing their job?"

"I highly doubt it. I hadn't taken those things in a while," she stated as I laid across the bed, on my back.

"What is a while?" I probed, gazing at my beautifully naked woman.

"Close to two-and-a-half or three weeks now," she replied, strolling towards me with the medical supplies in her hand.

"Can we make a baby when you are done puttin' that bag on me?" I seriously asked, rubbing her stomach.

With a smile on her face, she loving replied, "Yes, we can."

"Fo' real?" I excitedly asked while she prepped the bag to be placed over my stoma.

"Yes, for real."

She didn't know how happy she made me. It was past due for us to start our family. If anyone deserved to have a happy family, it was Tashima. She would be the best mother any child could have. There was no need in me tooting my own horn, but any child would be blessed to have me as their loving and doting father. I was going to wear that word out and show niggas how to be there for their kids.

After Tashima softly pressed the colostomy bag in their desired place, she crawled on top of me, gently stroked my face, and said, "You will be an amazing father, sir."

"An' you will be an amazin' mother an' wife. Get ready," I voice as I brought her head towards mine.

Biting her bottom lip, she said, "Indeed, I will."

"Before we get into our baby makin' session, I need to ask you this," I softly asked while rubbing her back.

"What's up?"

"How did things go wit' Dom Dom an' them?"

"Just as I planned. They are on board wit' what I suggested that they allow me to do."

"Which is?"

"Infiltrate Bo Jack and his crew."

"But you declined his offer," I stated, confused.

"Of course, I did. If I didn't decline on the first go-round, there was a high possibility that he would've red-flagged me. Even though I meant everything I said to the nigga, I still have to play my cards right. My worry is this ... that he will get in your head, which will cause you to do something stupid. Do you have enough power within yourself to not allow him to get the best of you, concerning Dom Dom?"

Back to that, huh? How many times I gotta tell her ass I ain't gonna fuck wit' that nigga? I thought as I asked, "When was the last time you fucked him?"

"Three days after he was released from the hospital," she answered, biting her bottom lip.

Not like her response, I growled while slipping my stiff dick inside of her juicy, hot pussy, and sternly said, "That better be the last time he ever taste, touch, kiss, or stick his dick in you. Do I make myself clear?"

"Mmm," she whined, eyes rolling in the back of her head.

That's not the answer that I wanted to hear; therefore, I grabbed a handful of hair and drilled Tashima's gushy coochie all the while asking, "Did I make myself clear about you not lettin' that nigga touch you?"

Weakly, she stammered, "Ye ... yes."

I didn't believe her, but I had to give her the benefit of the doubt.

"Well, then, Bo Jack can't fuck wit' my mind concernin' Dom Dom," I voiced as I flipped Tashima on her back and slowly dug into her core.

With teary eyes, Tashima said, "I know shit fucked up all the way. If I've brought you shame or humiliation, I deeply apologize. At the moment, I can't help how I feel concerning the two of you. Maybe in time, those feelings will change, but I need you to know that I love you, Dyon with everything in me. I need you. I'll never do anything intentionally to hurt you, minus me shooting you for something that you did. Please believe me. Okay?"

I wonder if I tell her that Dom Dom and I are cousins would that cause her to change her mind about him, or would it deter her away from me? I thought as she began to cry.

Immediately, I stopped stroking her and held my baby tight. Tashima was in a fucked up place. She wasn't like most females. She wasn't like the chicken head bitches in the streets that had the hots for dope boys. I knew she was the one hurting behind the fact that she loved two street niggas that would go to war about her. Without a doubt, I knew that Tashima was the one ashamed and humiliated. I knew that a part of her felt disgusting for loving Dom Dom and me with her entire soul. Also, I knew that Tashima was going to slip up and have sex with Dom Dom again. It was only a matter of time before she did. When that time arrived, she better be ready for the consequences.

After I placed a kiss on Tashima's forehead, I looked into her wet, round eyes, and softly said, "Aye, baby, stop thinkin' 'bout other shit. Okay? Focus on us right now. Feel the love an' affection that I'm givin'. There is no need to feel the way you do. Shit happens. You are not at fault. I promise you ain't. Know that I got you. I will always have you. I can promise you that. After I dry yo' eyes, Daddy going to make love to you. From this moment on, we need to be in a happy, lovin' zone, we are in the process of creatin' our family. Can you not think 'bout any bullshit that'll cause you to be sad?"

Slowly nodding her head, she replied, "Yes."

"You promise?" I asked before kissing her lips.

"I can't promise you anything, but I can certainly try."

"That's good enough. I love you, Tashima Winn," I spoke slowly as I began to stroke her goodies.

"Me love you, Dyon," she replied before sucking on my bottom lip.

Seal the deal on pullin' her far away from Dom Dom. You've noticed that she hadn't been 'round him lately. Something happened between the two of them. This is yo' chance to solidify shit fo' good, nigga.

CHAPTER SEVENTEEN

Tashima

At three a.m., my mind was on a whirlwind as I lay in Dyon's arms while he snored like a damn bear. I couldn't peacefully sleep nor rest because I had a lot to think about. I needed to make sure that my plan of having Bo Jack knocked down several inches was secured. I had to ensure that I had eyes on them at all times. Setting up false plays had to be executed with precision. I wouldn't be able to rest until I knew that I had Bo Jack wrapped around my fingers.

In need of thinking freely without a black bear snoring loudly, I quickly slipped out of the room with my phone in my hand. As I quietly sashayed my naked behind out of the cozy room, I placed myself in business mode. Everything that Sonica and Dom Dom had taught me, I rehashed. Every lesson was important. The delivery of my message was important to everyone involved—never to underestimate a woman, a Black woman at that.

Before I made my way downstairs, I stopped by my office. I hadn't been focused on my personal "legal" business, something that was rare on my end. I had to tighten up my personal matters and illegal dealings so that I could focus on the legit money. As I took a seat at my large, black, personalized designed desk, I powered on my desktop. While patiently waiting for my device to load, I powered on my cell phone. Ten seconds of my phone being on, that fucker did numbers. I had several text message notifications from Catalina and Dom Dom. My heart raced as I saw their names in bold.

Quickly, I clicked on Catalina's name. As I read her sensual text message, my body relaxed as I softly purred. Ever since we had our first sexual encounter, Catalina didn't hold back on the knowledge of how she wanted to have my legs spread eagle on her jet, in her exquisite home in Ecuador, and other exotic places in the world. Every morning and night, she would send me a text that had me blushing and rehashing about our time together. I had never thought that I would enjoy being around a woman that didn't mind eating pussy, ass, and sucking on my body as if her life depended on it. One thing I did know, that sexual shit between Catalina and I had to cease. My life was chaotic enough. Yeah, she was overly cool with being in the background, but I felt that being flirtatious was terrible for business.

After I re-read her messages several times with a purring kitty, I shook my head and sighed. I didn't respond to any of her messages. It was time to stick to what I told her.

As I opened Dom Dom's message, my heart raced. Quickly, I looked at the door to ensure that Dyon wasn't there. Pleased that he wasn't, I dropped my eyes to my phone and read.

First Hubby: So, that's how we do? You gonna ignore my texts?

With a puzzled facial expression, I read the next text.

First Hubby: Mane, look, I'm sorry fo' what I said. A nigga was all fucked up in the head. You know I got mad love fo' you. I always have an' I always will. None of these bitches in the streets matter to me. That chick that you saw me wit', she just a jumpoff. Something to do since we weren't on good terms. I know how you feel 'bout a nigga, an' you should know how I feel 'bout you. I'll make it up to you. I promise, an' I'll never hurt you again wit' my ruthless ass mouth.

As I slowly read that text message, I wasn't moved by his words. Yeah, he had a temper, and I understood why. However, he didn't have to say the things that he did. To make sure that he knew how to control his mouth, I would continue to give his ass the cold shoulder. All those times I reached out to him, he denied me. What Dom Dom failed to realize, I was a woman who was taught by the best of the best—him and his mother. He would have to really see how I moved. That was the only way to gain his respect, entirely; until then, we were dead.

First Hubby: So, you just ain't gon' respond, huh?

"Damn, did it ever occurred to your silly ass that maybe I was sleep or some shit, sir," I mumbled as I read the next text message.

First Hubby: *Yo' ass got me on block or somethin', Tashima?*

Shaking my head, I read the next text.

First Hubby: *Yo' ass gon' make me act a motherfuckin' fool! Respond to me damn it! You know my mind get to trippin'. I would advise yo' ass to respond. I don't give a fuck if you is layin' up wit' that nigga! I was wit' yo' ass first. I am yo' fuckin' first everythin'!*

"Niggas, don't like that same energy that they dish out. Typical males. He get on my nerves with that bullshit," I mumbled as my phone dinged, a new text message from Dom Dom.

First Hubby: *Since yo' ass ain't responded to a call or text message, I'm at you an' that nigga's crib. How you like these motherfuckin' apples?*

My motherfucking legs were weak as I quickly hopped away from the desk with my phone in my hand. Not willing to allow it to ring, I placed it on silent. One thing I know about Dom Dom, he wasn't the type to lie about being anywhere or doing anything. Shit was starting to cool down between him and Dyon, and the last thing I needed was for some shit to pop off when I wasn't prepared to deal with either of them. Immediately, my nerves were shot.

As I scurried down the stairs, I prayed that Dyon didn't wake up while I tried my best to get Dom Dom away from our home. They weren't ready to live underneath the same roof yet; therefore, I had to be very careful in how I handled their asses. Pressing the issue was not the route to go.

While I skipped into the laundry room to put on some clothes, my phone rang. The caller was Dom Dom. On the second ring, I answered.

"Oh, so now you wanna answer the phone," he nastily said as if he had been drinking.

"Dom Dom, what do you want at this hour of the morning?" I inquired as I shoved my head through the hole of the oversized black T-shirt.

"I want you. Fuck that, I need you."

"Nawl, you good, sir," I spoke through my pretty, white teeth.

Chuckling, he replied, "You must didn't get my texts?"

In need of lying, I said, "No. When you called, I had just powered on my phone."

"You's a damn lie," he laughed.

Rolling my eyes, I replied, "What I have to lie for? It ain't like you my man. Remember?"

Growling, he spat, "Keep fuckin' playin' wit' me an' I'mma set y'all pretty ass house on fire. By the way, I'm outside. Brang yo' ass out, or I'm gonna ring that motherfuckin' doorbell."

"Why are you doing all of this fuck shit, nigga? Didn't you tell me that it was over? What you thought I was going to wait for you to get your mind right? Or you thought I was going to cry and beg you? Dude, it's too early in the morning for that bullshi—"

"I need yo' legs behind yo' head while I eat that pussy up. I need to hear you squeal my name as I snake my fingers into that juicy, delicious pussy of yours while my tongue doing numbers on yo' clit. I need my naked ass dick wet by yo' juices. I need to feel yo' nails scratchin' my back. Most importantly, I want that super soaker of a mouth on my man while you knead my balls. Now, if you don't brang yo' ass out that damn door, I swear befo' the good Lord, that I'mma break into that house an' fuck you on every fuckin' piece of furniture you an' that nigga purchased. Think I'm playin'? Try me!" he seductively barked.

With wide eyes, I ended the call and ran towards the door. When I placed my hands on the doorknob, I realized that I didn't have on any panties, shorts, or socks. I was going to turn around and head back to the laundry room until I heard a car door slam.

"I know this bastard did not get out of his damn car," I stated lowly as I prayed that Dyon was still sound asleep.

Quickly and quietly, I opened the door and saw Dom Dom walking towards me. On panic mode, I stepped across the threshold. With a shaky hand, I closed the door behind me. I didn't know if I jogged, ran, or walked to Dom Dom. All I know was that we were faced to face; I was nervous about him being on property that he had no business being on.

"You must think I'm a joke or som'?" he inquired as he pulled me towards him.

"What are you doing here, Dominick?" I sighed lowly.

"Don't make me repeat myself, Tashima, you know I hate doing that shit," he growled as he pinched my nipples.

"Oou," I cooed as my knees buckled.

"You got on any pannies underneath that nigga's shirt?" he asked aggressively.

"No," I heard myself say.

"Good. Get yo' ass in the car."

"Dom Dom, I'm going to go get dressed, and I'll be at your house within twenty minutes. Cool?" I asked, pulling out of his embrace.

Shaking his head, he grabbed my hand, placed it on his hardened dick, and replied, "Nope. I want you right here. Right now."

"Not here," I moaned.

"You don't want that nigga to catch you face down, ass up wit' me ... his cousin," he chuckled.

Not seeing shit funny, I aggressively removed Dom Dom's hands from my waist. As I backed away from him, I shook my head. I was pissed at his comment; I was pissed because of how I looked, concerning those two males. Feeling nasty, I told Dom Dom to go home and never to return to this property. My pleas went unanswered.

In a matter of seconds, that foolish man was holding me tightly as his hands explored my body. Feeling weak, mentally exhausted, and turned on, I didn't have a say so in the matter as he teased and pleased my purring kitty. One finger followed by another was inside of my hungry pussy as Dom Dom began licking and sucking on my neck. It seemed as if I was floating on water; in reality, he walked backward all the while pulling me with him. Every time I allowed him to touch me, he took my mind to another realm.

As I made a mess on his fingers, my body shook. I knew that I was playing a dangerous game, but the way Dom Dom worked his fingers all that I could say was, "Dom Dom, not here. Please not here."

"I want that nigga to see how I do yo' body. One of us has to bow down, an' it sure as hell ain't going to be me. Like I said, I had you first an' that means I will always have you. You will always weigh heavy on a nigga's soul, heart, an' mental. It's 'bout time he realize that shit too," he whispered in my ear before sucking on my earlobe.

The way shit had been playing out since Dom Dom returned home, I had been really disrespectful towards him and Dyon. If I wanted them underneath one roof, the shit that Dom Dom was doing wasn't a good move. I had too much respect for Dyon to have sex with Dom Dom on a property that I shared with him and vice versa. Now, fucking the daylights out of Dom Dom on his land, I would do that any and every day of the week.

As Dom Dom bit his bottom lip, he sexily shoved me against the warm hood of his car, all the while tapping on my G-Spot. Loudly, I groaned. I didn't know which motioned had me intrigued the most: the warm hood, him fingering me, or the shoving. Either way, a sister was turned on and ready to disrespect Dyon. That was until my angel of an imp spoke loud and clear. I had to get Dom Dom away from my damn house!

"Dom Dom, we gotta leave but in separate vehicles," I stated sternly as he slowly descended to the ground.

"Nope. That ain't gonna happen," he quickly spoke while lifting up the T-shirt.

Rapidly, I removed his hands off the shirt and became serious when I spoke to him. "Look, you decided that things were over between us. You decided to say hateful things to me when, in reality, I had your back and Dyon's. You wanted that chicken-headed hoe. So go be with her. I'm doing motherfucking fine this way."

I thought he would be pissed at my comment; instead, I fueled that nigga. Before I could blink my damn eyes, Dom Dom had me spread eagle across the hood of his car and having the time of his life as he dragged his tongue across my starving kitty.

As I gripped the back of his head, every piece of common sense that I had was gone. Everything I said about not disrespecting Dyon went out of the window. I didn't give a damn if the neighbors saw what was going on, and I surely didn't care about the fuckery that could pop off if Dyon was to witness what the hell I had going on—in the fucking front yard.

"Dominickkk," I cooed as he spat on my pussy only to suck it up.

"Oh my fucking god! You's a nasty motherfucka!" I sexily growled while sliding my hands towards his jet-black beard.

"All fo' yo' motherfuckin' ass," he voiced as he placed my legs behind my head.

You gotta get him out of here, I thought while moaning, "Not here."

Breathlessly, I shoved Dom Dom off me and barked for him to get the fuck in the car. On command, he sneakily rose and did precisely what I asked, all the while carrying me along with him-- his fingers stuffed in my core.

At that moment, I hated that handsome bastard because he had too much power over me. Instantly, I knew that I had to find a way to get that power back. Dom Dom was the type of nigga that like to handle people, but his motherfucking ass was not going to handle me.

Upon us getting into the car, I had a slick move to make, and I wasn't quite sure it was going to work. However, I had to try. The moment Dom Dom sat in the driver's seat, I sexily snaked underneath the steering wheel as I pulled out his stiff dick.

"Fuck, I missed you. No other female compare to you, an' I mean that shit," he groaned as I slowly jacked his dick while getting my mouth as wet as I could.

"Um, how much you missed me, baby?" I cooed before licking the head of his dick.

Before he could respond, I deep throated his juicy, black dick several times while tightly holding onto his balls. I gave that bastard the suckling of his life as he bucked in the front seat. I could tell that his toes curled in the all-white Jordan's. His balled hands were on my shoulders, trembling. He couldn't stop groaning my name and saying that he loved me.

Now, is the time to hop out of the car and run into the house, I thought as I aggressively yet passionately sucked and licked on that nigga dick and balls.

"I love you, Tashima Winn, I swear I do," he whined, which was so not Dom Dom.

Right then, I knew that I was in deep shit because Dominick Rodgers had never sounded defeated. I was at a crossroads as to what to do. It didn't take me long to figure out what I had to do.

"Close the door, and let's leave here," I gently spoke as my eyes became teary.

After he closed the door, I climbed on top of him, sat on his monster, and rocked us as he started the engine and reversed out of the yard, poorly.

My God, what am I doing? Things are not going as I had planned. Please don't let Dyon wake up and realize that I am gone, I thought as Dom Dom spoke, "I need you to come home, Tashima. I need my one an' only beside me every day an' night. I need what I always have needed at that's yo' love. I'll do whatever it takes to have you in my presence every-fuckin'-night an' I mean that."

While he slowly thrust inside of me, I matched his thrust and buried my face into the crook of his neck. Mischievously smiling, I thought, A*nd then, only you God come through for me. Now, I need you to come through for me on two more things: make sure Dyon stays asleep through the night and let him say the same words Dom Dom just said.*

ΩΩΩ

"Ugh, do y'all always have to talk about the streets? Can we have one damn day without the dope game following us?"

Desaree spoke lowly through clenched teeth as she aggressively stabbed the Bourbon glazed ribs.

"Well, thanks to your sister, Desaree, serious shit is going on, and we need to discuss those issues," Nixon voiced as he rubbed his temples, evilly glaring at me.

"Why in the hell are you looking at me as if I killed your best friend, Nixon?" I shot back while picking a banana pepper out of my salad, only to place it into my mouth.

"Because you are going to fuck 'round an' get my brother murdered. Not to mention, all this unnecessary shit y'all are into because of them Jackson niggas," he scolded, shaking his head.

"Nigga, calm the fuck down. This shit between Bo Jack an' Marc Jack doesn't have shit to do wit' Tashima. Like I told you, you'll lay low off sellin' drugs. I don't want you into any fuckery. Shit finna get real sticky, Nixon," Dyon huffed while eyeing his brother.

Nixon and Dyon bickered about Dyon's involvement in bringing down Bo Jack and his crew. What Nixon didn't know was that Bo Jack was Dyon's father, which meant that he didn't have the slightest clue that Dyon and Dom Dom were cousins. Honestly, I was thankful that he didn't know. He would be on my ass more than ever, and the only way to get him off was to shove a gun in his face. I didn't want to do that; our relationship was strained from the last time I did that.

Ignoring the fellas talking, I focused on my glowing, beautiful pregnant sister. With a smile on my face, I asked, "So, how's the knocked up life treating you?"

"It's actually been good. No morning sickness. However, I eat all damn day long. It seems like I'm never full," she replied, dapping the corners of her mouth with the brown napkin.

Snickering, I replied, "I can tell. You ordered quite a significant amount of food."

"It's like that every-damn-where we go," Nixon chimed in, attitude better.

"Oh, hush up, dude. Don't act like your appetite hadn't increased," Desaree spoke softly while gently pushing Nixon.

"See what had happened was," he spoke, causing us to laugh.

The sight of them being happy and in tune with one another had me wishing that I had that with Dyon and Dom Dom, together not separately. One day, I was going to have that happily ever after with the two men that held my heart in the palms of their hands.

Finally, we began to enjoy each other's company. Inside of the small, hood diner that was owned by a married Black couple, our little table was filled with laughter, jokes, and discussions of old memories. We frequented the place often and had been for the past ten years. Nixon was the one that put us onto the soul food joint. We made it our business to visit the eatery once a week together. Today was the first day in weeks that we had sat at the table, closest to the door, and enjoyed our meal--like we usually did. Moments like this were life to me. I could be with the people that I loved and let my hair down.

"What's wrong?" Dyon asked me while grabbing my hand.

With a weird look on my face, I replied, "Nothing. Why you asked me that?"

"You zoned out wit' a serious expression on yo' face," he voiced as Nixon cleared his throat in an agitated tone.

"I was just thinking about how happy Desaree and Nixon are and the past years of us visiting this place. How peaceful it is to be here with y'all," I smiled, staring into each of their faces.

Dyon and Desaree smiled as Nixon shook his head and said, "That's a bunch of bullshit. You are up to somethin'. You never think 'bout good memories. You always have something up yo' sleeve."

Tired of his ass, I spat, "You are constantly up my ass. I wish you would get out of it before I get fucking mad, and that's the last thing anyone in this damn diner wants to see, especially you and Desaree. The issue you have with me better cease. Tired of yo' fuckin' mouth, Nixon."

"Don't y'all start that shit," Dyon and Desaree spoke as Catalina and two of her guys stepped into the diner.

Immediately, my little coochie and nipples were eager to be placed in her mouth. Shaking away the overwhelming feeling, I set my attention on Nixon and sincerely spoke, "As much as you don't like me right now, trust and believe that I'm battling with demons that you could never imagine tagging on your ass twenty-four seven. I love your brother as you do, but trust I will *never* allow anything to happen to him. No need to say anything about me shooting him because everyone at this damn table knows why I did what I did. Now, we continue going at each other it's only going to upset Dyon and Desaree. I sure as hell don't want her pregnancy to turn into a horror show. Do you?"

Profoundly sighing, Nixon shook his head and replied, "Nope."

"Then, we need to let the past be the past. Most importantly, you need to trust me. I've had a long talk with myself earlier this morning, and shit will be over sooner than you think."

"What do you mean?" Dyon inquired with a raised eyebrow.

"Just know that things will not be strained or frustrated for long. I've made sure of that," I told him as my phone dinged.

Retrieving my phone from the table, I looked at Catalina's name. Using my peripheral vision, I saw that Dyon was looking at me. I knew that I had to quickly read the message and respond equally fast.

"Before you get deep off in that phone, tell me what you mean by shit being over quickly, Tashima," Dyon spoke, giving me his undivided attention as customers entered the increasingly noisy diner.

"Bo Jack and the others won't be a problem for long," I replied while opening the message from Catalina.

Catalina: *The bait has been set like you wanted. Now, it's showtime.*

Me: *Showtime.*

Clearing his throat, Dyon said, "You better answer me."

With a raised eyebrow and stern facial expression, I sweetly and seductively announced, "I love when you are stern and bossed out with me. That shit turns me the fuck on, honey."

"I'm not finna play these games wit' you, Tashima."

"Who said anything about playing games? You want to know something that I'm not willing to tell you. All I can say is, trust me ... like you have been for years."

For ten minutes, we went back and forth about what I had up my sleeves. I was glad when he shut the fuck up; however, it wasn't because of me being firm with him. It was because Bo Jack, Tello, and his crew sashayed into the diner as if they were the big bad wolves. Just as I had planned for them too.

"I guess they are the issues at hand, huh?" Desaree spoke, slamming a wad of napkins on the plate filled with rib bones.

Our table was quiet as Bo Jack glared at us before flashing the fakest smile I had ever seen on a person. With an ugly expression on his face, the handsome, fuck nigga strolled towards our table and began introducing Dyon to the crew, his family. I wasn't expecting that at all. For sure, Nixon would know that Dom Dom and Dyon were first cousins. I was far from embarrassed about the situation; I didn't want anything to happen to Nixon because he said some foul shit out of his mouth.

"What's up, bro?" Tello voiced in a jealous tone as he dapped up Dyon.

"What's up?" Dyon replied as he eyed his brother.

From there, a string of weak ass 'what's up' took place between Tello's crew and Dyon.

"So, y'all bros now?" Nixon asked, chuckling.

"Apparently, Bo Jack is my dad," Dyon spoke, shaking his head.

"What the fuck?" Nixon and Desaree asked in unison as they looked between Dyon and me.

I was thankful that I noticed the niggas of Tello's crew looking at me with as a disgust expression was on their faces. In need of a distraction, I laughed and asked them, "I took a shower or two today, so I know I smell great. So, what's up with those ugly ass glares?"

Bo Jack chuckled before telling the guys to place several tables together. Upon his command, those niggas scurried like the rats that they were. Sitting a few inches away from us, the fellas talked in hushed tones, all the while stealing looks our way. They were up to something; therefore, I knew that I had to keep my eyes on them. They were known for doing sneaky shit. What they didn't know was that I was known for spotting that shit out.

"Um is anyone going to say anythin' 'bout the shit we just learned," Nixon spoke as Desaree agreed.

Before Dyon and I said a word, shit certainly became weird. Dom Dom's sexy, fine ass strolled in with his parents behind him. My pussy awakened more the second he placed his eyes on me and raised that one damn eyebrow. As thoughts of us fucking all over his house took me into a realm I had no business being, in the public that was, I rubbed my hands together and prayed. I was on a path that I needed to change and fast. My situation became odd the moment I learned about Dyon and Dom Dom.

Sonica's giggle and Marc Jack's sultry, deep voice snapped me into reality; not only did they snap me into reality but everyone inside of the diner, minus the snitch crew. Literally, they shut that bitch down! Every old head in the restaurant that was minding their business was no longer doing that. Workers of the restaurant and customers glared at the couple, happily. All eyes were on them, or it could've been on Marc Jack.

While everyone looked astonished, a series of 'welcome home, Marc Jack' and clapping sounded off as Nixon asked Dyon and me questions, which we ignored. Quickly, I looked at Bo Jack; the expression on his face wasn't a pleasant one. That nigga was upset, and everyone at his table knew that.

"It's good to be back," Marc Jack spoke as Bo Jack sauntered towards him with outstretched arms.

Look at this fake shit here, I thought while chuckling, causing all eyes to be on me.

"'Bout time I see yo' ass. It's been a long-time brother. When did they let you out?" Bo Jack inquired as Marc Jack was hesitant to hug his brother.

"Now, wait a gotdamn minute. Y'all really finna talk to me. I'm wonderin' why Tashima ain't lookin' shocked. I need to know how fuckin' crazy y'all are," Nixon shockingly stated while looking between Dyon and me, mouth opened.

Dyon nor I didn't say anything; we were locked into the fuckery between Marc Jack and Bo Jack. As Desaree and Nixon talked about what they learned, I was eager to peep something between the brothers.

"I ain't been out too long ago, Bo Jack. I was surprised, giving that we had another five years to complete. I'm still amazed that I'm on the streets early when I know I have no business being free. Funny, huh?" Marc Jack stated coolly.

TN Jones

"Nawl, brother, that's the work of God. We paid our debts. Now, it's time to enjoy the fruits from our groins," Bo Jack chuckled as he placed his eyes on Sonica, who quickly grabbed Marc Jack's hand.

"Hey, Sonica," Bo Jack softly said as if he was a puppy dog.

"Hi, Bo Jack," she replied, placing a kiss on the back of Marc Jack's hand.

And that's one of the reasons he's jealous of his brother, I thought as Dom Dom shook his head and walked towards the lunch line.

"There are my beautiful daughters," Sonica happily stated as she sashayed towards our table.

"Hey, Sonica," Desaree and I spoke in unison.

"How are y'all?" she asked, hugging me before hugging Desaree and rubbing on her belly.

"We are good. Trying to enjoy the day without bullshit," Desaree replied unhappily.

"You will," she spoke before whispering into Desaree's ear.

With a sad expression on her face, Desaree nodded her head and replied, "I will do."

After Sonica left, all eyes were on me, but this time I didn't like it. While prying eyes were on me, Nixon asked Desaree what Sonica had told him. Of course, I didn't know, and I sure as hell didn't pry. If Sonica wanted me to know anything, she would've told me; however, I was sure that she told Desaree that she should be leaving soon.

Quickly, I glanced around the restaurant. I was paranoid and felt that people were talking about my situation with two guys. Without a doubt, I knew people had our names in their mouths; I wished that they didn't. I assumed ever since Dom Dom returned, we were the talk of the town. As long as they didn't say a piping word to or around Dom Dom, Dyon, or me, they would be in great standing.

"I think it's time to take my shit off safety. I know it's going to be som' shit up in here. The vibe all the way off," Nixon spoke as he slowly reached underneath the table. Following suit, Dyon did the same. I didn't have to because my weapons were never on safety.

Odd looks from Desaree and Nixon had me ignoring them. I couldn't take too many of their stares before I bucked my eyes and asked, "Why in the hell are y'all looking at me like that?"

Nixon looked at his brother and lowly said, "Bruh, you an' that nigga are cousins, an' y'all fuckin' an' in love wit' the same chick. Not to mention, the same Jackson's we are out to get … you are fuckin' related to them."

Shaking his head, Dyon responded, "I gotta focus, Nixon, not now."

"Fuck that shit. Tell me how long have you known?" Nixon inquired as the restaurant resumed somewhat normal.

"Fo' a minute."

"An' you still fuckin' wit' her?" he voiced, pointing at me.

"Yep. Now, get focused. It's a lot of animosity in this motherfuckin' place," Dyon stated as he observed our surroundings.

"This is som' crazy ass shit. When in the fuck were you going to tell me? How in the fuck can you still deal wit' her knowin' how she feels 'bout yo' cousin, bro?"

Through clenched teeth, Dyon sternly spat, "Chill the fuck out an' focus."

"Dude, we are in the center of bullshit because of her. The only reason I am not leavin' is because you are in this shit for the simple fact that you don't know when to shove yo' dick elsewhere," Nixon spoke angrily, causing me to growl as I reached underneath my shirt.

Dyon calmly talked his brother into shutting up. Upon him doing so, I noticed that everyone was eating and talking. I tried to read Bo Jack's lips, but I failed miserably. In between talking, he shoved food into his mouth. Turning around to look at Dom Dom, he nastily glared at me all the while mouthing that he was going to punish me.

Ten minutes later, Desaree announced, "It's too awkward in here for me. I think I'm going to leave. Y'all, please don't do shit that will have me stressed out. Tashima, the second you leave here ... your ass better call me. I think you have officially lost yo' damn mind."

I was on the verge of replying to my sister when Bo Jack stretched, stood, looked at me and loudly said, "Today has been an intriguing good day. All of my family is in one spot. Much love to y'all. My daughter slash niece-in-law is looking grand as ever as she's found the golden rule to have two, first cousins in the same damn building not causing a disturbance and loving on her. Damn, Tashima, you gotta teach me how to do it. I wish I had known how to perfect that move; maybe I wouldn't have gone to prison."

Unwanted attention was at an all-time high for me. From there, shit went to the left. Dyon and Dom Dom hopped away from the tables, growled, and barked, "Don't start that fuck shit wit' Tashima, nigga. That's the last female you want to start a gotdamn war over!"

The entire restaurant came to a halt; hell, even I stopped and looked at them, one at a time. I didn't know how to feel, but panic wasn't anywhere in my body. As Dom Dom and Dyon briefly looked at one another, not in a menacing or hateful way, my heart pounded.

What in the fuck is going on? Are they finally coming to terms with what I want? I thought as Nixon tsk'ed.

"Look at this shit here. Mane, these niggas stupid as fuck," Nixon spoke in an unpleasant tone before continuing, "Baby, leave now. I'm sure som' shit is really finna pop off."

"Y'all can calm down. Ain't nobody gunnin' fo' Tashima. She's a smart an' gorgeous lady. Y'all are lucky to have her," Bo Jack spat as he and the crew walked towards us.

Quickly, I stood because a motherfucker would never sneak me and live to talk about it.

"Bo Jack, you might want to chill because it sounds to me that you are gunnin' fo' Tashima. Like my son *an'* nephew said, that is not the move. Too many innocent people is in this establishment. Fo' once in yo' damn life don't be an asshole. Today is not the day fo' that," Marc Jack spoke loud and clear.

"It would sound like that to you, huh? Shit sounds familiar, brother?" Bo Jack asked with much attitude.

"Like I said, you don't want to do this shit today," Marc Jack spoke through clenched teeth.

With a smirk on his face, Bo Jack bowed and said, "You are absolutely right, brother, today is not the day."

In the proximity of me, Bo Jack looked at Dyon, then looked at me before planting his eyes on an angry Dom Dom and snickered, "You should stay up late nights, Son. There's no tellin' what type of shit you will witness."

Immediately, my heart fell into my butt as Dyon replied, "And *Dad*, you might want to use yo' own advice."

In my heart, I knew that Dyon understood what Bo Jack was saying. I was prepared for him to question what Bo Jack meant. I was ready to tell him the truth that Dom Dom had shown face at our home earlier this morning and that some things took place. However, I wasn't ready for the shit that could possibly happen because of it. At that moment, as everyone glared into each other's faces, I prayed that Bo Jack didn't have evidence to support his claim; however, being the hood nigga that he was; I was sure that bastard had evidence.

Stepping close to me, Bo Jack gazed into my eyes, brought his mouth to my right ear, and whispered, "My nephew ate an' fingered that pussy good earlier this mornin' on the hood of his car, huh? I couldn't lie as if my dick didn't get hard watchin' yo' thick, beautiful ass wrestle wit' the back of his head while fuckin' his mouth. Let me not speak on the way you sucked his dick. The thought of it makin' my dick hard right motherfuckin' now. No wonder them niggas going crazy over yo' ass; hell, I would too. You haven't seen war 'til being in one wit' me. It's apparent you don't hate that nigga like you put on yesterday."

Before I could control my rising temper, I had guns shoved into Bo Jack's sides. Low murmurs escaped the mouths of those that witnessed my weapons. I didn't give a fuck; I was starting to see red. From a short distance, Sonica calmly talked to me; eventually, her soothing voice was no longer falling on my ears. Dyon and Dom Dom were behind me, trying to de-escalate the situation.

As I glared into Bo Jack's face, I spat, "You have zero chances to fuck with me. I am not your weak ass sons and daughters. Bitch, I will splatter your nothing ass and guess what ... I won't do a lick of prison time. Why? Because you are a snitch bitch. You've ratted on so many people that they want to see you dead, including law enforcement. You see, I do what the fuck I want ... when I want. With that being said, you need to move along, stay the fuck out of areas that don't belong to you. As of this moment ... you are fucking dead in the streets. You see those tall, pale-looking motherfuckers to the right of us?"

While looking directly into my eyes, I could tell that Bo Jack wasn't focused on me. He was scoping out the scene. With a wicked smile on my face, I loudly shouted, "Leak the press, please."

A series of harsh coughing took place as Dom Dom growled, "Tashima, pipe the fuck down!"

Ignoring him, I asked Bo Jack, "What guys were coughing, sir?"

With balled lips, he slowly replied, "Those motherfuckin' pale dudes."

"Right. That means that my job is complete. You have a good day trying to take some shit that didn't belong to you in the first place. Everyone in the city will know you and the rest of those bitches that run with your son are snitches," I stated as the colors in Bo Jack and his crew's faces, minus Tello, drained.

"Cuzzo and bro, y'all better get y'all's bitch. She cappin'. Tellin' lies on us," Tello stated angrily.

"Mane, I know damn well you ain't call my guh a bitch," Dyon and Dom Dom angrily spoke in unison as they began walking toward Tello as the remainder of his crew moved out of the way with their hands outstretched.

"Tell your son to apologize, Bo Jack," I stated, shoving the guns further into his sides.

"Tello, apologize," Bo Jack spoke through clenched teeth.

"Nawl, fuck that gu—"

His sentenced was incomplete as Dom Dom kicked Tello in the knees as Dyon slammed a fist into his face. Shit didn't go according to plan, thanks to my temper, but at least Tello got an ass-whooping. None of his people helped, which was expected; hell, they never helped Tello in anything other than snitching.

The double-teaming didn't last long; Nixon pulled Dyon as Marc Jack pulled Dom Dom. Patrons of the hood restaurant didn't scream, holler, or any of that shit. They glared at the scene, all the while eating. I didn't see how they weren't afraid for their lives. Hell, I was sure they knew that anything was liable to happen, but then again, I figured their calmness had a lot to do with Marc Jack being on the scene.

Aggressively, Dom Dom spat, "Tashima, you just fucked up big time."

"No, she didn't," Catalina spoke, sashaying her petite frame towards us. "She did what was best for everyone. I'm actually glad that she listened to me, or quite a few of you wouldn't be alive within the next six months. My guys will take things from here. Tashima, I will be in touch. Soon, real soon."

I had some shit to explain, and by the look on Marc Jack, Dom Dom, Sonica, and Dyon's faces, they were going to curse my ass out. Each of them wanted to place a nail in Bo Jack's coffin, and I was the reason they wouldn't be able to do that.

The angry people stated in unison, "It's time to go. Now."

Nodding my head, I looked at Catalina and said, "Will you please make sure that Bo Jack pays our tab?"

"Of course," she stated with a sneaky smile on her face as Bo Jack sighed deeply.

Removing my guns and tucking them into their holsters, I stood on my tiptoes, patted the burly man's chest, and said, "You don't look too tough now, huh? My pussy is super wet at the thought of what will happen to you and your weak ass crew. Have a good one."

The second I stepped into the humid air, Desaree looked at me and shook her head. Dyon and Dom Dom eyed me as I tried not to look at either of them. Marc Jack shook his head and mumbled. Sonica angrily yet lowly spat for me to ride with her. Upon nodding my head, I strolled towards her truck. Once I hopped in the front seat, she grilled me out.

"Do you know what the fuck you have done?" she yelled.

"Yeah, I made sure there were no casualties that would've crippled me."

"No, what the fuck you did was put us on the gotdamn map. So, when those motherfuckers come up missing, guess who will be knocking at our damn doors, Tashima? You made a wrong move without consulting with us. You are not the sole runner of things anymore. You are in the background as it was supposed to have happened if my damn son hadn't killed that boy at that store. You were not meant to be upfront and damn center. That position was giving because Dom Dom had to do fifteen years, which turned into twenty-one long-ass years. So, basically, what I'm saying is that you don't make no damn calls. You suggest, and we, as in Dom Dom, Marc Jack, and I, say yes or no."

As I opened the passenger door of her vehicle, I flagged Catalina's men down. The second they stopped, I looked Sonica in the face and spat, "You didn't do shit but teach me. Marc Jack most definitely didn't do shit. I was the one that got Catalina on board with halfway working with y'all. That was until she realized who Dom Dom's people are. As I see it, y'all need me to stay afloat. It's my knowledge, compassion, and dedication that have motherfuckers working with us. It's my pretty, fat pussy that has Catalina at my beck and call. With that being said, I do run shit. Like I told Bo Jack, have a good one."

CHAPTER EIGHTEEN

Dom Dom

While my parents fumed at the shit that went down at the diner, I was in thinking mode. Tashima was all for battle. I didn't understand why she copped out so quickly instead of waiting for the trap to be set for Bo Jack and his crew. One thing that I could say about that woman was that she loved to handle threats herself. Something was off, and I had to find out why she decided to keep her hands clean.

"She had no damn right going over our heads!" Momma angrily spat, a little too angry for me.

"Lil' bitch thank she got the muscle but really don't know a fuckin' 'thing," my father spoke, walking into my living room.

"Aye, mane, watch yo' mouth. Either you gon' respect Tashima willingly or I'mma make you," I voiced, glaring into my father's face.

Hostile, he spoke, "Nawl, nigga, you gon—"

Smirking, I placed my gun in my lap, all the while eyeing the man that had a lot of shit to say behind bars. I still owed my father an ass whooping for putting me in a position that I never wanted to fulfill.

Through clenched teeth, I said, "I'm tired of repeatin' myself. I thought you saw that I meant business at the diner, concernin' Tashima. She did what she did. It was a reason why. Momma, you of all people should know how we trained her to be. If she didn't fall through, it was because of a larger picture that we don't see."

As she paced the kitchen floor, my mother grew quiet. She was thinking about what I said. I was sure that she thought of the person Tashima was before and after her father died.

My father, on the other hand, had a lot of slick shit to say about everything that went down. From day one, he was afraid that Tashima would get the big head; I was slightly fearful of that as well, but for another reason. I didn't want her to get hurt or caught up in some shit that she was never meant to be in.

"What in the fuck are we going to do 'bout the shit that girl did? Does she know how the Feds work? There is a reason why Bo Jack an' them other niggas snitched. They are workin' wit' the Feds. Not to mention, why in the hell is Nick Jack alive instead of dead an' what is his role in this fuckery?" my father angrily stated aloud as he stood in my living room, glaring into my face.

"The first thing we need to do is figure out what Catalina plans to do wit' them. Next, we need to figure out why Bo Jack an' them other niggas snitched. What was at stake an' what will they gain by cooperatin' wit' the Feds," I voiced, retrieving my cell phone.

Marc Jack looked at me for several seconds before saying, "Stop, playin' wit' that damn phone. Get yo' head in the game an' help me an' yo' mother solve this shit. If you don't do yo' job an' get yo' organization back, there will be problems between us!" my father hollered, spit flying everywhere.

With a raised eyebrow, I spat, "Mane, you better lower yo' damn voice when speakin' to me. If you hadn't gone to prison, you would still be over som' shit I never wanted to begin wit'. I ain't finna worry 'bout a damn thing at the moment. I'm thinkin' an' that's all I'm gon' do. Truth be told, you the best one to find answers. Them yo' folks mo' so than mine. Hell, I didn't deal wit' them. You an' Momma did."

Marc Jack and I went back and forth before my mother stepped in and told my father that it was best to leave. Agreeing with her, I saluted them. I had bigger fish to fry, and it had nothing to do with those stupid Jackson people. I needed to know why Tashima flaked out on the plan of infiltrating Bo Jack's organization, just to set bait for them.

"If an' when you decide to step up to the plate, call me. If you talk to Tashima, call me. I really want to know where her head is," Momma softly replied at the opening of the front door's hallway.

"Okay. Be sure to lock the door behind you," I told her as I received a text from Tashima.

"I will. Love you, Son," she spoke as Marc Jack exited my home, sighing heavily.

"I love you the most, Momma," I replied quickly while briefly looking at her.

The second my mother closed the door behind her, I opened the text from that chocolate woman of mine.

Dat Baby: *Are you upset with me? I did what I had to do. Too many people that I care about are involved. The last thing that I needed was for something to happen to Desaree and the baby all because of us not moving swiftly. I don't trust Bo Jack or anyone in that crew. Nick Jack isn't accounted for. Catalina nor I can't locate him. He has plans, and I need to know what they are. Your family has some influential people that are in the backgrounds, pulling strings. Bo Jack is not the biggest fish to fry. Whoever the head is …. orchestrating shit to the T, they are very, very precise. How well do you know your father's parents?"*

Me: *No, I'm not upset wit' you. I didn't understand why you chose to go the other route when we discussed the plan, but now I know. The other shit you asked 'bout I'm not finna discuss over the phone. Where you at?*

Dat Baby: Two houses down from you. Walking to your home.

Me: LOL. So, you scopin' me out now? How long have you been there?

With a rising dick, I hopped away from the sofa, ambling towards the front door. Upon me approaching the rectangular object, my phone dinged. Dropping my head, I read the text from Tashima.

Dat Baby: No. Just didn't feel like arguing and possibly shooting Marc Jack. Didn't want to talk to Sonica. I'm almost to the front door.

Rapidly, I placed my phone on the long, dark brown table before opening the door. Once I opened it, I glared into the sexiest face that I had the pleasure of looking in. Tashima looked defeated; she was tired. Everything weighed on her shoulders. It was time for her to rest peacefully, and I was going to help her with that.

"Talk to me," I told her as she walked across the threshold of the door.

"I'm tired, confused, and frustrated, Dominick," she spoke, walking into my outstretched arms.

"I know it's mo' to that," I voiced, glancing at her.

"It is, but I'm not willing to speak on it ... at the moment, that is."

"My folks in an uproar 'bout you steppin' over what we agreed on."

"I know. Sonica made sure to tell me that."

"An' what was yo' response," I voiced, pulling her back so that I could look into her eyes.

Tashima's eyes lowered to the ground, prompting me to command that she placed her eyes on me. When she did, I knew that she said some shit she had no business saying. Trying not to become angry, I sighed several times heavily before telling her to speak.

"Tell me what you said, baby."

Clearing her throat, she softly said, "I told Sonica that without me the organization wouldn't be shit and that I do run things since every plug that I acquired while you were in prison decided to work with us was because of me. I mentioned that if it weren't for my pretty, fat pussy, Catalina wouldn't be at my beck and call."

Taken aback at her statement, I stared at the woman before me. At first, I didn't know what to say. Then, I had one question.

"Did something sexual happen between you an' Catalina?"

"Yes."

"How do you feel 'bout that?"

"I'm not proud, but I'm not angry that it happened either. Let's just say that the experience was wonderful, but I don't like mixing business with pleasure. I feel that shit can get sticky if I continue to allow Catalina to take off my clothes and place her mouth on my sensitive spots."

With a stiff dick, I groaned as I envisioned Catalina's small, pale hands traveling up Tashima's thick, chocolate thighs. The thought of my baby sexily cooing with her back arched had me grabbing my dick. Explicit thoughts after thoughts had me wanting to know things that would have me jealous as hell, which it didn't take me long to experience that emotion. As I glared at Tashima, I pondered did Catalina sucking on Tashima's body better than I did.

"Why are you looking at me like that, Dominick?" she asked, looking at me.

"Because you got a nigga fucked up on so many levels," I told her while rubbing on her nipples.

With a raised eyebrow, Tashima gently asked, "You aren't mad at me for what went down between Catalina and me?"

"Nope."

Confused, she replied, "Why not?"

"Because I love woman-on-woman action. Now, what really gets the best of me is the fact that I know you are still fuckin' 'round wit' Dyon. Even though you know that nigga is my cousin," I seductively spoke through clenched teeth as I gripped her throat and slid my hands underneath her gray shirt.

"Ah," she cooed as her legs grew weak.

Licking my lips, I gently pinched her nipples. Tashima lost it, and it turned me on. While softly moaning my name, Tashima shoved my head toward hers, ran her fingers through my thick beard, and sucked my bottom lip into her mouth, all the while unbuckling my belt. Saying that she was eager for the dick was an understatement. That woman took control, and the only thing that I could was let her handle her business.

Before we made it into the living room, we were naked in all of our glory. The only sounds that sounded within my home were the humming from the refrigerator, smacking of our lips, Tashima cooing and whimpering, and my hands connecting to her beautiful, oily ass. The moment that bossy ass woman aggressively shoved me on the sofa, I knew that I had to change the course of things.

"You ain't finna fuck me like you did when I first got out. I was dead ass serious when I told you that you will never get on me again," I voiced as I snatched my love by her thighs and placed her on her back.

Giggling, she said, "Dominick, that was a one-time thing. You pissed me off talking to me like I was an average bitch."

Knowing exactly the tone that I used on her that night in Auburn, I placed my hands on the sides of her face and gazed into her eyes. The look in those beautiful peepers told me everything that I needed to know. My baby was exhausted, mentally, physically, and emotionally. She had many things to handle over two decades, and it was my mission to erase that exhaustion from her.

"I was disturbed 'bout the Julio situation. I felt like Dyon was going to push me out the way ... from my contact, that's really personal to me, an' from the only person besides my mother an' Desaree that matters to me. So, I was thrown off by Dyon workin' wit' Julio," I softly said before continuing, "I need you, Tashima. These other bitches are just toys when you piss me off to the max, concernin' Dyon. Me not being able to touch him the way I want irks my nerves, but out of respect fo' you ... I won't deaden the nigga. One thing I can honestly say, I respect that nigga fo' standin' up against our folks when Bo Jack tried to step down. I liked how he didn't side-eye me when I looked at him fo' jumpin' up just as quickly as I did. I can promise you that I won't hurt him, physically, that is, but I will not stop 'til you have my last name. I won't stop pesterin' you to be mine before I make shit real hard in these streets. I love you mo' than life itself. I hope you know that."

Sincerely, she replied, "I do."

"What can I do to make things easier on you?" I voiced, rubbing the sides of her face.

"Take the reins of your company. Stand behind me that I made the right decision to throw Bo Jack and the crew to Catalina. Not pressure me so much as to which one of y'all I need to be with."

Exhaling sharply, I nodded my head and said, "I was going to stand behind you on that front as well. I wasn't in the mood to go up against those fuckas anyway. That was all Momma an' that nigga Marc Jack's idea. You know me, straight dome check them niggas an' keep it movin'. As far as me on yo' ass 'bout choosin', I'mma give you yo' space to figure it out, but like I said, I will pester you but not by talkin', but by actions … like this."

With my eyes on her, I snaked my tongue from her neck towards her pretty titties. As I inhaled her left nipple into my mouth, I sneakily slipped two fingers into Tashima's hot cave. With my free hand, I toyed with her other nipple.

"Fuckk, Dominick," she cooed while gripping the back of my head and slowly shaking her head from side to side.

"What, baby?" I asked as I gently scraped my teeth around her hard nipple.

That damn woman went crazy, and I loved it. While she stuttered, Tashima's body trembled as that beautiful pussy permeated heat as if it was an eruptive volcano.

"Fuck me, Dominick," she whimpered while wiggling her juicy monkey on my elongated member.

"I don't wanna do that wit' you, baby."

"Whyyy?" she whined.

"Because I need to make love to you," I voiced while removing my mouth off her nipple only to kiss and suck on the other one.

"I need that dick slammed in me something awful. I'm too stressed for you to make love to me, Dominick," she whimpered as my mouth traveled south.

The moment my mouth landed on that little pink bud, Tashima loudly and provocatively said, "Oouu."

Her body went rigid, and that was my cue to indulge in that twat of hers. Instead of going at it the thug way, I took the gentleman's route. I passionately sucked and licked on my baby's pussy as if it was an exotic fruit from a tropical island, all the while gazing into her beautiful face. As I looked at Tashima, I knew that I had to do everything in my power to make her mine forever. I didn't want her to need Dyon for a motherfucking thing. All she needed was a man that would stand firm behind her, whether she was wrong or right. Tashima needed a nigga that was going to move hell and heaven for her without complicating her life. She needed a nigga that would wine and dine her just because the day was a Monday. It was time to show Tashima just how much she needed me and me only in her life and vice versa.

"Dominickkk!" she loudly screamed as tears streamed down her face.

"Yes," I seductively voiced with a mouth filled with her sweet juices.

"I love youu," she sobbed.

Trailing my tongue from her wet box, I slid it upwards. Her hands shook on the back of my head as she firmly held onto it. The second my mouth was on hers, we got lost in a wet, loving kiss that blew my mind. Every emotion that Tashima felt, it soared through my body. My frame had never tingled from a kiss, even with her, yet at that moment, it did. With an amazing sensation flowing through my core, I slipped my member into Tashima's starving cat and made love to her like I'd never done before. Every promise that I made her, I meant it. Every passionate thrust that I delivered, she felt and held onto me tightly. As I made genuine love to my girl, I knew that I had chosen the right one to be there for and with through the thick and thin.

When we finished, we were lying across my bed, glaring into each other's faces with a loving look in our eyes. While rubbing the sides of her face, I noticed a bit of sadness in my baby's peepers. I had to know what was wrong with her.

Therefore, I pulled her on top of me, stroked her back, and asked, "What's wrong?"

"I can't do this. I ... I thought I could, but I can't," she sobbed.

Thrown, I questioned, "What you talkin' 'bout?"

"I thought I could make you and Dyon see that I needed both of y'all, at the same time. I don't. My heart lies with you more so than with him. How can I tell him that I need you more than I need him? How can I hurt him like that? I'm not a bad person. I am not," she cried as I held her tightly.

Planting kisses on the side of her neck, I sincerely said, "No, you ain't a bad person. You just got caught up wit' two niggas. As far as how you tell him ... you just do it, Tashima. Don't get frustrated when he tries to win you over. Just be firm an' genuine wit' him. Either he gonna come fo' me or he gonna be a man, hold his head up, an' leave you alone."

"How did I make a big mess of my love life?" she questioned.

Seriously, I replied, "That's something that y'all women do. Instead of y'all fuckin' wit' a nigga fo' the hell of it; y'all emotional creatures catch feelin's an' shit. Start tellin' the nigga y'all love him an' all types of shit. I guess it's in y'all DNA to get caught up when it comes to the matters of that big thing called heart."

Silence overcame us as I looked at the ceiling. My mind was blank as Tashima sighed and breathed heavily.

"You do know once I leave here, I'mma have to go talk to Dyon, right?" she lowly spoke while rubbing my chest.

"In one of my whips, at that, an' you better not take all damn day either," I sternly replied, looking down at her.

"I know that."

"You better," I voiced as I kissed the top of her head.

While I held Tashima, quietness surrounded us, and for the first time, I enjoyed it. The steady beat of her loving heart, the flickers from her long, natural eyelashes as they grazed my chest, and the soft, milk-chocolate skin that plastered a portion of my six-foot body were all that I needed in the world of chaos and destruction. Tashima sneezed, and a glob of our nut escaped her tunnel, only to land on my dick and balls.

As I laughed, Tashima looked at me and said, "Well, I guess that's my cue to be carried into the bathroom, huh?"

"Yep."

In the process of exiting my bedroom, our cell phones rang. We didn't worry about our devices. My mind was somewhere else as I knew Tashima's thinking was all over the place. I wasn't going to disturb her while she thought how things were going to go down between her and Dyon. Therefore, I left her alone. Did I feel bad about what she was going to do? Not at all; however, it did matter to me because she was conflicted about the situation.

Tired of the brief silence, I genuinely asked, "Is there anything I can do to make yo' mind less boggled?"

"No. I brought this upon myself," she sighed as I stepped across the threshold of the bathroom.

"When I first got out, you were hell-bent on havin' both of us. What changed yo' mind?"

"Honestly, it's what Bo Jack whispered into my ear at the diner today that really opened my eyes to this delicate situation," she voiced as I placed her on the ground.

With a raised eyebrow, I probed, "What did he say?"

It took her a while to speak; by the time she spoke, I had turned on the water and shower knobs. While she talked, I grew angry. I wasn't pleased with a single thing that came out of that nigga's mouth. His inappropriate remarks had me itching to place a bullet in the back of his head. At that moment, I hated that Catalina had her hands on him. Catalina had to release that nigga or let me see him for six minutes.

"I need you to call Catalina, now, and tell her that you want those bastards alive. Understood?" I bossily demanded through clenched teeth.

Nodding her head, Tashima replied, "Okay."

After she exited the bathroom, I hopped in the shower, shook my head, and bathed my body. Bo Jack had a way with women, a way that had me wondering why one of his women hadn't killed him yet. Upon his entry into the free world, Bo Jack had caused more issues than before he was placed into the federal prison system. The more I thought of my father's brother, the more I envisioned how I was going to cut his damn tongue out of his mouth before shooting him in front of his son and crew.

"What the fuck do you mean?" Tashima loudly spat.

With a body filled with soap suds, I stopped cleaning myself. Several agitated sighs escaped Tashima's mouth, causing me to hop out of the shower, cautiously. When I approached the bathroom's door, an angry Tashima tightly held her phone above her head while shaking her head several times.

"What's wrong?" I growled, slowly walking towards her.

"Bo Jack, Tello, an' them other niggas are unaccounted for. Catalina has no idea where they are."

"How in the fuck did she let that shit happened?"

"I have no idea, but I can tell you what she told me," Tashima stated, walking towards me before continuing, "Catalina's main men had Bo Jack an' the rest of the crew in three SUV's. Catalina and her two drivers went a different route to one of her holding houses, which were the instructions that she had given her other guys. Well, apparently, Bo Jack was ready for some shit ... like I had pulled ... to happen. A shooting occurred on the Boulevard."

There was some fishy shit going on. There was no way in hell a shootout was supposed to have happened with a top-notch supplier and Bo Jack. Someone was in the process of being set up, and that someone was Catalina and us.

"Baby, think 'bout what you said. Some shit don't sound right at all. If her other guys were killed, how does Catalina know what happened an' where?"

"From what Catalina told me, Bo Jack made sure to keep one of her guys alive to tell her before shootin' him in the head."

Angered to the max, I sternly said, "Something is off. Who all knew of yo' plan fo' today?"

"Catalina, her men, and me."

"She got a snake in her camp, Tashima. There is no way that any of that shit was supposed to have happened," I spoke, shaking my head before saying, "Get my parents on the phone now! Tell them to get here ASAP. After that call is complete, tell Desaree to meet you at the airport in Montgomery. I don't care where y'all go but get far away from Alabama an' the surroundin' states. Y'all will not come back 'til you receive word from a trusted source that it's safe fo' y'all to return. Som' shit is 'bout to go down, an' I don't need y'all in the mix. If I know Bo Jack, like I assume I do, he's going to play dirty. Real motherfuckin' dirty."

"Dom Dom, I'm not going anywh—"

Yelling, I said, "Don't fuckin' debate me on this shit, Tashima. This is not a fuckin' game anymo'. You are not qualified to play in this round. Truth be told, you ain't qualified to play at all! You or Desaree will fuckin' die, an' I can't allow that to happen. Now, please do what the fuck I say!"

CHAPTER NINETEEN

Dyon

After I left the diner, my house was the only place that I wanted to be. I needed to think in peace; however, I couldn't do that because Nixon's ass wanted to bitch and gripe about the news he learned. Shortly afterward, Desaree strolled her pregnant ass through the door, complaining about being at home by herself. Therefore, I told her that she could stay with Nixon since his ass wouldn't go home.

While they talked, I thought about the significant violation that Tashima did by shoving Bo Jack and them niggas on Catalina. What Tashima didn't know was that Bo Jack had a back-up plan for the back-up plans. He was a snitch through and through, but that motherfucker knew how to get himself out of a jam.

"Honestly, I thought you would be okay with the smooth move that Tashima made concerning Catalina. Shit could've gone an entirely different way, if y'all would've stuck to whatever plan y'all had up y'all's sleeve," Nixon voiced as Desaree hopped away from the sofa, aiming for the bathroom.

"Tashima's moved without consultin' wit' me. The shit she pulled can have a serious backlash behind it. I don't trust Bo Jack fo' many reasons. His vibe throws me the fuck off. That nigga ain't to be trusted on no levels. He'll finesse his way into an' out of anything he sees fit. Tashima's last-minute plan was not the right move to make an I know this fo' a fact," I stated as I heard the toilet flush.

With a disgusting expression plastered on my face, I asked, "Damn, Desaree, don't believe in closin' the bathroom door?"

"Nope. She does that shit at the crib an' it drives me fuckin' insane," Nixon sighed, shaking his head.

While we chatted about the bullshit that happened at the diner, Desaree strolled into the living room, wiping her hands on a napkin. With a raised eyebrow, I looked at her and then looked at my brother.

"Why are you lookin' at me like that?" Nixon inquired.

"I need som' peace an' quiet. I don't know a polite way in askin' y'all to leave," I voiced.

Giggling, Desaree announced, "Just say that you need your space, and we are gone."

Nodding my head, I said, "A'ight. Well, I'mma check on y'all later."

Ring. Ring. Ring.

"I'll let you know when we make it home," Nixon spoke as we dapped while Desaree answered her ringing device.

"Bet," I replied.

After Desaree said hello into her phone, several loud bangs sounded off around my home. Briefly, Nixon and I glared at each other as we drew our weapons. Desaree was stuck in place. She didn't know what to do.

"Go hide an' don't come out 'til—"

My brother's words to Desaree fell on deaf ears; several different types of guns sounded off before slamming into my crib. Nixon rushed towards Desaree, knocking her on the floor before covering her frighten body. I was on the floor, crawling towards the large windows. Intrigued to know was slanging bullets through my home, I peeked through the bottom of the blinds. I was surprised, shocked, and pissed to see Bo Jack sitting on the hood of his car, smoking a cigar as those damn dummies of Tello's sprayed my shit. I didn't have the necessary guns to retaliate. At that moment, I wished I had've listened to Tashima when she told me that we should have tonka toys in every room of our home. No, my ass was naive to think that a nigga wouldn't step foot on our property with the dumb shit. I was dead as wrong!

After the gunfire ceased, my front door was kicked open as Bo Jack loudly and sternly spat, "Son, I would advise you an' Nixon to put down whatever lil' weapons y'all got. This is the type of shit that goes down when you don't do what I've commanded nicely of you. I'm here to make shit right, an' you want to side wit' that black bitch that sucked and fucked yo' cousin in yo' front yard, earlier this mornin'. His fingers was in her pussy while she sucked his lips damn near off his face! Oh, not to mention, his dick was deep down her throat before she left *y'all's* crib to go to his spot! You going against the grain fo' a bitch that has no respect fo' you. You really crossed the wrong motherfucka; however, I'm going to give you one mo' chance to turn into the type of Jackson that you need to be ... a ruthless, cold-hearted, and downright with the fuckery!"

I wasn't bothered about any of the shit that Bo Jack spat concerning Tashima because she would never disrespect our home in that manner. Bo Jack liked to stir up shit like a bitch. I wasn't falling for his fuckery. I wasn't weak like those he had underneath him. Standing, I tucked my gun in the back of my jeans.

"Son, you better say somethin' before I have these trigger happy niggas spray towards yo' brother an' his bitch," he laughed.

"I'm right here," I told him as I stepped into his line of vision.

"Did you not hear a thing that I said after I made a grand entrance into yo' spot?" Bo Jack spoke as I saw Tello and four of his partners walking down my hallway.

"I heard everything that you said. That shit you speak of don't bother me at all," I told him as Tello opened his mouth to speak.

"Tashima ain't here," my brother on my father's side spoke, shaking his head.

"Go figures. Either she's gettin' her pussy ate by that Catalina bitch or that fuck nigga Dom Dom," Bo Jack announced before ordering Tello's crew to put their weapons down.

"Dyon, so you say, that the shit I speak don't bother you, huh?"

"That's what I said. You can't finesse me how you finesse everybody else," I spat as he walked closer to me while the other clowns ambled behind him.

"An' why is that, Son?"

"Because you are the type of nigga that lie to get motherfuckas to do what he wants. I'm not fallin' fo' none of yo' tricks, Bo Jack," I spoke, glaring into his blackened face.

As he chuckled, I badly wanted to place a bullet in his head. I would've been a dummy to do so since I was outnumbered. While the nigga continued to laugh, more unwanted guests filed into my home with angry facial expressions.

Deeply inhaling, Bo Jack reached into his back pocket, all the while looking into my eyes before saying, "Since you think I'm lyin' ... peep this shit out, Son."

"I'm not finna watch shit. Get the fuck out of my spot. You came over here makin' all that damn noise fo' what? To have me in som' shit that has nothin' to do wit' me? Yo' beef wit' yo' family is on you. Now, all of a sudden, you want me to be a part of yo' family. Mane, fuck that shit. I don't give a damn what you thought, *Dad*, but I'm not a sucka ass nigga. I don't make deals wit' the Feds because I envy my brother or because someone else is pullin' the strings over my head."

Through clenched teeth, Bo Jack spoke, "Watch yo' motherfuckin' mouth, lil' nigga. You have no idea what you speakin' on. The only reason I won't kill you or that lil' nigga over there wit' his bitch ... is because y'all auntie suck a mean dick an' knows how to throw that ass on my pipe. Wit' that being said, you ain't gon' keep talkin' out the side of yo' neck to me."

As I growled, Tello and his crew began to joke and laugh. I didn't find shit funny. While I evilly eyed the nigga that aided my mother in the creation of me, he shoved his phone in my face and barked for me to look at it. Shaking my head, I briefly looked towards Nixon and Desaree. The look on her face told me exactly what she thought; she was disgusted and frightened. Nixon's facial expression was self-explanatory; that nigga wanted to kill, but who I wasn't quite sure. It could've been Bo Jack or Tashima, or it was both.

"Look at how she's on the hood of that nigga's car while his face is between her legs. I'm sure you was in the house sleep ... after gettin' the same pussy, he was playin' in," Bo Jack spat, causing me to look at him.

Growing angry, I slapped the phone out of my face before nastily saying, "Get that shit out of my face, Bo Jack, I told you I care nothin' 'bout the shit you spittin'."

"Mane, this nigga ain't gon' move nothin' ... let's go 'head wit' the plan, Dad," Tello spoke in an agitated timbre.

"A'ight, Tello," Bo Jack spoke without looking at his son.

Fuming, I decided to keep calm in front of an enemy. Satan must've known that because I was caught off guard when Bo Jack shoved his hand against my throat before pushing me into the wall. Nastily and slowly, he spoke for me to look at the phone.

"You ain't stupid, boy. I know who raised you, an' I know fo' a fact she didn't raise you to be a crash dummy of a nigga! You weak as hell fo' som' pussy, but you are not a gotdamn crash dummy! Look at this damn video, Son. It will open yo' eyes to the type of bitch you are dealin' wit'!"

I didn't want to look at that video because I knew I was going to do something horrible to Tashima. The last thing I wanted to do was hurt the one person that had been hurting me badly lately. The moment I saw my crib and the sensual and loving way that Dom Dom had Tashima sprawled on the hood of his car before carrying her towards the driver's seat of his whip, I knew that he had her heart more than I ever could. The moment she violated our home by having open sexual encounters with him for the world to see, we were finished—for life. There was no need to fight over her anymore.

Evilly looking at Nixon and Desaree, I told Bo Jack, "I don't need to see anymo'."

"So, what you gon' do 'bout those disrespectful motherfuckas?" Bo Jack inquired.

"Let them be. Karma is a motherfucka," I told him as I pondered was I going to let them get away with disrespecting me like that.

Shaking his head as he released me, Bo Jack spat, "You are one dumb ass nigga. I should have a DNA test done on you. At this very moment, I really don't think you are my son. Shit, how stupid can you really be, boy? At this very moment, the mo' I look at you, the mo' I wished yo' Momma would've aborted you like I told her ass to do. You shouldn't be carryin' my blood in yo' veins at all. I swear. Mane, you need to thank yo' auntie fo' keepin' you an' that nigga in her mouth while my dick was deep down her throat."

Shaking his head while backing away from me, Bo Jack turned his attention to Tello and hollered, "Snatch that pregnant bitch off the ground. Word 'round town, Tashima don't play 'bout her. Let's see how much of that shit is true!"

"What? Fuck no!" Nixon hollered as he stood. Tello aimed his gun at my brother, and I envisioned a scene that I didn't want to see.

Not willing to see my brother die, I calmly voiced, "Nixon chill. Desaree, go willingly an' quietly an' you'll return unharmed."

I was too damn calm for my likening, which meant I was not the loving, caring, and compassionate Dyon; I was a monster that no one wanted to see. At that moment, I was a nigga that didn't give a fuck about Desaree's well-being. I wanted her dirty ass sister in my face.

"What the fuck, Dyon?" Nixon loudly spat, standing. He was ready for war; that was until Tello placed his gun on the back of Nixon's head.

"Tello, put that gun down. Dyon an' Nixon knows not to fuck wit' me or us fo' that matter. After all, we finna take a precious individual that they love. Now, grab her ass so we can roll up outta here before the cops get here," Bo Jack spoke before making his way towards the hallway that led to the front door.

As one of Tello's niggas reached out to Desaree, she hollered, "No, don't touch me. I can get up by my-damn-self!"

While Desaree put on her big girl draws, Nixon nastily looked at me and spat, "Desaree, baby, you will be alright. Nothin' ain't gon' happen to you."

"I love you, Nixon," she sadly voiced as tears welled in her eyes.

"An' I love you," he spoke, placing his eyes on his woman.

The hustle and bustle of niggas in my home faded quickly. While the last of the crew exited my house, I zoned out. My thinking was on another level.

Upon hearing tires skirting off, I calmly yet nonchalantly voiced, "You are going to get her back, an' I promise you every last one of those niggas going to die fo' takin' her in the first place."

Standing inches away from my face, Nixon barked, "We better or that bitch, Tashima, is dead, an' I'm gonna be the nigga to pull that motherfuckin' trigger. Now, that shit you can fuckin' believe."

As my brother walked away, I was stuck to the wall, rehashing what I had seen on Bo Jack's phone and what he said about Auntie Mesha. I couldn't focus on my aunt's fake ass ways for the thoughts of Dom Dom and Tashima. The more I thought about the disrespectful actions, the more I was eager to see Tashima's beautiful face so that I could put a bullet in the center of her fucking head. Fuck that. I was going to choke the life out of her with a sinister smile on my angered face.

I didn't know how long I was against the wall, or why the police hadn't shown. However, I was glad when they weren't present because I heard Tashima's voice, yelling my name.

"What!" I shot back angrily as I looked towards the kitchen.

"Where's my sister?" Tashima inquired in the proximity of me.

Rapidly, I placed my hand around her neck, kicked her in the leg before shoving her onto the ground. She tried to fight me, but I lost it. I had no idea what happened until I had come to and observed my body and hers.

I was standing over her with my zipper undone. She didn't have on an ounce of clothing. Dried tear stains were on her face as tears slid down her face. Her beautiful eyes showcased sadness and fear. The corners of her mouth were white and crusty. My face burned; there were scratches on them. I was breathless, incredibly.

As I looked at a distraught, helpless, and soulless Tashima, sprawled on the ground, shaking as if she was hurting, I spat in her face before gently placing my dirty shoe on her throat. There were so many things that I needed to say, but I didn't utter a damn word.

"Dyon," she cried.

"Fuck you, bitch! I'll never forgive you fo' what you did earlier this mornin' on the property that we own! You are dead to me, an' to make sure you understand what the fuck I am sayin'..."

"Dyon, I didn't mean—"

I refused to let her speak a single word to me; therefore, I unzipped my shit bag and dumped that motherfucker all over her face.

"Good riddance, you shitty, fucked-up bitch."

Walking off on the broad that I had been dumb over, I heard the police sirens. Quickly, I snatched my keys out of my pocket, all the while walking out of the home I once loved with one thing on my mind, revenge.

A lot of motherfuckas finna see me in my raw form. It's finna be a lot of bloodshed along wit' fires. Satan, I came to you one time befo', an' I'm back. Help me crush those that think I'm a pussy ass nigga......

ABOUT THE NOVELIST

TN Jones was born and raised in Alabama, which she resides in her home state with her daughter. Growing up, TN Jones always had a passion for and writing, which led her to writing short stories as a young teen.

In 2015, TN Jones began working on her first book, *Disloyal: Revenge of a Broken Heart*, which was previously titled, *Passionate Betrayals*.

TN Jones writes in the following Urban/Interracial genres: Women's Fiction, Mystery/Suspense, Fiction/Romance, Dark Erotica/Erotica, and Paranormal.

Published novels by TN Jones: By Any Means: Going Against the Grain 1-2, The Sins of Love: Finessing the Enemies 1-3, Caught Up In a D-Boy's Illest Love 1-3, Choosing To Love A Lady Thug 1-4, Is This Your Man, Sis: Side Piece Chronicles, Just You and Me: A Magical Love Story, Jonesin' For A Boss Chick: A Montgomery Love Story, That Young Hood Love 1-2, Give Me What I Want, If My Walls Could Talk, A Sucka for a Thug's Love, Her Mattress Buddy, Chocolate Enchantress, I Now Pronouce You Mr. & Mrs. Thug,

Disloyal: Revenge of a Broken Heart, and *Disloyal 2: A Woman's Revenge* .

Collaboration novel: *Dating a Female Goon* with Ms. Biggz

Re-releases: Two books (*If You'll Give Me Your Heart 1-2*) will be re-released. Dates TBA.

Upcoming novels by TN Jones: Disloyal 3:Revenge of all Revenges, I Now Pronounce You Mr. and Mrs. Thug 3, Soulless: An Infatuation with Love, and The Lost Dhampir Princess (trilogy).

Thank you for reading the second installment of *I Now Pronounce You Mr. and Mrs. Thug*. Please leave an honest review under the book title on Amazon and Goodreads.

For future book details, please visit any of the links below:

Amazon Author page:
https://www.amazon.com/tnjones666

Facebook: https://www.facebook.com/novelisttnjones/

Goodreads:
https://www.goodreads.com/author/show/14918893.TN_Jones :

Google+:
https://www.plus.google.com/u/1/communities/115057649956960897339

Instagram: https://www.instagram.com/tnjones666

Twitter: https://twitter.com/TNHarris6.

You are welcome to *email* her: tnjones666@gmail.com

Chat with her daily in the *Facebook* group: *Its Just Me...TN Jones*.

I Now Pronounce You, Mr. and Mrs. Thug 2

DID YOU ENJOY THIS BOOK?

Leaving an honest review is beneficial for me as an author. It is one of the most potent tools used as I seek attention for my books. Receiving feedback from readers will increase my chances of reaching other readers that haven't read a book by me. Word of mouth is a great way to spread the news of a book that you've enjoyed.

With that being said, once you reach this page, please scroll to the review section and leave an honest review. Be sure to click the box for Goodreads as well as Amazon. As always, thank you for taking a chance on allowing me to provide you with quality entertainment.

Peace and Blessings, Loves!

TN Jones

CPSIA information can be obtained
at www.ICGtesting.com
Printed in the USA
LVHW091735191219
641092LV00002B/137/P

9 781697 907148